A Loyal Betrayal

A Loyal Betrayal

N.R. SCARANO

Paperback: 979-8-9871935-0-1
Hardcover: 979-8-9871935-1-8

Cover Designed by Fay Lane
Interior Formatting by Nicole Scarano Formatting & Design
Character Illustration by @Cebanart
Proofread by Cassandra Chaput

CONTENTS

AUTHOR'S NOTE

This book was written under N.R. Scarano, which means this romance is meant for mature audiences. If you do not like this style of romance (or even if you do!), please see her books with Nicole Scarano on the cover instead. Nicole's books are still meant for mature audiences, but the romance is YA-appropriate.

If you would like to go into this story blind, feel free! But for those who like CWS, here they are:

This 3rd person POV reimagining takes many liberties with the original legend and contains graphic love scenes, violence, language, and a quick mention of infertility. The original Camelot Legend deals with cheating, so in this reimagining, I do work that into the plot BUT I change what is really going on. I think you will like how it is worked into this story, especially since I am a huge soulmate trope lover. But for those of you who dislike cheating in books (like me), I encourage you to keep reading and wait for the plot twist.

Thank you for reading this note. You are such a good girl ;)

ONE

Blood and failure. They coated Arthur's tongue and ensnared his soul, drowning him in their bile and filth. They would be his constant companions on this long journey home, and Arthur leaned over the side of his horse to spit crimson onto the dirt. His blood sank into the earth until it was nothing but a memory, but its bitterness lingered as he rubbed his aching jaw. Once again, Mordred had escaped his clutches. The mage taunted him on all sides, worming his way into Arthur's subconscious, yet he remained always out of reach, just beyond his grasp. This battle had been no different, and hatred riddled Arthur's gut. Hatred of himself. How had he allowed this monster to taunt him with such cruelty? He was no king if he could not end a tyrant, for that's what Mordred was. A mage born of evil, bred of darkness, he fought tooth and sweat and nail to destroy the peace Arthur had bled so viciously for… still bled for. Camelot would never be safe while Mordred walked free, and this battle was supposed to have ended his reign of fear. Arthur led an army to confront the mage's followers, but as the tide turned in their favor, Mordred vanished. Distracted, Arthur faltered, his men following his lead, and the cost had been great. The dead watered the grass with their blood, the field stained forever red, and even though his knights rallied and brought him victory, Mordred was gone. And while the mage lived, Arthur failed.

"My king?" Tristan's voice pushed through his dark haze, and Arthur looked up with hardened eyes. He should welcome the interruption. It dragged him back from the abyss, but darkness had already embedded its icy claws in his veins, and not even the sight of one of his knights brought him relief.

Tristan ignored Arthur's foul mood and gestured to an approaching rider. Arthur stared at the newcomer. He was barely a man, having never felt the blade against his beard, and his presence stirred confusion within the king. The stranger was too clean to have come from his army, but nothing inhabited this barren land except for dirt and disappointment.

"He brings word from Sir Leodegrance," Tristan whispered as the boy approached.

"Who?" Arthur did not bother to lower his voice. Tristan shrugged, and Arthur sagged in relief. Born into poverty, thieves and the whores had raised the future king. An orphan, a mere gutter rat in the eyes of the nobility, he survived by lying and stealing and eventually by killing. His rough childhood had forged a harsh man, a warrior bred of steel and flame. He did not understand every aspect of court as a king should, for his life was one of war. He fought for everything he had, for each day he survived, and when the oppression grew unbearable, Arthur rose from gutter rat to rebel. It was not long before his name spread. The wicked feared him. The hopeless worshiped him, but still, injustice reigned. Camelot was a writhing cesspool of filth, a dark stain marring the continent. Its rulers were corrupt, its people dying, and when all hope of salvation slipped through their fingers, he met a young mage. Merlin told of a sword fused within a stone at the heart of Camelot. It was prophesied that whoever could withdraw the blade was the kingdom's true ruler, but it had sat entombed for so long that most forgot it existed. Merlin had not, though, and he pledged his allegiance to Arthur, promising to help him fight their way to the weapon. Merlin believed in the young revolutionary, and Arthur was so desperate to staunch the bloodshed that he put his faith in a legend.

Many lives were sacrificed as they forged a bloody path to the stone, but the moment Arthur's fingers grasped the hilt, a shock of power coursed through his veins, and the blade slipped free. Excalibur was his. Arthur was king.

It took years of pain and hardship, but Arthur brought peace to Camelot. He was a kind and honorable ruler, his reign the first in centuries to bring happiness and prosperity, and while he had learned much over the years, he was a warrior at heart. Brutal and efficient, he cared more about the practicality of his rule than the pompous affairs most deemed necessary. He was often at a loss when it came to the ceremonies presumed important. Not that he purposely ignored them, but it wasn't who he was. He would never be a flamboyant or eloquent king. Arthur was a reserved man, and if not for his sheer size, no one would notice him enter the room. He kept to the shadows, humble and always watching, but he preferred it that way. He wasn't better than his people just because Excalibur chose him. The moment he forgot that was the day he became his predecessors, a rot to be carved out and burned.

It was not uncommon for him to not recognize a lord's name. His missteps sometimes embarrassed him, but Tristan seemed equally baffled, which put Arthur at ease. Of all his knights, Tristan was his most eloquent. Raised at court, he had pledged his allegiance to Arthur's rebellion at its start. Tristan, along with Gawain and Percival, were the men Arthur relied on most.

"My king," the young stranger bowed as low as his horse permitted as he halted before them. "My lord, Sir Leodegrance, has an estate just beyond that ridge." He gestured to the rolling hill to his left. "Hearing news that the king and his army would pass through the borders of his land, he sent me to offer his hospitality. He invites you to his home to rest before you continue your journey."

Arthur stared at the young man without speaking, causing the messenger to shift uncomfortably under his glare. He deserved to sleep on the cold ground for his failures, but his men needed the comforts of civilization. The fact that not even Tristan recognized this lord gave him pause, though. This invitation sounded like a blessing, but it could as easily be a trap.

"Leodegrance," a soft voice soothed in his ear, and he flinched at the interruption despite recognizing the tone. Merlin was the only man who could sneak up on him, and regardless of how often it happened, it unnerved Arthur.

"Old family name," the mage's melodic voice continued. "Respected once for their great wealth and contributions. I have not seen it written in the histories as of late, which points to the falling of their household. Nevertheless, the name is of good standing. I see no reason to refuse the invitation."

Arthur grunted at Merlin's answer to his unasked question, and the mage slipped backward as if on the wind.

"Tell your master we accept," Arthur said. "We'll stay the night and return to Camelot in the morning."

"Yes, my king." The boy's smile quickly morphed into a grimace at the king's bloodstained frown. "Thank you. Sir Leodegrance will be most pleased."

Leodegrance greeted them at the gate with such enthusiasm, Arthur's teeth ground together in annoyance, his jaw aching at the pressure. Deep down, he was grateful for the hospitality, but this was what he hated most about ruling. Everything was pomp and ceremony. Men clamoring for his attention, craving any blessing he might grant. He was in no mood to cater to this man's unwavering attention. In no mood to stroke egos or be used to elevate statuses. He wanted to sleep. He wanted to find Mordred and end the bloodshed. He wanted to be welcomed as simply Arthur and not the king. That was something he would never grow accustomed to. Everyone craved a piece of him, to carve out a pound of his flesh to mount on their walls as a trophy, but no one truly cared for the man. He missed the days of his youth. At least then, when someone smiled at him, he knew the expression was true.

Arthur scowled. He felt annoyed by the groveling, but mostly he was annoyed with himself. He should be kinder, better with his words, but he was no poet, no great orator. He was forged of blood and steel. A man of action, forever different from the king the world expected of him.

He needed to eat and bathe. Perhaps that would wash away his foul mood, but Arthur refused to go inside until his army settled. He claimed it was because he couldn't rest until his men were cared for, and while it was mostly true, he really craved the quiet. He needed to center himself. Bitterness hovered over him like a storm, and despite being uncomfortable in court, he would not be rude. Whatever the lord's agenda, he had opened his home to starving and weary soldiers.

The sun had long since set before Arthur scrubbed the filth from his skin and ventured inside. He had not changed, but at least the blood and sweat had been washed away. A servant tried to offer him fresh clothes, but nothing fit him. At six feet, five inches, Arthur was all coiled violence and hardened muscle. A mountain among men, his size along with his dark hair, nearly black eyes, a nose broken one too many times, and an array of scars woven into his flesh like a brutal tapestry caused most to both recoil from his presence and beg for his approval. No, the lack of clean dress wear didn't bother him. Blood stains and torn fabric suited him.

"This ale tastes like shit," Gawain said as Arthur slipped into the dining hall unseen by all save his friend, Excalibur strapped across his back. Not a king who made an entrance, he preferred to enter rooms unnoticed. One could learn a lot from those who did not realize he was present.

"But it's strong as fuck," Gawain continued, shoving his mug in front of Arthur's nose. His statement, along with Arthur's observations, confirmed Merlin's initial assessment of the Leodegrance household. Once a respected name, the house no longer claimed the same power it once had, well maintained and comfortable as it slowly slipped into oblivion.

Gawain tilted the mug, reclaiming the king's attention. "Have some."

Arthur leaned against the table at his back and glared at the knight. His icy stare held his friend's taunting gaze, and then finally Gawain sank to a half seat beside him.

"It wasn't your fault," he said, and Arthur hated how easily his friend read his emotions. "Mordred is not some madman bent on making your life miserable. He is one of the most powerful mages our generation has faced. He was there when you took Excalibur. You know better than anyone what those mages were capable of."

Arthur grunted but said nothing as he swiped a loaf of bread from the table. No one had noticed him yet, and he prayed it stayed that way. He wanted to stay long enough to eat and then slip unseen to bed. He needed to get back to Camelot. To plan his next attack.

"Stop blaming yourself." Gawain took another sip of the ale and coughed. "Damn, you really should try this."

"Go bother Percival," Arthur growled.

Gawain laughed, completely unbothered by the king's sour mood. "You will corner Mordred, and when you do, I'll be there, protecting your back." He pounded Arthur's shoulder blade. "All right. I need more of this shit."

He strode off, and Arthur bristled, shoving food into his mouth. A mug of ale strong enough to knock his self-doubt unconscious tempted him, but he refused to lose control here. Too many unknowns, too many people. He would let his men enjoy their night, but his restraint never faltered. The ale would make him tolerable, but at what cost? Always have an exit strategy. Always be mindful of your surroundings. Growing up on the streets had taught him that the hard way. It was a lesson he never forgot.

Arthur grabbed a slice of meat from behind him and tore off a bite. This table hovered forgotten at the edge of the room, intended merely as overflow, but the vantage suited him. No one noticed the hulking yet hunched warrior in the corner while he observed the crowd with perfect clarity. Merlin stood at the center of the floor, undoubtedly regaling the diners with the tale of King Arthur and Excalibur. Gawain and Percival seemed intent on discovering which of them could drink the most ale. Tristan had found a pretty girl to impress with his heroics and charm, and Arthur wondered if it would be rude to grab the serving platter and slip away to find an empty hiding spot. The fantasy was so tempting he almost tasted the solitude, but he could already hear Merlin ordering him to get his shit together and act his station. Camelot had flourished under his reign, but he wasn't the storyteller Merlin was, nor the carefree life of the party Gawain and Percival were. And he was decidedly not the charming romantic Tristan was. He felt far more comfortable with a sword than his words.

Arthur groaned and pushed himself off the table. He would thank his host and say a few kind words to the guests, but before he could emerge from his solitude, a dark flash captured his eyes. He shrank back into the shadows and stared, awestruck, as a woman emerged from behind a group of older couples. Her midnight black hair caught the firelight, glinting as if it were a precious metal, and every muscle in Arthur's body coiled tight at the sight.

CHAPTER TWO

Arthur stood mesmerized by that hair. He had never seen anything so intoxicating, and the sudden urge to run his fingers through it, coiling the thick strands in his fist as he pulled back her head, hit him like lightning in a storm. His breath caught in his lungs, and suddenly his skin felt too tight, too raw. He couldn't move as the girl turned, oblivious to his pain, and when he saw her face, it increased tenfold.

Her profile was stunning, as if an artist painted her perfection to life. Her blue eyes contrasted her black hair, two oceans he wanted to drown in. What he would give to have her turn her gaze to his, to have her peer up at him through thick lashes. She was tall for a woman, yet he still towered above her. She would have to look up to meet his gaze, even more so if she was on her knees, and Arthur's cock twitched at the image. Big round eyes stared up at him. Gorgeous red lips parted in anticipation. He pictured the way they would trail across his skin, tasting every inch of him.

"Fuck." Arthur stepped back as if he had been slapped. He

needed to stop. The woman before him was young, too young for him. At thirty-two, the king was not old, but this girl couldn't be older than twenty. Someone that youthful, that perfect, would not want a brute like him. He was more scar than skin, and he was not a romantic or a poet. He was gruff and to the point. Introverted and harsh. That exquisite creature deserved beauty and seduction, a handsome man to write sonnets about the way her laughter lit up a room. How her grace put all others to shame. She did not deserve him staring at her from the shadows, wondering what it would feel like to have such marble smooth skin beneath his calloused palms. Would she enjoy their roughness as he slid his fingers up her thighs? Would it make her wet? Would her voice escape her in a soft moan or a hungry scream when he pushed a finger inside her?

Arthur snarled and shut his eyes. What was wrong with him? He was not a virgin, but he rarely pursued women. Not that he didn't crave a wife to cherish, but most only coveted his title. He understood he would marry for the good of Camelot and not for love, and he had promised himself his marriage would be an equal union. He would bring his future bride and her people the same benefits that she brought Camelot. Respect could grow from such an alignment of equality, and while he was resolved to that fate, the darkest recesses of his soul longed for someone who saw past his status to the man. It was why he seldom spent time alone with women. They wanted his crown, and every time he bedded one, a piece of his soul chipped away. He had ignored his desires for so long that he barely acknowledged the females vying for his attention anymore. His days were too consumed with the weight of his rule to worry about his loneliness, yet as he stood there staring at the girl who had not noticed him, he could not stem the desire coiling in his belly.

The room was suddenly too hot, his clothes too small. He should have drank that ale. *Goddamn it, why was he so stubborn?* He should leave and stop glaring at her, but then she moved, her red dress clinging to her as she shifted. Arthur leaned back uncomfortably as her delicate hand grazed her leg. The thigh he so badly wanted wrapped around his waist as he thrust deep inside her, the thigh he craved to run his tongue, his lips, his fingers over.

Arthur clenched his teeth so hard he feared they would shatter. He needed to get control of his body. She was too young. His crown might tempt her, but that would be as far as her interest would extend. Divine beauty like her would not choose him, and he only wanted a woman who genuinely wanted him in return. He could never be with someone that beautiful, knowing she longed to be anywhere but with him. Still, he could not stop staring. Her smile was soft and kind, her laugh a song on the air, and then she twisted again, her eyes falling on his. It was a fraction of a second. A single breath, but their gazes met. She barely noticed him, her features without recognition, but an excruciating blow pummeled Arthur. He stopped breathing and would have stumbled if not for the table digging into the backs of his thighs. He could not explain it, but he had experienced this sensation before. It had happened the moment he laid his sight upon Excalibur.

Fate.

ARTHUR NEEDED to leave this damn room. The air was too hot, the floor too hard. The guests were loud, too damn loud, and his skin felt as if it belonged to a stranger. Women never affected him like this, and annoyance flared in his chest as embarrassment tinged his cheeks. He needed to get outside and breathe in the fresh air. Arthur clenched his eyes shut and groaned, forcing thoughts of Mordred and Camelot through his brain. It took a few moments, but eventually, his thundering heart slowed enough to allow him to flee in safety.

Arthur opened his eyes and shifted toward the exit when he saw Leodegrance scanning the crowd, undoubtedly searching for him. It was now or never, but before the soles of his battle-worn boots peeled from the floor to deliver him to oblivion, he froze. His host's hand rested on the young woman's back, corralling her slowly through the throng of guests. The similarities struck Arthur as his gaze drifted between the pair. The same bone structure, the similar coloring. She was Sir Leodegrance's daughter, and dread seized his gut with its icy fingers. He had lived through this scene before, more times than he cared to admit. A man would see the crown and throw his unwilling daughter at his feet, hoping to maneuver her into a prime position to be crowned the next queen. Arthur cursed under his breath, the lord's enthusiasm at housing the army suddenly painfully obvious. He planned to sacrifice his beautiful daughter before the king with the ambition of raising his station, and the food roiled in Arthur's stomach. This dance sickened him. More so now, since the woman had evoked such a violent reaction. He yearned for her to glance at him, to talk to him, to touch him, but he wanted it to be genuine. It made his stomach sour thinking that the only reason she would speak to him was because her father demanded it.

Leodegrance spotted the king, and escape impossible, Arthur folded his arms over his well-muscled chest and watched the lord push his daughter forward. The closer she stepped, the more beautiful he realized she was. Her soft skin glowed in the firelight, her thick eyelashes becoming visible. The sleeves of her red dress hung off her shoulders, leaving her neck gloriously bare. It was the kind of dress that invited a man's lips to press against the slender column of her throat, to drag them over her collarbone and down to the swell of her breasts, to grab hold of the crimson fabric with his teeth and pull down just far enough to capture a perfect nipple in his mouth.

Arthur swore under his breath and silently begged her to look at him, to show any sign of excitement at meeting him, that this introduction was at her request and not her father's insistence, but her eyes remained demurely down as Leodegrance pushed her to a halt before him.

"My king." Leodegrance bowed. "Long may you reign and prosper. You grace my home with your presence." Arthur forced himself not to grimace and offered a smile that failed to reach his dark eyes, but the man didn't seem to notice his uncomfortable expression. "May I present my daughter Guinevere?"

Guinevere. Gods, even her name was beautiful. She sank in a respectful curtsey, her eyes tilting up for the briefest of moments, but that was all she gave him. She was there out of obligation, and that fact only solidified Arthur's restraint. He would not pursue her regardless of her father's intentions or his own desire. He wouldn't bring unhappiness to this exquisite woman with his unwanted attention.

"Guinevere was only just speaking of your exploits today and how you are the wisest king Camelot has seen in generations," Leodegrance continued, but the expression on Guinevere's face told Arthur that was far from the truth. "Isn't that right, my dear? Did you not mention how you longed to make his acquaintance?"

"Yes, father," Guinevere said softly, and Arthur clenched his teeth to keep from groaning. The sound was the sweetest melody. He wanted to ask her to speak again, to say anything just so he might hear it, but he kept his mouth firmly shut.

"Imagine her excitement when your army passed, and we could offer you accommodations," her father continued. "It must have been fate, a blessing from God."

Fate. There was that word again, and Arthur stilled, staring at Guinevere. He had felt it the moment their eyes met, but she refused to meet his gaze now, face downcast in respectful disinterest. He wished she would return his stare so he might read the thoughts churning behind her demure expression, but she hovered before him as if she was merely a servant to be examined. The entire time her father talked, she stood respectfully by, and Arthur studied her closely, drinking every inch of her in, knowing that after tonight he would never again witness anything so lovely. He vaguely registered her father's droning voice as he listed his daughter's most appealing qualities and her age. His guess had been correct. She was only twenty years old, and Arthur decided to end this conversation. Leodegrance was blatantly pushing her on him, and she clearly had no desire to be used as a bargaining chip for men's ambition. Forcing her to stand here just so he could study her was selfish. So, Arthur tore his gaze from her and looked at his host. He opened his mouth and—

Crash! The room exploded in chaos, and Percival dove for a statue Gawain knocked over.

"No, not—" Leodegrance flew across the floor, abandoning his daughter, and Arthur suspected Gawain did that on purpose to provide him with an escape. The knights might be drunk, but they never stooped so low as to embarrass their king.

Arthur breathed in relief and turned back to Guinevere to say goodbye before her father returned to corner him, but the instant their eyes met, Arthur's feet rooted to the floor. His boots were stone, his mouth dust, his heart a vicious storm, and all he could do was stare at her. Gone was the demure daughter. Gone was the reluctance and disinterest. Not a single guest watched them as they gawked at Gawain, granting Arthur and Guinevere a moment of unadulterated privacy. And she was a wholly different woman. She stood tall and strong, her confidence coloring the air with its power. Her irises seared heat into him without hesitation, no longer hiding the tempest raging in her ocean blues, and what he found in her gaze almost knocked him to the ground. Desire. It coiled around her like a ravenous flame, reaching between them to wrap him in its burning embrace. The brazenness of her expression shocked him, and her lips quirked as if in a challenge, as if she was testing what he would do with her truth. She had saved it just for him, refusing to allow anyone else to know, and Arthur longed to grab her by the throat and accept her challenge with a kiss she would never forget.

But he could not move. Could not speak. He was completely under her spell, and he never wanted to leave. They stood locked together, letting their eyes shout for them as their words failed, and then slowly Guinevere leaned forward. The movement was subtle, her feet still rooted where her father had left her, but her chest drifted closer to his, offering him an uninhibited view of the soft skin straining against her bodice. Without breaking his gaze, her palm tensely trailed up to her stomach, where she fisted the crimson fabric until her knuckles paled white, and Arthur growled. He understood her meaning. She was struggling to remain in control just as violently as he was, and his fist twitched. He ached to rip that hand from her dress, to push his fingers through hers and let her grip him until he lost all circulation.

"All is well, thank God," Leodegrance interrupted as he appeared back at his daughter's side. Guinevere snapped upright, her gaze falling, and as suddenly as it had disappeared, the demure picture resumed control. Gone was the lust, the brazen challenge, and Arthur exhaled with a slight cough. Her spell was intoxicating, and he clenched his fists so hard his short nails dug painfully into his callouses. Gods, he wanted her to look up again. He almost snarled at her father for interrupting, but the damage was done. The innocent, disinterested girl had returned, but knowing the fire those blue eyes held choked Arthur, and he could no longer make small talk with his host.

"Thank you for your hospitality. You are a true servant to

the crown," he said, struggling to keep his gruff voice even, and Leodegrance crooned at the praise. "I am grateful we happened upon your land, but I'm sure you understand my weariness from the battle. After checking on my men, I will retire for the evening. I must bid you goodnight."

"Of course, my king." Leodegrance bowed, and Arthur noticed the man's disappointment, but he physically couldn't stand here any longer. He refused to embarrass himself. To embarrass that tempting angel draped in sinful red.

"My king." Guinevere curtseyed as he walked away, a palpable tension coiling between her and her father, and Arthur's fists clenched even tighter. That voice. That goddamn voice. It could convince him to do anything.

He stormed across the room and grabbed the ale from Gawain. The knight jerked in surprise, but as Arthur drained what little remained, Merlin stared at him with a knowing expression.

Arthur shoved the empty mug back at his friend and said, "I'm going to bed. Don't drink any more of this shit."

"Are you—?" Percival started.

"I'm fine," Arthur snarled. "You all should get some rest. Tomorrow will be a long day."

"Arthur." Gawain drunkenly threw an arm around the king's much larger shoulders. "You should smile more."

"I will hit you if you don't let go of me."

The knights burst into laughter, and Gawain only tightened his grip. "I know you hate when fathers do that to you," he mumbled, annoyingly observant despite the alcohol. "But she is beautiful. It's all right to talk to her."

"She would never want me." He didn't need to elaborate. His friends knew what he meant.

"You never know," Gawain's words slurred. "You don't know what fate has in store for you."

Fate. That word needed to stop fucking with him.

"Get some sleep." He slapped Gawain's cheek lightly in an affectionate gesture. "I can't have you all feeling like shit tomorrow."

"Yes, my king." Tristan bent in a mock bow. These men were fortunate he loved them. They were pushing their luck.

"Merlin," Arthur grunted, "have fun with these fools." The group erupted in laughter, but Arthur turned and strode out of the room without so much as a glance at Guinevere, his powerful steps delivering him to a solitary freedom.

CHAPTER THREE

Arthur's arm curled over his head, his other pressed flat against his ribs. The room was warm in the weak firelight, and the blanket hung low, barely covering his hips. He blamed his inability to sleep on the heat, but the lie held little conviction. It would be a long night imprisoned within these walls. Morning and his return to Camelot could not come soon enough.

He shifted uncomfortably, the blankets too rough against his bare skin. Leodegrance had gifted him his finest room, but the bed was slightly too small for his hulking frame. Or maybe it was his skin that was too small? He couldn't tell. All he knew was he needed to get away from here, from Guinevere. If a single look had him so thoroughly under her spell, he worried what an entire conversation might do. He would rise early and take care to avoid her in the morning. If he was fortunate, he would not see her—

A soft click interrupted the silence, and Arthur stiffened, every battle-hardened muscle coiling with anticipation. The ornate four-poster bed frame with its draped curtains blocked the door from his view, but there was no mistaking the sound. Someone had slipped almost silently inside. Perhaps he had misjudged Leodegrance's intentions earlier. Perhaps Mordred had gotten to him first.

Arthur snagged the dagger from beneath the pillow beside him and rose to a seat, slowly rising to a kneel on one leg while the other extended to the floor. The blanket slid low, barely covering his nudity. He would have to fight naked. He had survived worse.

A soft footfall sounded, and his body coiled, poised to strike as a figure slipped through the shadows. Arthur's torso shot forward; his aim perfect as his blade flicked to the intruder's throat, but he did not push the metal into flesh. Not yet. He wanted to look his assassin in the eyes and watch them realize how fatally they had failed.

The assailant barely reached to his chest, and a warning rang through his brain. The stranger was too short, too small to defeat him. The scene before him was wrong, all wrong, and shock froze his veins. Blue eyes stared up at him, not in fear nor in anger, but in bold acceptance, as if they welcomed the challenge. The taste of metal against flesh. Dark hair glistened in the dim light, and Arthur's mouth went dry as recognition settled in his chest. Guinevere.

"I almost killed you," he growled, but she said nothing. She merely stared through her eyelashes at him as if she knew he would never, could never, harm her. Arthur's heart thundered against his ribs with such force he was sure she heard it, sure she felt it vibrating the air. He vaguely recalled that he was naked, half kneeling on the bed, covered by a blanket that hung dangerously low. He should lower the blade from her throat and cover himself, but before he could move, he made the mistake of glancing down. Arthur swore, the sound harsh as if his voice dragged over gravel.

Guinevere had changed out of the exquisite red dress and into a sheer robe tied between her breasts. The fabric left little to the imagination, clearly intended to be worn over another gown for added flare, but she wore it and nothing else save her beauty. Arthur tried not to look, but he couldn't stop himself. Her body was both strong and soft, her curves intoxicating but not voluptuous. Her breasts would fit perfectly in his calloused palms, in his mouth. *Gods.* He twitched involuntarily at the sight, and the blanket slipped precariously low. Peaked and blush pink, her nipples strained against the fabric, begging him to step closer, urging him to throw caution to the wind. The curve of her hips called to his hands, craved to be gripped tight as he pulled her close, and despite everything within him screaming not to tilt his gaze down, his will was weak. His eyes drifted over the dark curls between her thighs. She had trimmed them short, as if she anticipated that he would want to see her through them, and she was beautiful. No woman had the right to be this perfect.

"What are you doing here?" Arthur snapped his gaze back to her challenging eyes. "Someone might have seen you."

"No one saw me," she said without an ounce of fear, despite the dagger still kissing her skin.

"Although, I'm sure that was your father's intention," Arthur spat. Guinevere's eyebrows pinched together in confusion, but he barely noticed her expression. Revulsion roiled in his gut, and he felt sick at his reaction to her. She was so beautiful. All he wanted was to wrap his fingers in her hair and make her his until her voice was raw from her screams of pleasure, but he understood the bitter reality of what this scene meant. It disgusted him. How could a father stoop so low as to whore out his daughter to improve his station? The brutal scars woven into his chest and arms were a stark comparison to the soft skin before him. It was impossible that she was here to satisfy her own hunger. He was too old for her. Too savage. The only other explanation was that Leodegrance planned to sacrifice her innocence to ensnare the king. It was not unheard of for a man to catch a lord in a compromising position to force an engagement. Here he was, the blanket slipping off him, his dagger pressed to Guinevere's practically naked form. How many more seconds until someone burst through the door and caught them? When that happened, Arthur would have two choices. Marry the poor girl who was forced into this embarrassment, or refuse her, shaming her entire future. In the end, it was no choice. He refused to ruin this girl's life. She deserved honor and romance. A lover to shower her with flowers and read to her the great romantic poems. She did not deserve a marriage born of shame. He had to get her out of here.

"Get out," Arthur growled. "You have nothing to fear." Guinevere lifted an eyebrow at him as if in question. "Tell your father I will not bring you shame, and even though I want to throttle him for compromising you, no one will hear of this. I have no interest in a woman forced to seduce me by her own family. I promise you, I never touch women who do not wish me to."

"But I—" Guinevere said, her voice honey and wine and lust.

"Get out." The words sounded too harsh, too cruel, but his control was a fraying thread. The way her body sang a song his soul recognized drove him further into madness the longer he resisted. She could not be here when the last shred of his discipline snapped. "I won't say it again. I will not lay a hand on you. I'm too old for you, anyway."

"My father doesn't know I'm here." Guinevere stood completely unbothered by his snarled words. "He expressly forbade me to give into you, no matter how hard you begged." Arthur froze, barely able to breathe at her declaration. Danger danced in her eyes, pulling him close, dragging him under, rendering him powerless. "You are correct in assuming my father planned to use me to elevate his social standing, but he wanted me to seduce you while remaining innocent. He said no king wants a whore for a bride, so he made me swear to remain chaste even if you ordered me into your bed. He knows I am beautiful and has received offers for my hand already, but you are the man he set his sights upon. If he knew where I was, he would drag me out by my hair."

"Then why..."

"Am I here?" Guinevere finished for him. Arthur swallowed, and she leaned forward slightly, pressing against the blade, not hard enough to break the skin but enough to form an indent. "Because I am not naïve. My family name once held meaning, but we are so ensnared in debt that marrying me would be a mistake in your reign. My youth and beauty are not worth our debts, and you are an intelligent man. My father may have exaggerated my words earlier, nevertheless, they hold true. I believe you are the greatest king Camelot has ever seen. You are brilliant and courageous and wise. You saw through my father's ploy, and eventually, you would have discovered the extent of what this household owes. There is nothing I can offer a king. You won't marry me. I am resolved to that truth. My fate is to wed a rich fool who will settle my family's affairs in exchange for a young and fertile wife. Love is not destined to rule my future, so I will marry for my family, but I am under no delusions. The husband I will be cursed with will never be you. I did not realize how devastating that would be until I caught sight of you."

Arthur's cock jerked at her last confession, and the blanket slid off his thigh to the bed, baring him completely to her. Her eyes flicked down for a second, and when they returned to his gaze, heat burned in her irises.

"I refuse to play a part in my father's scheme to fool you," she continued. "I respect you too much for that, but the moment I laid eyes on you, I knew I would never have you. That realization hurt more than I expected. I will not insult you by confessing to love you, but I cannot describe what happened to me, what I felt deep in my spirit. It is why I am here, doing something I recognize is foolish. King Arthur, I have to have you at least once in my life. I am here to ask you to be my first and my greatest, to grant me a memory that shall stay with me all my days until I take it silently to the grave. I don't care about the risks, and after tonight, I shall marry whomever my father orders, knowing I will never love him. But I will have this memory to warm my lonely nights. I need to know what it is like to be with someone who captured my soul, who made it impossible to breathe."

"Guinevere." Arthur's throat was so tight he could barely utter her name.

"Please, my king." Gods, she was perfect when she begged. "Before you walk out of my life forever, let me have you at least once."

"No one has ever touched you?"

"Never."

"Fuck, Guinevere." Arthur's control was slipping, but every fiber of his being raged against the beast within, driving it to its knees. "Tell me again that you desire this. That no one is forcing you. That you want me."

"I can't explain it, but I want you more than I have ever wanted anything."

Arthur practically roared as he lowered the blade, slicing through the ribbons that tied her robe closed. She gasped in surprise, but before she could react, he cast the dagger to the chair beside his bed and ripped the sheer fabric off her. It pooled on the floor as he grabbed the back of her neck with a rough hand and yanked her against his hard body, reveling in how soft her skin felt against his scarred flesh, how her voice moaned before his mouth slammed against hers.

CHAPTER FOUR

Arthur's kiss was rough as his fingers curled in her hair, tugging her head back as his other hand slipped around her waist. Guinevere gasped, her lips parting slightly, and his tongue slid into her mouth, taking everything she offered and pouring his desire into her with his every desperate breath. Guinevere had never been kissed, and Arthur seemed to sense her inexperience as he moved, guiding her, coaxing her, teaching her. His lips were both rough and gentle, and he kissed exactly how she imagined he would, all fire and dominance and savage passion. She let him show her how to move against him, matching his longing until she was sure she no longer stood on Earth.

After her mother died without birthing a male heir, Guinevere understood with painful clarity what her future held. Her father would force her to marry to better the family name, and without a great title or wealth, her innocent beauty was all she had to offer. She would undoubtedly wed a man she didn't love, which was why she avoided the handsome men her age. It would only bring disappointment. She didn't want to risk loving someone she could never have.

Noblemen had shown interest in her before tonight, and she was well accustomed to being paraded around like cattle to be sold, so when her father told her King Arthur would be dining with them, she resigned to play the part duty demanded. She had no interest in the king twelve years her senior, even if he was the greatest ruler Camelot had seen in decades. He would be another older man, intelligent enough to avoid being tricked into accepting her family's debt just for her beauty, yet she nodded and smiled when her father lectured her on how to behave. She simply wanted to survive the evening without his ambitions embarrassing the household, but everything changed the moment Arthur stepped into the dining hall.

He had slipped in silently, no one noticing the impossibly tall king, but Guinevere had sensed the change in the atmosphere the instant he entered. She hadn't seen him, but she had felt him, his alluring presence thick as it coated her skin and settled its delicious weight on her soul. It was something she couldn't describe. She likely would never be able to, but she knew he had come, and everything within her ignited. Without drawing attention to her desperate curiosity, she had searched the guests, and when her eyes landed on the king, the earth tilted below her feet.

He was the tallest man she had ever seen. His body forged by blood and steel and pain on the battlefield. His clothes were still stained. Excalibur hung strapped to his back, and even hunched in the shadows, he owned the room. He was all harsh lines and sharp angles. Severe. Brutal. A vengeful storm, and Guinevere's blood froze as her skin ignited. He was not beautiful, his broken nose, jagged scars, and thick thighs too ruthless to be pretty, but he was everything Guinevere wanted. She realized why she had never tried to kiss a boy before that moment. They were not him. No one would ever be King Arthur. He exuded power and sex, raw masculinity, and as his broad hands clenched into fists, Guinevere couldn't stop picturing what they would do to her. The way they would cage her in, hold her down, grip her throat as he trapped her against his solid frame. She wondered if they would leave bruises if he fucked her, and she had to clench her legs at the thought. She would love to be marked by such a man.

Her visceral reaction wildly embarrassed her when her father forced an introduction. The king seemed annoyed and disinterested, so she kept her eyes downcast, hating her father for tainting their first meeting. Arthur clearly saw through his intentions, and she fought the urge to scream. She wanted no part in his tricks. She longed for Arthur to see her, truly see her, but he wouldn't after her father's obviousness. It was why she told him the truth about her family's debts when she came to his room. She wished, no, needed him to understand that this was not a trap. She wanted nothing from him beyond his hands on every inch of her skin, possessing her until her body was fully and unadulteratedly his. She had tried to fight his gravity dragging her toward his commanding presence. Tried to stay locked away in her bedroom, but before she realized she was moving, she was at his door, unable to stop herself.

Guinevere gasped as Arthur claimed her mouth, and she captured his bottom lip, tentatively exploring the way its fullness felt between her teeth. Arthur growled against her kiss and slid the hand on her back down to seize her ass, dragging her up his body until her belly pressed against him. Gods, he was beautiful, tempting against her soft flesh, and she bit his lip harder. When the blanket had fallen, it had taken every ounce of control to not drop to her knees and take him in her mouth, a primal need dictating her inexperienced lust. He was long and thick, but not so large as to cause her fear. It was exactly how she pictured he would be. Perfect. Hard. Sculpted, begging to be gripped in her hands, and wetness dripped down her thighs. For a moment, her obvious arousal embarrassed her as he shoved his knee between her legs. Wetness coated his skin, but before she could pull away, he groaned into her mouth, their breath mixing, becoming one.

"You are so fucking wet, pretty girl. Put your hands on me," Arthur ordered. "I am yours."

Guinevere slid her fingers into his dark hair, curling the strand into her fist as she gripped hard. He meant only for tonight, but what she would give to be his, truly his. Emboldened by his demand, she tentatively reached her other hand behind him. His thick thighs pressed against her smaller ones, the swell of his ass too large for her small palm, and she moaned so loud she would have been mortified if she hadn't been burning with need. He was a mountain of a man. So much larger than her, yet they fit together flawlessly.

"I am going to ruin you for other men," Arthur growled against her lips, his voice gruff as if it had been dragged to Hell and back. "I am going to fuck you until I leave an imprint within you that no man will ever be able to fill. I promise not to hurt you, but you will never forget the way I feel deep inside your gorgeous little cunt."

Guinevere wanted to beg as she slid her leg around his, desperate for more contact, but Arthur pulled her hair tight until she looked up at him. His dark eyes were almost black with lust, and he smelled like soap and sweat mixed with the perfume from her skin. It was intoxicating, and she breathed in deep, her nipples brushing teasingly against his chest as she inhaled.

"Tell me you want this," he ordered. "Tell me again this is your desire and no one else's."

"Please." Guinevere pulled on his hair, trying to close the distance between their lips. She needed more. She demanded his all. "Please, my king."

Arthur smiled a wicked smile and then hauled her back toward the bed as he said, "Gods, you are perfect when you beg."

He grabbed her hips, and she expected him to throw her to the mattress, but he lay down, dragging her on top of him until she knelt above his face. A moment of panic flashed through her, unsure of what he was doing, but the sight of the King of Camelot between her thighs made her ache.

"I want you to sit on my face until you cannot stand," he said, voice shaking with restraint as he wrapped his broad hands around her thighs and pulled down. "Grab onto the bed frame, Guinevere."

Excitement coiled in her chest, and she obeyed, letting him guide her down as her fingers gripped the wood. Arthur smiled up at her, and Guinevere realized what her life had been missing. His expression wrapped her in its warmth and desire. Embraced her. Ignited her. Ruined her. His harsh face softened, the smile reaching his eyes with glorious beauty. This was where she wanted to be for the rest of her existence. Above him. Below him. Beside him. For a second, neither of them moved. He simply studied her, and for a panicked moment, she wondered if he didn't like what he saw, but then he groaned so loud she thought he might be dying.

"You are so fucking beautiful," he moaned as he dragged his tongue over her, and Guinevere jerked in both shock and pleasure. She had never experienced anything so intense, so delicious. His tongue flicked out again, slipping deeper, and she pulled away slightly, nervous she would suffocate him. Afraid of the electricity raging through her blood.

"Guinevere, I said, sit on my fucking face." His hold on her legs tightened, and he yanked her back down. She sucked in a breath at the pleasure, which only encouraged Arthur. He pulled her thighs harder, guiding her until she was riding him, every lick, every kiss, every stroke of his jaw building the intensity within her until she thought she might explode. She stifled a cry as she gripped the headboard with white knuckles, her mind spinning, spinning, spinning as sensation ravaged her core.

"No," Arthur snarled. "You do not stifle your cries when you're with me. I want to hear how desperate I make you."

Guinevere lost all control at his words and bent over the headboard with a soft scream as she came on his tongue. Gods, he was better than she expected. This was better than she had prayed for. He was not lying. He would ruin her.

Guinevere struggled to regain her breath as she pulled away from his face, but Arthur held tight, refusing to part with her.

"I said I was going to make you come until you couldn't stand. Your legs are working fine, so be a good girl and sit back down."

Guinevere gasped as he yanked her against his mouth, his fingers bruising on her thighs. The sight of her indented muscles stole the air from her lungs, and she released the headboard long enough to brush her fingertips over his. She wondered if his grip would leave a mark. She prayed it did as she seized hold of the bed frame again. A lingering reminder even after he was gone, after his scent washed from her skin. Her heart thundered with such intensity she feared her ribs would break apart with anticipation, and he wasted no time stoking her fire. His tongue moved forward along her entrance until he reached her clit, and as he flicked it, she bucked against his jaw.

"Good girl," he murmured against her. "You are so beautiful riding my face." Their eyes met as he sucked the bundle of nerves between his lips, and Guinevere let go of the headboard to fist his hair. She wanted to touch more of him, hold him close as he devoured her. Her fingers slid between his locks, gripping him so tight she worried she might rip strands out, but she didn't care. She needed more of him, all of him, and she ground down on his face until his teeth gently bit her clit. Her climax was immediate, rolling through her endlessly, beautifully, brutally. Her heart raced, and her voice screamed, but Arthur did not stop. He was determined to drag every ounce of pleasure from her, and her third orgasm hovered on the edge. She pulled his hair harder, and one of his hands left her thighs.

In a haze of blissful lust, she twisted to watch, her breath catching as he gripped his cock. He dragged his hand up his thick shaft, twisting slightly at the head. Pre-cum dripped from him as he slid his fingers back down to the base, his movements controlled but rough. Guinevere's mouth watered at the sight. His fist moved slowly with each stroke as if to show her every glorious inch of him, to let her see what was hers, and the way his hand jerked hard should have embarrassed her, but it only stoked her fire. She had seen nothing that intoxicating, and she watched mesmerized as he stroked himself, all the while licking her, sucking her, kissing her. It was too much. The sight of the king between her thighs, his soft lips on her, his fist pumping his cock with powerful strokes. She couldn't stop watching him as she lost all control, her climax so forceful she almost shattered in tears.

ARTHUR LET her ride out her orgasm, and then he released his aching dick. She was divine, her body so responsive to his every touch, and he worried his actions would disgust her, but instead, watching had made her drip onto his tongue. She tasted delicious. He could feast on her all night, and he felt drunk, the effects of her arousal stronger than wine, sweeter than honey. He would live between her thighs and drown there if she allowed him. Arthur captured her hips and pulled her off his face until she rested on his stomach. Her arousal spread over his abs, and it was enough to make him feral.

"I need to be inside you," he moaned, fighting for restraint as his grip dug into her untouched skin. "But I need you to take charge. If I do, I will fuck you hard and raw, until my cum leaks out of your tight little cunt, and I refuse to hurt you. You are so perfect, Guinevere, that my control is hanging on by a thread."

Guinevere swallowed, her beautiful eyes wide with anticipation as she nodded, and he lifted his back off the bed, leaning on one hand so he could grab the base of her neck with the other.

"Are you all right?" he asked. "If you don't want this—"

She leaned forward and kissed him, silencing him as she drifted backward. She didn't want his protests, only his pleasure, and seeing him fist himself had nearly driven her to insanity. Arthur hissed as she slid against him, and he gripped her neck tighter.

"Slow," he ordered as he possessively guided her back and forth over the underside of his cock. "Coat me in your wetness. Show me how badly you want me to fill this pretty pussy. How badly you want me to fuck you until my cum drips down your thighs, marking you as mine."

Guinevere gasped, her entire body convulsing as she slid against his impressive length, and a wicked smile spread across her lips. She inhaled, suddenly nervous, but then again, so was he. He'd never felt this way about a woman. He had rarely bedded women in his thirty-two years. He had been raised by thieves and whores, and those wonderful women made damn sure he knew how to please his partners. But this woman? He had told her he would ruin her, but he feared that wasn't the truth. He was afraid she would utterly destroy him.

"I won't hurt you," he encouraged. "You're in control." Guinevere sucked in a breath, her eyes nearly rolling back into her skull at his encouragement, and her hand gripped his chest above his thundering heart until her nails bit into his flesh as the other slid along his strong jaw. He still smelled like her, and she leaned forward, the knowledge that he wore her scent driving her insane. They paused. Eyes and hearts and skin locked together, frozen in time, and then slowly she slid her opening against him and sank.

"Don't be nervous," Arthur said through gritted teeth, barely keeping still. The urge to thrust into her was unbearable, but he wouldn't ruin this for her. No, she needed to remember this moment for the rest of her life. "You can take it." She shot him a look filled with nerves and adrenaline, and he lurched forward to bite her bottom lip. It was so soft, so full, and she moaned as she pushed him inside her a bit further.

"Good girl," he encouraged against her mouth. "You can take it. I know you can. Look what a good job you're doing." He drew back and pulled her hair to shift her gaze. "Look at me. I want your eyes as you take all of me. I want to see every gorgeous face you make as I fuck you."

Guinevere hissed at the pain, but the moment the sting shot through her, Arthur let go of her neck and wrapped an arm around her waist. Leaning on his free hand, he yanked her close, sucking a rosy nipple into his mouth. Pleasure seared her core as his tongue flicked the hard nub, and wetness flooded her cunt. Inch by glorious inch, her body welcomed him, possessed him, owned him, and his lips left her nipple to kiss the other.

"You're taking me so well," he praised as he kissed and nipped her breast. "Gods, you feel like you were made for me."

Guinevere moaned and pushed further until his full length slipped inside her. It had been painful, but he let her take control, forced her to go slow until she adjusted around him, and an unbearable need replaced the prick of pain. She needed to come, to feel the king inside her as she orgasmed, and her arms ensnared his neck, clutching him tight against her breasts as she stilled. Arthur tilted his head up, breathless at the goddess wrapped in his embrace, their hearts thundering as one.

"Such a good girl." He kissed her, biting her bottom lip to encourage her as she slowly began to move. "Fuck, Guinevere. I am barely holding on. I need you."

"You have me," she moaned, picking up her pace. With every thrust of her hips, her clit brushed against his skin as he cemented her to his chest, pleasure replacing the sting. They were silent as they moved. His mouth devoured her, their slow movements morphing into desperate thrusts.

"Do you like how full you are?" Arthur bit her nipple, causing Guinevere to yelp, and then he licked it to soothe the pain. He couldn't keep quiet. He needed her to hear every thought racing through his mind. Every emotion she dragged out of him. He would never be the same after this.

"My king…" She was barely coherent as she slid against him, her tongue licking the seam of his mouth as she cried out.

"Good girl, Guinevere, come on my cock."

"My king…" Her voice was loud, but she didn't care if she woke up the entire household. Her climax was so close within reach that she almost tasted its sweetness.

"Come for me, pretty girl." He thrust into her hard, unable to control his madness. "Now, Guinevere."

She screamed as she came undone, and he captured her mouth, swallowing her pleasure with greed. She was so beautiful, and her warmth pulsed around him so strongly that he almost blacked out. He wanted to follow her over the cliff, to pour himself inside her and mark her as his, but he wasn't done. Not yet. If he only had her for one night. he demanded more.

Arthur threw her to the bed, shifting so that he knelt between her thighs before grabbing the back of her neck, propping her up.

"Watch," he ordered, and Guinevere met his gaze with wide eyes. She was not surprised or disgusted. She was hungry, she craved more, and Arthur almost came just from her expression. Had he finally met his match in this woman? Someone as bold and ravenous as him? The thought made his brain fog with desperation. "I want you to watch me fuck you, to see how well you take me."

"Please." She grabbed his wrist and looked up at him with a challenge, knowing exactly what begging did to him. "You are so handsome, my king." She reached out and brushed her fingertips over his abs, over the scars he let no one touch, the scars no one wanted to touch, and he flinched at the contact.

"You don't have to lie," he growled.

"I will never lie to you," she gasped, propping herself up on her elbow to place a hand over his, their fingers becoming one. Together, they stroked her clit as they both watched him slide in and out of her. Guinevere's heart raced at the sight of their joined bodies and hands. This is how they were meant to be. How they were always meant to be. And as she teetered on the brink of the abyss, she gazed at the king with molten heat. Their eyes met, and she knew he sensed it. Something neither of them could explain passed between them, and then Arthur lost control.

"Come, now." His words shoved her over the edge, and she writhed beneath him as pleasure like she had never experienced consumed her body, her hand gripping his as he skillfully massaged her until her knuckles turned white.

"I can't come inside you," Arthur grunted, his voice desperate, his movements feral.

"I know. I'm not here to trap you with a pregnancy." He heard the truth in her words, which only made him thrust harder.

"I can't."

"I know." Guinevere wrapped her legs around him. He could break free if he wished to, and she meant every word. She wasn't trying to trap him, but she wanted to experience everything with him. To experience having him in every way a woman could have a man.

"Guinevere, you feel so good." He collapsed on top of her, and she wrapped her arms and legs around him tight, kissing him deeply, letting him know she wanted him. All of him. She did not let go, her heart racing against his, and then he thrust one final time, coming with a raw and feral roar. Warmth spread inside her, and she pulled him tighter, hoping he recognized just how blissful he had made her.

"You are perfect," he whispered against her mouth as their hearts thundered against each other in a melodic harmony.

"No. I am simply perfect for you."

CHAPTER FIVE

Neither of them spoke. Neither of them moved. Arthur lay atop her overheated body, pushing her into the mattress with his reassuring pressure. Her arms and legs stayed wrapped around him. He did not want to pull out. He didn't want this to be over. Her words rang between them on a melodic loop. *I am just perfect for you.* Fate. That goddamned word again. He had only endured its weight once before when he had seized hold of Excalibur. Holding her was even more intense, and he pulled back slightly to meet her gaze.

Guinevere could not catch her breath, and as Arthur tore his chest away, she wanted to tug him back, to forbid him from leaving her. She felt young and foolish, but a single night would never be enough. Tears threatened to spill down her cheeks as he peeled off her, as a rush of unwelcomed emotions bathed her spirit. She could not leave his bed now and sleep alone. The thought of enduring a lifetime absent his weight, his heat, his possession carved into her soul like a blunt knife. It hacked and sawed and ripped her heart ragged, but then he cupped her face in his calloused palm. He stared at her for a long moment. The confusion and surprise in his eyes mingled with an emotion she couldn't place. There was a gentleness to his rough features he had not shown her before, and then he lowered his lips to hers. Unlike their first kiss, this one was gentle. It was reverent. It was holy. He lingered against her mouth, worshiping her softness as his tongue stroked hers. Truth passed between their spirits, braiding them together, and Guinevere wound her arms tighter around his neck. Neither of them possessed words for how they felt, so the kiss spoke for them. They poured their desires and fears into each other. Their unspoken longing, and when they finally broke apart, breathless and gasping, both understood. They wouldn't say it, but something changed that night as King Arthur kissed Guinevere with more tenderness than he knew himself capable of.

In a daze, Arthur lifted himself off her body and surveyed her now that the haze of lust had cleared. He took his time studying every aspect of her soft flesh, proud of how flushed it was from his hands and mouth. She was flawless, so marked and disheveled by him. He would keep her like this for an eternity if she allowed it.

He rolled to his side and pulled out of her. She gasped slightly at the sudden emptiness, and Arthur watched with pride as she blushed with arousal. Gods, she was demanding, and it was his duty as both man and king to satisfy her.

Arthur propped himself up on his elbow and slid his fingers against the apex of her thighs, groaning as his cum flooded over his skin. He had filled her to overflowing, and for a second, he wondered how she would react if he told her to stand so he might watch it drip out. He didn't want to frighten her, though. He had already pushed her virgin body more than most men would, but unable to ignore the heady power coursing through him from the knowledge of how thoroughly he had taken her, he drove two fingers inside her. He slowly scooped up the liquid, careful to brush her sensitive walls with his knuckles, and then he brought it to hover over her chest.

"Do you see how hard you made me come?" he growled, and her cheeks burned red. So innocent. So brazen. So perfect. *His.* The declaration screamed through his mind. *His. His. His.*

"Look what you did to me." He swiped a finger across her nipple, leaving a streak of cum on her breast, and she jerked off the bed at the contact. "Is this what you wanted?" She nodded. "Say it, Guinevere."

"Yes," she moaned.

"Then take all of it." He pushed his fingers back inside her, stroking her into a frenzy, pushing his cum deeper. "I want you to take every last drop." But what he really meant was, *I want you to take all of me.*

"My king." Guinevere bucked against his hand as his palm pressed against where she needed him most, grabbing his biceps as if trying to remain anchored to the earth. Arthur normally didn't like when women called him that. It reminded him that his title was the only reason they fell into his bed, but on her voice, it was erotic, as if she was so desperate for him all she could do was beg. He leaned down and sucked her nipple between his teeth, but she grabbed his hair and dragged him to her mouth.

"Kiss me," she demanded, and he was helpless but to obey. If he had not witnessed her innocence earlier, he would have assumed her boldness came from experience. It lit a fire in his chest, knowing that she had never been touched, yet was unable to control herself in his arms. He loved how she took what she wanted without shame. It made him long for this night to never end. She kissed him roughly, biting his lower lip, writhing in pleasure beneath him, and when her pussy gripped his fingers, Arthur thought he might pass out.

"I..." Guinevere couldn't speak. She couldn't form sentences. All she knew was his heavy body pressed deliciously against hers. His mouth claimed her lips as he pushed his cum so deep inside her that she would never be free of him. She didn't want to be free of him. This man, with his scars and his scowls, would be her undoing, and she kissed him harder as she climaxed. He swallowed her cries, and when she finally stopped spasming, she collapsed to the bed.

"I would say now your legs cannot stand." Arthur's voice was thick as he teased. "I cannot get enough of you." He was suddenly serious. "Did I...?"

"Ruin me for other men?" she cut him off, cupping his face. She refused to let him go there. There was no room for regret. Not after how he had made her come alive with vibrant colors. With gentle fingers she traced his healed nose, crooked but strong after the breaks. "Irrevocably."

Arthur smiled with pride, and she was once again struck by how magnificent the expression was. It was so uncharacteristic of his features. She wondered if she was one of the few he had graced with it. She prayed she was. She coveted that for herself.

Arthur bent and kissed her forehead as he withdrew his fingers. She grimaced slightly at the movement. He knew she would be sore tomorrow, but the thought pleased him. Every time she moved, she would feel him still inside her. He never wanted her to forget that sensation.

He dragged himself off of the bed, his body screaming to return to her side, and he snatched her sheer robe off the floor. Fear flickered through her features that he intended to send her out into the cold alone, but Arthur was far too selfish to allow the night to end. He poured some of the water sitting on a table into a mug before dumping the rest onto the robe. He handed her the cup, and as she drank, he gently brushed the cool, damp fabric between her thighs. He took his time, careful not to hurt her. Careful to worship her. Careful to show her she was his. He noticed her watching his every movement from over the cup's rim. He loved how much she enjoyed looking at him. He knew he wasn't handsome, but under her heated gaze, he felt almost beautiful.

When he finished, Arthur threw the ruined robe to the floor, and Guinevere handed him the water without breaking eye contact. He drank every drop she had saved for him, placing the mug on the table before wrapping a massive forearm around her waist. He lay down without a word and pulled her spine to his heart, trapping her in a warm embrace. She didn't fight him, pushing herself into him until they were no longer two bodies. With reverent fingers, she grabbed the wrist clinging to her belly and held on, afraid if she let go, he might disappear. She fit perfectly against his chest, in his arms, around his cock, and suddenly Arthur couldn't stop himself.

"Stay with me?" he whispered in her ear. He meant for tonight. He meant forever. He didn't know what he meant. This wasn't him. He was not so easily seduced, but a nagging thought tugged at his brain. This wasn't seduction. This was fate. She was destined for him.

Guinevere remained silent, and Arthur gave up waiting for a response. Perhaps his request had scared her, but she hadn't left, so he accepted that. He settled behind her, burying his nose in her fragrant hair. His breathing slowed, and just as he drifted off, her voice whispered into the darkness.

She thought he was asleep, her confession safe. Hidden. A secret. But Arthur heard it as sleep claimed him.

"Always."

A SOFT KNOCK sounded at the door, and Arthur groaned. He would murder whoever it was. It was too early to be disturbed, and Guinevere still lay trapped in his arms. He wasn't ready to give her up yet.

Guinevere.

Arthur sat up, untangling himself from her warm body with a kiss to her shoulder. He couldn't let anyone find her here. He would get rid of the intruder and then sneak her to her room. Padding naked across the floor, he cracked the door to see who interrupted his peace.

"My king." Gawain's voice was low but urgent. Too urgent. Something was wrong. "He's been spotted not far from here. If we leave now, we should be able to catch him."

Mordred. As fiercely as Arthur longed to go back to bed, he had to leave. He could not allow the mage to escape, and with a pain in his gut, he glanced over his shoulder at the sleeping Guinevere. She had asked for only one night. He had granted her that request, and his normally harsh demeanor settled over his features, replacing the temporary peace she had brought him. He was king. His title demanded responsibility.

"Ready the men," Arthur said coldly, and Gawain nodded, choosing not to acknowledge the harshness in his king's tone. He left obediently, making it halfway down the corridor before Arthur's voice sounded again.

"Fetch me a maid and gather the household in the dining hall."

The knight stopped and twisted around, squinting at the anger on his friend's face. The entire household this early? He had assumed news of Mordred would lift the king's spirits, but it appeared to bring him pain. He was upset about something, but Gawain could not fathom what, so he simply nodded.

CHAPTER SIX

Guinevere woke. The absence of the strong warmth surrounding her jarred her back to reality. Arthur was gone. Her one night with the king had vanished into memory, the only proof was the soreness between her legs. Guinevere drew in a shaky breath. She hadn't expected the fall to reality to be so unforgiving, but lying in the solitude stirred an ache in her chest. She almost wished Arthur had been boring and uninspired. At least then she could walk away without a backward glance, but the knowledge of how he played her body like a musician, how he ignited a forest fire in her bones, combined with the unnerving sense of foreboding that had passed between them made waking alone painful. The bitter-sweet aftermath clung to her skin, and she clenched her eyes shut to keep from crying. She rarely shed tears, her lack of hope for her future forging her into steel, but this new dawn was a slap to the face. She hated how her chest ached. She didn't believe in love at first sight, but Arthur's kiss had felt like home. Like the final piece of her heart clicking into place, and she wanted to scream at her naivety. To scold her traitorous organ for believing she could have more out of life. That she could have him.

Guinevere exhaled slowly and unclenched her eyes, thankful no tears slipped free. The soft sunlight surprised her. It was early. Too early. Something had driven the king from her side, and that fact stung more than waking alone. He clearly could not wait to escape her. Had she made a mistake coming here? Had he woken this morning and been revolted by how she flung herself at him, seeing her in the light as just another desperate woman eager for the king's favor? Perhaps it was for the best. She would never see him again. Maybe it was better if he left disgusted and did not prolong her heartache. At least at this hour, no one should be awake, especially after consuming her father's ale. She would wrap the blankets around her and flee to her room. No one would have to witness her shame.

Guinevere pushed herself up, wincing at her aching muscles, and then turned around. She jerked at the sight, gasping a short, unattractive sound before clamping her lips together. Arthur sat fully dressed in a chair, staring at her. Excalibur hung strapped to his back, the same blood-stained clothes and ruthless scowl from last night adorning him. A thread of fear flickered through her at his gaze. Gone was the desire, the kindness, the worship. All that remained was the savage warrior and a swath of crimson fabric. Her fear doubled when she realized what lay draped across his lap. Her red dress. She had not brought it with her, which meant he had requested a maid deliver it. If one maid knew, then they all would come evening. Word of her lost innocence would spread, and even if the servant took this secret to her grave, the fact that he held last night's gown was proof he intended for all to discover her indiscretion. Why request that dress unless to prove she hadn't slept in her own room?

Guinevere threw a panicked look into Arthur's cold eyes. Had she been so mistaken? He would not forsake his duty and marry her, a girl who offered the crown nothing, but she had not expected him to be cruel. Bile rose in her throat, but she shoved both it and her tears down. She would not cry. She would not give him that satisfaction.

"Get dressed." Arthur thrust the dress at her but made no move to stand, making it clear he intended for her to vacate the bed. For a moment, Guinevere considered refusing. Considered denying him the pleasure of seeing her one last time, but the look on his face wiped any urge to rebel from her. She scowled instead and threw back the blankets. Let him try to humiliate her. He could not rob her of her dignity without her permission, and she clung to it as if it were armor.

She rose completely bare and snatched the dress, stepping into it with aching muscles. Thankfully, his gaze did not drop to her body but lingered on her face as she dressed. As soon as the fabric covered her breasts, he stood and moved behind her, helping her with the small buttons, and the action surprised her. He hovered so close that she felt his heat, the roughness of his fingertips, the softness of his breath. She hated herself for it, but gods, she wanted him to slip his hands around her waist, to lower his lips to her neck, to tell her she was never allowed to leave him. But when the last button popped into place, he stepped away, taking her longing with him.

"Come." Arthur grabbed her biceps and dragged her out into the hallway. His grip was firm but not painful, his hand simply meant to keep her from fleeing his control, and Guinevere ordered herself not to cry. No matter what he did, no matter what he said, she would not cry. Even as her heart sank with every step, his determined grasp so different from his hold on her last night, she would not shed a single tear.

Arthur led her through the dimly lit corridors and pushed her into the dining hall. The sight that greeted them made Guinevere's stomach heave, and she bit the inside of her mouth to keep from crying out. The entire household, along with her father and Arthur's knights, stood waiting for them. Waiting as the king dragged a disheveled Guinevere behind him, wearing last night's dress. Despite their wildly hungover stares, she saw the realization hit the room's inhabitants at the same time. They all understood what this meant, and she made the mistake of meeting her father's gaze. Disgust riddled his features. She was his only child, but by the rigid line of his frown, she had lost that right. He would never forgive this humiliation.

"Did you send your daughter to seduce me? To trap your king with a pregnancy?" Arthur stormed to her father, pulling her against his body. His hand still lingered on her biceps, but he plastered her back to his chest, his thighs pressed firmly against hers as if they were one flesh. The intimate touch and protective stance warred with his bitter tone, but she was thankful for the support of his large frame. If he had not been holding her, the sheer revulsion on her father's face would have plunged her to her knees.

"My king," Leodegrance stammered. "I would never dishonor you so."

"I would choose your next words carefully," Arthur warned. "Do not lie to the king."

"I would never do such a disgraceful thing," her father spat. "Anything that happened was the actions of my whore of a daughter."

Arthur flinched against her as if the man's answer slapped him in the face, and it gave her the courage to peer up over her shoulder at him. Rage simmered in his eyes, and his grip tightened on her slightly. She squinted in confusion at his reaction. Her father's outburst carved out her heart with agony, but the king's expression steadied her. She couldn't explain it, but by the way his muscles coiled behind her like a predator readying for the kill, by the way he pulled her closer even though she was already plastered against his skin, she wondered yet again if she had misjudged him. He seemed savage at the insults directed at her. Like he could barely contain his fury at the slander.

"So, you did not order her to trap me so that I would be forced to wed her and pay off your debts?" Arthur pushed.

"No... I could not bring this house such embarrassment... Guinevere, what have you done, you ungrateful "

"But you are in debt?" Arthur interrupted before he could fling the insult.

"Yes, my king." Leodegrance bowed his head in shame.

"And you knew I would never marry a woman with so little to offer?"

"I—" Leodegrance swallowed. "Of course not, my lord."

"You assumed the only chance of raising your station was to trap me with a scandal, then?"

"No, my king." Her father turned ferocious, lunging forward as if to slap Guinevere in his rage, but Arthur deftly pulled her behind him to block any blows, his massive body an impenetrable fortress for her safety.

"So last night was entirely your daughter's idea?"

"Yes, my king. And I beg you not to hold her disgrace against me. She acted alone, bringing shame to this house."

"Good." Arthur turned to Guinevere, his voice suddenly soft, his eyes kind, and Guinevere's emotions experienced a violent whiplash at the abrupt change in his temper. "That is all I wanted to confirm. That she truly meant what she said, and that she was not forced."

"My—" Leodegrance started.

"I would watch your fucking mouth," Arthur growled, whirling to pin her father with a vicious stare. "You have said enough. I expected you to defend your daughter and saddle yourself with the blame before admitting the truth, but you have shown your true colors. If I ever catch you talking about Guinevere like that again, I will rip out your fucking tongue."

The entire room froze in shock, and a rush of heat flooded

Guinevere's icy veins. Her mind was spinning, her stomach churning, and then Arthur turned back to her, grabbing her smaller hands in his rough ones.

"I am sorry." His mouth was moving, but Guinevere wasn't sure she heard correctly. She thought she might be sick, and the walls were spiraling. "I had to know." Her gaze snapped to his. He was still speaking. "People tell the truth when they are afraid of me, and I had to be certain your father wasn't forcing you."

"I..." she started, trailing off in confusion as he pulled her softly before him, gripping her hands reverently.

"Father," Arthur nodded his head. "You may proceed."

Guinevere hadn't noticed the priest, but suddenly he stood before them, his monotone voice droning on in prayer. She stared at his holy robes, not understanding a single word he uttered. She had not consumed alcohol, wanting to remember her night with the king with vivid clarity, but she felt intoxicated and out of control. Everyone was staring at her. Her father was scowling. Arthur was smiling. The tender expression just for her. Its beauty heartbreaking. The priest was speaking, but his words were a jumbled mess.

"Guinevere," Arthur whispered, and her gaze shot to his. The room was a blur, a hurricane of sounds and colors, but her focus settled on him, her anchor in the chaos.

"I'm sorry, I scared you," he repeated as the priest mumbled on endlessly, endlessly, endlessly. "Please forgive me. You deserve something more glamorous than this, than me. I am not a romantic. Not an artist with my words. I'm a warrior and a brute, but I needed to confirm you spoke the truth. That your father was not forcing you. I told you, I have no desire for an unwilling woman, and this morning, we received word of Mordred. I must leave immediately, and I will not be coming back."

Guinevere blinked up at him and swore she heard the priest

say marriage, but Arthur spoke before her brain could process the overwhelming noise.

"I know you felt it too, and I can't abandon you here. One night will never be enough, Guinevere. I said I would ruin you for other men, but the thought of anyone touching you makes me violent. I will kill any man who lays a hand on you because I can't fight this pull in my chest. It raged to life the moment I saw you, the moment I kissed you. You are my destiny, but I won't bring you to the city in shame to be devoured by the wolves. I never wish to spend another night apart from you, but if you arrive at the castle unwed, I will only continue to humiliate you by visiting your bed. I won't do that to you. You deserve to be there in honor and safety. Guinevere, I want you to come to Camelot as my wife."

Guinevere balked, reeling away from him in shock, his hands the only thing keeping her attached to the earth. Marriage? Her sight flung to the priest, and she suddenly recognized his droning. This was a wedding. Her wedding. To the king. Her eyes returned to Arthur's in panic. Surely, he was making a fool of her. He did not mean it, but his expression welded her feet to the floor. He looked at her as if she was all his hopes and dreams.

"I will not insult you by pretending I love you," Arthur repeated her own words back to her as the priest began a prayer. "I am not known for my charm. I am neither young nor handsome, but I promise you this. I will spend every second making you happy. It will take time, yet I have faith you will one day love me. I can't fight this overwhelming sense that you are mine. I could court you instead of marrying you today, but Guinevere, my desire won't weaken. Whether I marry now or in twenty years, I will never change my mind. I can't explain it, but I don't think I need to. You already understand."

She opened her mouth, but the priest's question rang loud like a tolling bell.

"I do," Arthur vowed.

"And do you, Guinevere, take King Arthur to be your lawfully wedded husband till death do you part?" the priest asked.

"Marriage?" Guinevere blurted. "You're marrying me?"

"If you'll have me?" Arthur smiled. Gods, that expression on his lips was perfect, and it made her want to give him everything, but she stepped back slightly, causing his smile to falter.

"Do I get a say?" she asked. "Or are you forcing me?" Her father hissed in disapproval behind her, but she couldn't stop herself. Something nagged at the recesses of her mind. She had accepted that any betrothal she entered would be forced upon her, and suddenly, standing before the king, terrified her. Anyone else, and she would endure the arrangement, but not him. She yearned for this to be real. She needed this marriage to be honest.

"I..." Arthur started, and every guest stilled. "I thought you chose this. Last night?" He dropped her hands as if they were hot coals, and his expression fell. "Of course, I won't force you. I am sorry I misread what you said. I must have dreamt it."

Always. He had not dreamt it. She meant it.

"You want your wife to want you," she whispered, stepping closer so that she had to crane her neck to meet his towering gaze. "I hoped for someone who wouldn't force me. If I say no. You won't punish me or my father?"

"Of course not," Arthur reached out involuntarily and brushed her hair behind her ear, surprising the crowd with his tenderness. "If you do not accept my proposal, I will pay your father's debts and find you a suitable husband, even if the notion of you with anyone else kills me. I won't make you unhappy."

"I do." Guinevere's voice was so loud she surprised herself, and Arthur jerked at her words, certain her broad smile would blind him. "That is all I wanted. Thank you for giving me a choice. You were my choice last night. You are my choice this morning." She grabbed his head and pulled him down to her. "I do. I do. I do."

Arthur seized her waist and hoisted her against his chest, silencing her vow with a kiss. Their lips sealed their promise, and Guinevere wrapped her arms around his neck, pulling him closer as his mouth claimed hers. She was his. Truly his, and tears spilled down her cheeks, coating his skin with her joy. She vaguely heard the priest pronounce them married, but in her heart, she belonged to King Arthur the moment she laid eyes on him. He was right. She couldn't explain it either, but she had felt it all the same. This man was her destiny, her future. She didn't love him. Not yet, but she would.

"Don't cry," he murmured against her lips. "I'll make you happy, I promise."

She kissed him harder, not caring they had an audience. Her voice was trapped in her throat, threatening to break if she unleashed it, so she curled her fingers in his hair and let her body speak for her.

I believe you.

CHAPTER SEVEN

Guinevere's kiss was like lightning ravaging his body, its searing intensity rendering him helpless in her embrace. The sensation of her lips devouring him, her tongue dancing along his combined with the way her fingers gripped his hair and her breasts nearly spilled out of her dress as she pressed against his heart had him worried he would lose all control and take her right here in front of the priest. He needed to put her down. He had already caused her enough humiliation for one morning.

With a groan of regret, Arthur lowered her down his body, careful to drag her seductively against his chest, slowing at his hips so she could feel every inch of his hard length, and he swallowed her gasps with a greedy inhale. Her scent drove him wild. The perfume she wore still lingered on her skin, and it mixed with the faintest hint of him, reminding him of how perfectly ruined she looked below him last night. Yes, he needed to release his new wife before he couldn't meet any of his friends' gazes.

"I have to go," he murmured against her mouth. The entire wedding took less than a quarter of an hour, but every minute he stayed with her was a minute Mordred slipped further from his grasp. He refused to allow the mage to escape. Not again. "Once I return to Camelot, I will send for you."

"No." Guinevere caught his wrist as he stepped back. "You cannot leave me on our wedding day."

"I have to."

"Then I'm coming with you." Her fingers dug into him until the bite of her nails stung his skin.

"It's not safe."

"I don't care."

"I will send for you in a few days, I promise."

"No." Her voice barreled out of her like a battle cry, and Arthur froze at her defiance. Her father lunged forward to pull her away, to quell her refusal, but Arthur tilted his icy gaze toward the man. Leodegrance recoiled instantly. No one was brave enough to challenge him when his eyes burned dark and his jaw clenched tight. The king was not a man of idle threats. A lesson too many had learned the hard way.

Arthur returned his attention to his bride and read the surprise plastered across her face as if her defiance surprised even her. He had the distinct sense that until he upended her life, she did as she was told. That she lived a subservient existence, resigned to obey the men in authority, but as if he had come along and unlocked her cage, the challenge resurfaced in her eyes. Arthur scowled and stepped forward, his looming height oppressive as it settled above her. He was not angry at her outburst. Quite the opposite. It turned him on to witness the passion flaring through her, to know that he had freed her beast, and gods, did he need to see it spread its wings and roar. He wanted to test how committed she was to this newfound confidence. If she would do what no man was brave enough to do. Defy him. He hoped she would. He didn't want a broken, submissive wife. He craved electricity and a zeal for life. An equal. A partner. He hoped she refused to surrender, but then the image of her on her knees flickered through his imagination, and he stifled a grin. Maybe he demanded a little submission. A few moments where he reigned in her fire and watched her blossom under his commands.

"You do not get to leave me on our wedding day," she said, stepping closer to him, accepting his challenge, and it took all his control not to fall to his knees and worship her. She was made for him.

"Is this how our marriage is going to be?" His voice was low and gruff, and the room recoiled at the tone, but they could not see his eyes. Only Guinevere had that pleasure, and the desire rippling through them told her exactly what answer he desired.

"Undoubtedly."

Arthur's lip twitched attractively as he groaned. "I am leaving now. Pack fast."

Guinevere flashed a smile of triumph and then turned on her heels. Before she took two steps, Arthur caught her skirt and wound it tight around his fist, jerking her to a stop. She threw a glance over her shoulder as he pulled the fabric in his grip, just as he had her hair the night before.

"Bring this dress," he ordered, his eyes molten lava. Guinevere nodded, and he released his hold. The instant she was free, she bolted from the room, and Arthur grunted as she disappeared. He already felt her gravity dragging him to the edge. It would take little to convince him to leap.

"Percival, send the army back to Camelot. We need to move fast. Only the knights will hunt Mordred with me," Arthur barked, and his knights jerked collectively, as if waking from a trance. They had watched the entire proceedings with shocked disbelief. Arthur was a man of blood and action, war and pain.

He had been with a few women in the past, but he was always level-headed around the opposite sex. They had never seen him look at a woman the way he stared at the young Guinevere, and Gawain was convinced he had drunk so much ale that he hallucinated the entire morning.

"Now." Arthur cocked his head at Percival when no one moved, and the knights scrambled from the room, thankful to escape the strangest morning they had experienced in ages. Only Merlin seemed undisturbed by the sudden marriage, and Arthur got the unnerving sense he had foreseen this. He wouldn't ask his friend. Merlin would deny it, but even if he hadn't expected Guinevere, he seemed to recognize the pull of fate braiding the couple's lives together.

"A beautiful bride, my king." Merlin clapped Arthur on the back with a wise smile. "May God bless you and your reign."

Arthur grunted his thanks and said, "Please see to it Leodegrance's debts are paid." Merlin bowed, and Arthur turned to his host. "I will be good to your daughter. I advise you to do the same. Do not abuse her position. She now wears my crown, and I expect you to serve it responsibly."

Leodegrance prostrated himself embarrassingly low, mumbling endless words of thanks and ass-kissing, but Arthur ignored him. It was more than he deserved. This was his wedding gift to his wife, but the way the man had spoken about his own daughter boiled rage in his gut. That was the last time anyone talked about Guinevere with such disrespect and lived to greet another day.

ARTHUR and his men had barely finished saddling their horses when Guinevere ran out into the warm morning air wearing a simple dress, a small pack slung across her back. She was still beautiful in the humble fabric, and the worn hem and fraying sleeves gave him the distinct impression that servants alone did not run this household. This woman was clearly no stranger to hard work, and that both surprised him and warmed his heart. Her speed also surprised him. Most women at court would deliberate half the day, but Guinevere had packed in minutes. His lips tilted in the faintest of smiles at her as she slowed to a halt, out of breath and flushed. She was so unlike anyone he had ever met, reminding him of himself when he was younger. Level-headed and primed for action. Willing to put her own hands to the difficult tasks. If this was any indication of her true nature, they would get along well.

"Do you have an extra horse?" she asked as he tugged the small pack from her shoulders. He peeled back the flap to confirm the red dress was inside and then attached it to his saddle. "My father needs his. I prefer not to take one if I don't have to."

Arthur said nothing. He merely slipped his muscled forearm around her waist and drew her to his chest, guiding her to his horse. It was a monster of a beast, bred for power and war. It would carry both of them with ease, and Arthur had no intentions of letting her ride anywhere else except before him. He hoisted her to the saddle and then climbed wordlessly behind her, wrapping the reins around his fist as his other arm remained curled across her belly. She was so small compared to him, fitting effortlessly in the hollow of his chest, and he couldn't stop himself from lowering his nose and breathing in the scent of her hair.

"I will send for the rest of your things once we reach Camelot," he said, thankful she did not protest his decision to have her ride with him, groaning softly as she shifted her hips to find a comfortable seat. He moved his hand from her belly and gripped her hip tight, stopping the movement. They had to leave. He didn't have time to make her his wife in every sense of the word, but so help him, if she did not stop moving—

"I need nothing else from here," she said as she ground backward. Her voice was steady, but he knew her movement was deliberate. There was no hiding how hard he was, and despite his increasing frustration, he loved how she pushed against him instead of shying away.

"Nothing?" Arthur leaned forward to look at her face, her words finally registering through the haze of lust. He wondered if she assumed that as his wife, he would furnish her with new and expensive belongings or if this home and her father had left such a bitter taste in her mouth that she couldn't bear to bring any of it with her.

"I don't have much, and I gave what I did to my maid." Her answer was not what he expected, and she shifted to peer into his eyes. "My father and the servants need my things more than I do. I only brought the essentials and some of my mother's belongings. I can't leave those."

Arthur grunted and urged his horse forward to where her father waited. Once again, she surprised him, and he vowed that when they arrived at Camelot, he would gift her everything she desired.

"I only wanted what was best," Leodegrance said as they paused before him, and Guinevere leaned down to take his hand.

"I know." She smiled, and Arthur pinched his brow at her. Despite his degrading words, she still felt kindness toward the man. He could learn a lot from his new wife.

"You will make a beautiful queen." Her father clutched her fingers.

"Thank you. I will see you soon. I'll send for you once I am settled."

"Of course, my daughter." Leodegrance glanced at Arthur as if afraid he would refuse him, but the king nodded his agreement. If Guinevere wanted to see her father, he would not stop her. He would make sure the man held his tongue, though.

"Safe journeys," her father continued as he released her hand. "Your mother would be so proud. I'll say a prayer for her."

"As will I." Sadness tinged her voice, and Arthur's arm tightened around her waist in comfort. Instinctively, Guinevere gripped his wrist. "I will write."

Leodegrance stepped back, and Arthur urged his horse forward, his knights and Merlin close on his heels.

"May God bless you and keep you," her father called as they rode off, and Guinevere peered around the mountain that was her new husband and waved until everything she knew disappeared.

GUINEVERE SHIFTED UNCOMFORTABLY. He had not hurt her beyond what claiming her virginity required, and she savored the ache between her thighs, the strong chest at her back, the entombing grip around her waist, but after an hour at this intense speed, she found herself shifting often to ease her stiff muscles.

Arthur seemed to sense her need for a reprieve and slowed his horse. Gawain caught his eye, and a wordless conversation passed between them. The knights pulled ahead before matching their pace, giving the newlyweds the appearance of privacy.

Guilt over her discomfort spiked through his chest, but if forced to be honest, Arthur longed for a moment alone with her. They had barely spoken during their brief acquaintance, and while he was not much of a conversationalist, he wanted to hear her voice. To learn about her and listen to her stories, her laugh, her thoughts. They needed to move fast if they were going to capture Mordred, but even the horses needed to catch their breath. They could afford a rest long enough for him to have his first genuine conversation with his wife.

"I apologize for this morning," he said as he adjusted her into a more comfortable position against him. "I didn't plan to scare you, but I'm not good at this. Talking. Romance. You deserved a grander wedding than that, and I should have handled your father with more grace. We were in a rush, and after that single word you gifted me last night when you thought I was asleep, I knew I couldn't leave you. One night would never suffice, and I believed you. I trusted you sought me out of your own free will, but I needed to ensure you hadn't been unconsciously manipulated."

"Can I ask you a question?" Guinevere twisted to glimpse his profile, his powerfully angled jaw and crooked nose begging for her touch, but she held onto the forearm circling her waist instead.

"Anything you want, I am yours."

"Why the red dress?"

"Because it makes me hard." The answer was so matter-of-fact that Guinevere burst into laughter, and Arthur grimaced at his bluntness. "My apologies. I told you I wasn't good at this."

"I thought you were trying to humiliate me by parading me around in last night's clothes." She paused and studied his face. "Although you announced I did not sleep alone, so the dress was irrelevant. In the end, your intentions were not to disgrace me, so I forgive you. I understand what it's like to have people demand something you're unwilling to give."

"I was all adrenaline and chaos. If you'll allow this confession, I've never woken up next to a woman before. You were in my arms, and then Mordred's sighting forced me to leave your bed, yet all I could think about was marrying you in that red dress."

Guinevere smiled, her cheeks blushing a beautiful pink, and Arthur couldn't stop himself. He leaned forward and pressed his lips against her soft neck. He gripped her hip tighter, drawing her back against him, and her skin flushed under his kiss. They lingered for a moment as if they had existed together for an eternity and not only a day, but then she twisted slightly.

"Speak your mind, wife," Arthur murmured against her throat before straightening. He practically heard her thoughts rattling in her brain. "Never hide from me. I want to hear your voice."

"I understand the desire to marry someone who genuinely wants you, but can I ask why it was so important to you?" She looked at him, and this time, she did not stop her fingers from tracing his face. She would spend a lifetime looking at him and never grow tired of his harsh lines and sharp angles. Most men had simple and expected faces. His was interesting, it told a story, and while some might look at it and find it severe or frightening, she wanted nothing more than to drag her lips across his jaw, to lick her way up to his ear before tracing his nose with kisses. "You could claim any woman. Money, power, beauty. Everything. Most kings would have taken that with no concern for the bride's desires."

"I assumed I would marry for Camelot, but I promised myself it would be an equal marriage, both of us offering what the other needed," Arthur said, shocked that he was about to tell her this. He never told anyone the true longings of his heart, but the way her fingers brushed his skin had him unable to resist. "Even without love, there would be respect, and a partnership could grow from that."

"I bring nothing to the table," Guinevere said, her voice faltering for the first time since they met, and he hugged her closer to his chest as if to force his conviction from his heart into hers.

"You bring everything to the table," he growled, angry that

she thought of herself as anything less than worthy. "I was an orphan, a thief no better than a diseased rat until a sword crowned me king. Your family name far outranks mine, so it is I who am unworthy of you," he teased into her ear, but his words did not remove the worry lines from her forehead. He took a deep breath and opened his mouth. It frightened him to be so honest with someone. He preferred a blade to emotions, but he needed her to understand. He needed to voice it for himself just as much as her.

"I know what it is like to be unwanted," his voice was cold, as if to detach himself from the truth. "I grew up on the streets, and no one looked twice at me save the thieves and the whores. They were far kinder than the nobles, and while I thank God for them, I still went to bed alone and frightened. During the day, I fought and bled, lied and cheated to survive, but at night, the emptiness flooded back. Men would spit on me as they passed me by, and then my rebellion against the oppression led me to Excalibur. Suddenly, because a sword found me worthy, I was king, and those same men who spat on me begged for my favor. They wanted my protection and my wealth, for me to marry their daughters. They forgot the boy in rags they kicked out of their way, but I did not. I remembered their cruelty."

Guinevere sucked in a breath and laced her fingers between his, leaning her head against his solid chest. Their embrace was intimate, comfortable as their breath fell in sync, and the simple movement echoed with profound unity. She knew Arthur led the rebellion before he seized the throne, but she had never known the truth of his childhood. It broke her heart. She was glad she sat before him, unable to look into his eyes. She suspected he wouldn't be able to tell her the truth if she watched him.

"Nights are the loneliest," he continued, his voice almost monotone as he fought to show her the dark parts of his soul he never allowed to see the light. "And as king, I could claim any woman, but I remember the disgust aimed at me. I recognize when a woman desires the crown and not the man wearing it. The thought of spending my days fighting for Camelot only to sleep beside someone unwilling to be there makes me sick. I longed for a wife that wanted the man alongside the throne. A woman who enjoyed my presence, who I could speak honestly with and ask council from. A lofty fantasy, and one I never expected to have fulfilled, but then lying next to you, waking next to you, I caught a glimpse of that dream. I wanted you to choose me. I hope this marriage grows into something real. You have everything to offer. Your wealth doesn't matter. You do."

Arthur fell silent, embarrassed by how much he revealed. Neither of them spoke for long moments, and with each passing second, he worried he had confessed too much. He never admitted these feelings to anyone, and fear clawed at his gut. He leaned forward and noticed tears gathering in her eyes. Sickness roiled through his stomach. He should have kept his mouth shut. He should stick to what he knew, death and the blade.

"You do not give yourself enough credit," Guinevere finally said as she swiped the tears from her cheek. Arthur's gut clenched at her movement. They were not even married a day, and he had already made her cry. "You say you aren't romantic, but I've never heard anyone speak like that." She twisted and pressed her lips to his jaw in a quick kiss, and he jerked in surprise. "I've received a few marriage offers, and each suitor talked about my beauty. About how my youth would grant me many years of childbirth and how their wealth would elevate my family's status. I knew I would never have a choice in who I wed, so their shallow words never affected me, but your proposal didn't mention how beautiful I am. You never alluded to my age or my ability to provide you with an heir. You did not use your crown to seduce me."

Arthur looked at her in confusion, not sure if he should feel guilty that he never complimented her beauty or thankful. She was intoxicating, a stunning angel he did not deserve, but her melodic voice continued, strangling his thoughts.

"You are the first person who truly saw me down to my very core. Last night, someone finally took note of the real Guinevere and liked her, and you believe I can be the partner to comfort you through the storms." She swiped at her eyes again. "I've always been afraid of marriage. I am well aware of the cruelty a man can inflict on his wife; of the force he can use against her. My father received proposals from some such men, and if he signed a contract with them, I would be theirs to torture. It is why I asked you if I had a choice. I can't explain it, but whatever this is, feels real, and I couldn't bear it if you had forced me. I wanted it to be genuine." Her voice was small and nervous. "Thank you for that."

"I do see you," Arthur pressed a kiss to her cheek, the salt of her tears stinging his lips. "I want to see all of you. Hide nothing from me. It's the only way we will learn to love each other."

"You say you are not a romantic." She rested her head against him, and he had the overwhelming sense that she felt safe in his arms. Pride welled in his chest at the thought. She was safe. All of her was safe with him. "But what you say is more important than how you say it, and I like your words, my king."

"Call me Arthur. Call me by my name. I won't pretend that my title wasn't attractive to you, and Guinevere, I don't care if part of your reason for wanting to marry me was because I am the king, but I am more than just the throne. That is all I ask. That you see all of me. So please call me Arthur, because that is who I am."

"Arthur." She tasted his name, and the sound sent a bolt of lust through his veins. He would never tire of hearing it on her lips, but then a memory flashed through his mind. How she had orgasmed with *my king* on her cries, and he pushed his mouth against her ear, his voice like thick smoke and smooth whiskey mingling on his tongue.

"The only time I want you to call me *my king* is when I am inside of you, so that everyone knows who is making you scream."

Chapter Eight

They spent the rest of the afternoon in relative silence as they rode, and by early evening, they rendezvoused with the scouts tracking Mordred. They had pursued him to the foothills just beyond a small hamlet, and Arthur slowed to a stop as its inhabitants gathered to catch a sight of the king.

"There looks to be an inn here," Arthur said as he leaped from the horse before helping Guinevere down, and she scowled at his graceful movements. She was stiff everywhere from the ride and envied his unaffected body.

"You will stay here with a guard until I return." Arthur stepped forward until he was towering over her, his features like etched stone. "I admire your fire. I want you to speak your mind, to challenge me, to be free and in control of your own thoughts and actions. Tell me no. Tell me I am wrong when no one else is brave enough to, but Guinevere, in times of danger or war, I expect your absolute obedience. I need you to listen to me and do exactly as I command. If I say run, you run. If I ask you to hide, then you hide. If you are not where you are supposed to be, I can't protect you, and if I'm worried about your safety, I won't be able to focus. It could get me or my men killed. Get you killed."

"You have my word." She captured his calloused hand in hers. "I will obey without hesitation."

A weight lifted off the king's shoulders, and he bent, placing a reverent kiss on her forehead. "Thank you."

He withdrew, but Guinevere tilted her head before he could escape and pressed her lips against his. Arthur's retreat halted as he savored her softness, debating a delicious idea.

"There is one other place I would enjoy your absolute obedience," he whispered, leaning forward until her dark hair brushed against his mouth. The grate of his voice electrocuted Guinevere's skin. "If I tell you to get on your knees. I expect you to do it."

He rose with the devil in his grin, taking her breath with him, and for a long second, Guinevere stood before him with wide eyes. He could almost see her heart thundering beneath her ribs, and every desperate gasp she took pushed her breasts against her dress as if they demanded his touch, his friction instead of the fabric. Her hands clenched at her sides, struggling to resist grabbing hold of him, and then, with the challenge in her gaze he was already addicted to, she exhaled.

"We shall see."

He smirked at her defiance. Such fight in her small frame. Her words were brave, but he could tell by the pink blooming on her cheeks and the darkness flooding her irises that she had every intention of submitting to him. That the idea of bending to his will and letting him control her body, her pleasure, pushed her arousal to its breaking point.

He turned away from her without another word and led his horse to Gawain, grabbing his friend's biceps and pulling him close.

"You will stay with her."

"My king?"

"I know you don't understand. I barely understand my actions myself, but that is my wife, and I trust no one more than you. Protect her in my absence."

Gawain met the king's gaze before throwing a quick glance over his shoulder. Arthur was right. He didn't understand, but he also knew his friend. They had fought side by side, their blood and sweat shed together, and Gawain would die for his king without a second's hesitation. Arthur had never steered him wrong, and if this young woman was his chosen queen, Gawain would not argue.

He gave a single nod, and Arthur returned the gesture as he silently mounted his horse. Gawain withdrew to where Guinevere stood and watched his king ride into danger without him to guard his back, his gut twisting. Arthur had never left him behind. Never asked him to protect anyone else. This girl had changed him in a matter of hours, and the knight studied her warily. He prayed she was worth it. If Arthur died, he would never forgive her. Would never forgive himself.

"SHOULD IT BE TAKING THIS LONG?" Guinevere asked as she stared into the night. After Arthur left, Gawain rented them a room at the small inn. To her intense gratitude, the innkeeper had drawn her a bath, fussing how she was the first to serve the new queen of Camelot. The heat had worked wonders on her stiff muscles, and when the water ran cold, the innkeeper had prepared them a simple meal. Guinevere tried to eat, but the longer Arthur was gone, the more worry gnawed at her gut, and every bite crumbled to ash on her tongue. She knew who

Mordred was. Knew the danger her husband faced, and for the first time in her life, genuine fear for the king crushed her chest. He had to return. She wanted him to return to her.

Thankfully, Gawain had no issues eating enough for the both of them, but the meal had long since passed with no sign of the knights. The sun set, and the hours crept by with icy dread. Unable to sleep until he returned, Guinevere huddled by the window, watching the darkness. But with morning fast approaching, her concern had morphed into an ugly, cruel monster.

"No," Gawain grunted too quickly, and Guinevere's eyes shot to him in alarm. As if suddenly realizing she sat in the room, he gestured placatingly. "I apologize. I'm not accustomed to traveling with women."

"It's all right. I prefer honesty." Her answer was clipped, but truthful.

Gawain tilted his head and studied the woman before him. She was so young compared to Arthur, yet there was a maturity about her. He guessed that as the only child in a household without a lady, its responsibilities had settled on her shoulders. There was something about her he struggled to identify, though. Something strange but strong. It made him wary, especially since the king had never once fallen prey to a pretty face. There was no denying Guinevere was exquisite, but she wasn't the only beauty Arthur had met. And while he regarded most women—and men—with cool indifference, this woman had changed his entire demeanor in a single day. It unsettled Gawain.

"Will he be all right?" His brain registered that she was speaking, and he jerked with awareness.

"He has Merlin," he answered coolly, but Guinevere stared at him, annoyed by his half answer. "Arthur is the greatest warrior I know. I hope it is a side of him you never witness, because it is truly terrifying. The man was forged for battle. He is one with

Excalibur, and the sight is haunting. But Mordred is no mere mortal. He was one of the mages who guarded Excalibur while it lived in the stone, and he did not take Arthur's freeing it lightly. If anyone can defeat him, it is the king, but not even Arthur is invincible."

Guinevere nodded, both pleased and nauseated by his blunt honesty as she turned to the dark window. "He will come back," she whispered, too low for Gawain to hear.

"You're not afraid of him?" Gawain's voice was suddenly behind her, and she jerked in surprise. How had he moved so silently?

"No." It was the truth. Despite his hulking size and permanent scowl, the king did not scare her. Her reaction to him made her nervous, though. It was visceral and scalding, a consuming fire that left nothing but scorches and ash in its wake, and she hoped her pull toward him would not render her blackened and lifeless. She prayed that agreeing to marry the most powerful man in the kingdom while he was a stranger did not leave her heart raw and bleeding till death stole her from him.

"He frightens most women," Gawain pushed, and Guinevere suddenly felt concerned by the direction the conversation had taken. "They become obsessed with the crown and his wealth. His power. They pretend to love him, to find him attractive, but deep down he scares them. They see the beast lurking within, and while he never hurts innocents or women, they fear the brute. If you ever saw him fight, you would too."

Guinevere glared into the knight's eyes, refusing to yield under his goading. He didn't trust her. If she was in his shoes, she wouldn't either, but she refused to back down. "He does not frighten me."

Gawain grunted as he sat on the chair opposite hers. He stared at her contemplatively before opening his mouth. "I cannot figure you out. There's something about you I've never felt, a touch of destiny weaving around you and Arthur. I find it unnerving because I cannot tell if you will be his undoing or his salvation."

"I will not be his undoing." Her voice was savage.

"I pray for both his sake and yours you are not." Gawain leaned forward, his gaze searing into her so that she would not mistake his meaning. "I am loyal to King Arthur. Everything I do is for him and him alone. I will die for him without hesitation. I won't allow harm of any kind to come to him."

Guinevere swallowed, her skin like cracking glass at his threat. He had not voiced it directly, but she understood all the same. He would kill her if he thought she meant the king harm.

"I am glad," she said, forcing her heartbeat to slow. "Arthur needs devoted men. I would expect your vow to him to remain true."

Gawain grunted, leaning back in his chair as if he had not just threatened his new queen. Guinevere mimicked his relaxed indifference, but unlike his cool demeanor, her heart rattled in panic. She knew his knights were loyal to the death. She wanted them to be, but fear still vibrated within her chest, pricking her skin like a thousand needles. If his most trusted knight was apprehensive about her intentions, how many others expected her to be the king's downfall? The thought made her spine stiffen. She would not be his downfall. Would she?

A commotion outside halted her spiraling thoughts, and Guinevere jerked to peer into the darkness. A group emerged from the night, a mountain of a man in the lead leaning dangerously on a smaller figure, and Guinevere's heart surged into her throat. Even with such a brief marriage, she would recognize that frame anywhere, and alarm turned her blood to icy shards.

"He's hurt." Her voice was panicked, and she leaped from her chair for the door.

"Guinevere, wait," Gawain warned, chasing after her, but she couldn't stop. The stain on Arthur's shirt was obvious even in the darkness, and it was all she could do not to trip down the stairs as she burst into the night air.

Gawain caught up, throwing his body before hers as she ran without concern for her own safety. He flung his arm out, blocking her from the men emerging from the blackness, but when he saw it was only the knights, he released her. Arthur collapsed to the ground, a hiss of pain on his lips, and before anyone could blink, Guinevere was on her knees, catching his collapsing torso.

"What happened?" Gawain asked, unable to keep the alarm from his question as Guinevere pulled her massive husband against her, her fingers already coated in his blood. He half expected her to scream, but the woman remained level-headed, pressing her palm against his side to staunch the bleeding.

"There was an ambush," a stranger answered, and both Gawain and Guinevere searched for the sound. She didn't know his knights well, but she hadn't heard that voice before. It was a song on the wind, a melody blessed by the gods, and she couldn't help but meet the gaze of the young man who supported Arthur's other arm. She tried to stifle her surprise. To swallow her uncontrollable reaction, but she could not stop the small gasp that escaped her lips when she peered into those perfect golden eyes. She had never witnessed beauty like his before. Never seen someone so graced by perfection. This newcomer was the most handsome man she had ever laid eyes on. He was tall and lean, his height nothing compared to the king's, though, and his skin was a splendid golden shade, smooth and unblemished. He was a few years older than her, his light brown hair an exquisite frame around the masterpiece of his face. His every line was sculpted elegance, his every muscle painted grandeur. Arthur was all masculinity and brutality, scars and dominance, but this stranger was sex and splendor, soft lines and crystal eyes. He was flawless, an angel fallen to grace mere mortals, and as he gazed at Guinevere, she recognized the hunger. He was as struck with her as she was with him, and as his intoxicating aura enveloped her, something settled in her gut. Something wrong. Something foreboding. She should look away. She needed to look away, but his gaze was a ravenous gravity pulling her in.

"Mordred knew we were coming," Arthur said, his voice a sharp and cruel contrast to the stranger's angelic melody. "He set an ambush. I would have died if not for Lancelot. He saved my life." Arthur's head leaned against Guinevere's shoulder as he tilted his sight to her face, only to find she was not looking at him. "Lancelot saved my life, and I finally defeated Mordred."

Chapter Nine

The earth tilted beneath Arthur's knees, his skin suddenly too cold, his blood too hot. If not for Lancelot, he would be dead, carved to grisly pieces in the dirt. As a reward for saving his life, he asked the young warrior to return with him to Camelot as one of his knights. But the moment the newcomer noticed the wife he had almost not returned to, his heart plummeted. She held his bloody side in her hands, supporting his heaving weight against her shoulder, but her eyes were on Lancelot as if he had trapped her in his orbit, drinking him in like honeyed wine. Arthur was not blind. He understood just how beautiful Lancelot was. He was the kind of man she deserved, his beauty equal only to hers, and a bitter thread wove through his mind, poisoning his thoughts. If he had not been so hasty in claiming Guinevere, would she have chosen a husband like Lancelot instead? Insecurity coiled thick and venomous through his gut. If she had only waited a few hours, she would have met someone far more worthy of her perfection than him, and Arthur was painfully aware of how coarse he was next to Lancelot.

Guinevere flinched against him, and as if Lancelot's hold on her broke with a sharp snap, she looked down at the blood coating Arthur's side. Panic replaced her dazed expression, and as if suddenly angry that the newcomer still touched the king, she heaved Arthur further into her arms.

"Fetch me water." Her voice was controlled as she pulled him unsteadily to his feet and toward the inn. "Clean linens and thread if you have it." She was so small compared to him, but she bore his weight effortlessly as she directed her request to the innkeeper. The woman obeyed without question as they moved inside. Lancelot followed behind them, arms outstretched to offer aid, but Guinevere simply jerked her husband further against her side and shoved him up the stairs, refusing the help. Arthur wondered if his mass was a shield against Lancelot's beauty or if she was afraid to allow the young man to come any closer. His heart pulsed erratically as he watched her struggle to climb the steps. He didn't want to fight to keep his new wife. He didn't want her to regret her reckless decision.

"Sit," Guinevere ordered, shoving his bulk against the table in her room, and he obediently slid onto the wood. Her hands shook as they reached for his shirt, and instinctively he captured them in his calloused fist. She stood frozen for a silent moment, letting him hold her unsteady fingers, and her expression nearly broke his heart. Fear. Fear for him. She couldn't stop staring at the blood stain oozing ever wider through the fabric, and he saw her terror. She was afraid to witness how badly he was injured, and her concern gave him hope.

"I need to see," she whispered, on the verge of tears, and Arthur released her fingers. Trepidation coated her skin as she peeled off his shirt to reveal a long gash running from the left of his belly button to the flesh above his hip.

"Thank God." Her tears flooded from her eyes at the exclamation, and she surprised him by wrapping her blood-smeared arms around his neck. She pulled his face to her breast, pressing his cheek over her thudding heart as her nose buried in his dark hair. "It's shallow. When I saw the blood, I thought..." She trailed off, and Arthur slid a broad palm to her lower back. She sank into his embrace, and he drank in her relief. Maybe he had misread how she had looked at Lancelot. There was no mistaking her worry as she held him against her heaving chest.

"My lady," a hesitant voice interrupted, and Guinevere jerked free of Arthur's hug. The innkeeper set a tray of threads and bandages down on the table beside them, and Gawain and Percival followed her with water.

"Thank you." Guinevere wiped her tears on her sleeve and then washed the blood from her hands.

"Would you like me to do it, my lady?" the innkeeper asked, gesturing at the needle waiting to pierce the king's flesh.

"No." Guinevere shook her head even though her eyes hesitated with confliction. "I want to do it."

The woman curtsied slightly and exited the room, saying, "If you need help, my chambers are downstairs next to the kitchen."

Guinevere nodded as the door clicked shut, leaving them alone for the first time since their fateful morning. Neither of them said anything as she cleaned his side, but when she threaded the needle, Arthur noticed how pale her cheeks had grown.

"Guinevere." He grabbed her hand. "You don't have to do this. The innkeeper or Gawain can instead."

"No." Her resolve shot out of her, and despite the paleness of her skin, her voice was steady. "I want to do it. This isn't the first time I've done this. I'm more resourceful than you think. It's only..."

"You never had to sew the king closed?"

"I've never had to tend to someone I cared about hurting," she corrected, and his heart swelled. He held her hand tighter, pulling her closer until he felt her body heat. "What if… what if I do a poor job?"

"Are you afraid I'll scar?" Arthur laughed so loud that Guinevere jerked backward and stared at him as if he had two heads. He rarely laughed, and he worried the sound scared her, but then she broke out in a smile, her skin flushing pink. He waggled his eyebrows at her, puffing out his chest slightly to draw her gaze to the tapestry of uneven flesh, and a soft chuckle escaped her beautiful lips at his teasing.

"How much of your father's household did you maintain?" Arthur picked at the fraying sleeves of her now ruined dress as she pressed the needle to his side, the question meant to distract himself just as much as her.

"You did not marry an idle lady." Her voice wobbled as she pulled the thread through his flesh. He flinched at the pain but kept his mouth shut. He was used to the sensation of severed skin being threaded and tugged back together, and he didn't want to frighten her. The color the laugh brought to her cheeks had faded, leaving her pale and unsettled again. "After my mother died, my father did his best to portray success to those around us. He wanted to appeal to my potential suitors, but it wasn't long before I realized just how far into debt he had fallen to keep up appearances. I taught myself to do most things so we could save our limited coin while maintaining the façade."

"The more I learn about you, the more I believe I was meant to find you." Arthur groaned his words to hide the pain in his voice, but he meant what he said. She reminded him so much of himself, knowing the worth of her hands and spirit. She was beautiful and not only outwardly. The goodness of her soul wafted off her in enticing waves, and he watched her sew him closed, marveling at how she was most likely the first queen in Camelot's history to face the blood and the gore for her king.

She leaned forward as she worked, and for a moment, Arthur wasn't sure what she was doing until her forehead hit his lips. Her fingers continued moving, but she rested against his mouth, and he granted her wish, reverently kissing her sweaty brow. The connection was surprisingly intimate. Her need to feel his support was so strong on her skin that he tasted it on his lips as he kept them firmly pressed to her head. Yes, he was meant to find her. She was destined for him. Beautiful Lancelot be damned. This woman was his.

"Is our marriage going to be like this?" Her question repeated his from earlier. "You leave me to face great danger, and I have to wait for you to return, hoping you will return."

"If you are waiting for me, I will fight harder than I have ever swung my sword to return to you." His mind thundered as he spoke against her skin. *Say you will wait. Say you are mine. Say I have you.* But she said nothing, continuing to close his wound with bloody fingers and pale cheeks. She did not remove her forehead from his lips, though, needing his reassurance and support. He could tell she fought to keep the nausea down, and unable to help himself, he pressed a kiss to her eyebrow and wrapped the hand opposite his wound firmly around her back. His large body entombed her as she worked, caging her in, protecting her from the world, and then he heard her whisper a word so low he thought he imagined it.

"Always."

THE SUN HAD REARED its lovely head by the time Guinevere finished stitching Arthur's side. She moved with careful precision, determined to gift him a more elegant scar, and then she had spent what felt like hours scrubbing the blood from both their bodies and the table. She was exhausted and nauseous, unnerved both by the sight of her bloodied husband and the arrival of the almost perfect male that had peered at her like he wished to consume her soul. Her fingers ached, and the stench of blood coated her nose. She longed to sleep, but the electrical storm surging through her nerves had her pulsing with awareness.

Guinevere sighed, rubbing her eyes with the back of her wrist before unraveling a clean bandage. With gentle movements, she wound the fabric around Arthur's wide torso, her fingers brushing his rough skin with each tie. When she knotted the dressing firmly in place, her hands drifted up his chest, coming to rest above his heart.

"You did well," Arthur praised, his voice thick as he spread his legs further and grabbed her hips, pulling her closer.

Guinevere nodded without a word. She was staring at his muscled chest, and Arthur followed her gaze. Her fingertips hovered right below a gnarled scar, barely a thread of air separating her from contorted flesh, and before she could stop herself, she dragged her hand up and brushed the uneven skin. He flinched at the contact, and she looked up at him with concern written on her features.

"Do they hurt?" Her voice was low and soft, seduction and exhaustion and care wrapped together in a beautiful braid.

"No." Arthur's hands tightened on her hips, and on instinct, Guinevere moved closer. Inches separated them, her alluring body so close to his, it made his cock throb and his heart ache. He wanted to watch her, not have her study his deformities. She would see how ugly he was if he let her look too closely.

"Then why did you flinch?" She pushed her fingers further against the scar, tracing it until she found a new blemish, her hand burning a trail of fire.

"They bother people and disgust most women." The admittance felt like choking, like dust and ash clogging his throat.

Guinevere's eyes shot to his, the exhaustion gone, replaced by rage. She stared at her husband, letting her defiance ripple through her, letting him see her disgust at how he had been treated, and then, without breaking eye contact, she lowered her mouth to one of his scars. She kissed it reverently. Slowly. Seductively. His grip on her hips tightened, his chest growing rigid, but she refused to stop. She held his gaze as she dragged her lips over the entire blemish. She moved deliberately, savoring the imperfections against her mouth, loving the contrast between his solid muscles, smooth skin, and jagged marks. Wetness coated her thighs as her tongue darted out to lick his skin.

"Fuck." Arthur yanked her fully between his legs, pressing his hard length against her, and she moaned against his chest as she dragged her kisses to another scar.

"Arthur," she protested as his broad hand slid from her waist to cup her ass. "You are wounded." She pushed herself away from him, bracing her palms on his ribs to force them apart, and Arthur stilled at her resistance. He searched her eyes as she tried to escape. Was it Lancelot? Had she seen true beauty and could no longer stomach the thought of bedding him?

"I have fought through worse than this," he snarled, hating that need coiled in his voice, displaying his overwhelming desire for her.

She looked down at his scars, her thumb absentmindedly brushing the blemish she had just run her tongue over. "I suppose you have," she whispered, and Arthur's hands dropped from her waist as she retreated. He wanted her more than he needed to breathe, but he wouldn't force her, and if he held her hips much longer, his control would snap.

"Arthur," she said, her voice almost a gentle reprimand as his words from earlier resurfaced in her mind. She couldn't allow that confession to go without her resounding response. "Never mention other women. I am not them." Then she was moving, her body pressed so close to his that her scent was all-consuming, her warmth a balm for his soul.

Guinevere pushed her lips against a scar and groaned. They didn't scare or disgust her, and she had the urge to strangle every woman in the king's life for making him think he was unworthy. It had taken every ounce of control not to kiss him lifeless when he returned. She had been afraid to touch him and worsen his pain, but ravenous hunger burned his eyes with such intensity that she almost felt his gaze caress her curves. The fear his wound injected into her heart was unlike any cruelty she had ever endured, and she needed to feel him against her, inside her, to know he was alive and here.

She traced a path of kisses across his chest, stopping at each strip of gnarled flesh. She would show this man just how much her body craved his until he believed he was not ugly. Until he believed he was the only reason for her unholy urgency. He was groaning under her lips, his ribs vibrating with the sound, and she loved how they rattled her skin. She wanted him louder, harder. She wanted to feel his every shudder against her mouth, and so she pressed a palm against his stomach, careful to avoid his stitches, and dragged it excruciatingly slowly down his chiseled abdomen. He flinched each time her fingers touched the deformities, but he didn't stop her. She took that as a small triumph. One day, he wouldn't flinch. One day, he would be so addicted to her touch that he would wear his scars with pride.

The top of his pants brushed her knuckles, and with a moan that rivaled his, she pushed her hand beneath the fabric to grab his thickness. It was velvet soft. Erotically hard, and she mimicked his movements from the night before, stroking its length base to tip.

"Fuck, Guinevere." Arthur coiled her hair around his fist and jerked her head back until she could see his eyes. They were dark and hooded, a dangerous storm brewing in his irises, and

Guinevere smiled. He had promised to ruin her, and she wanted to push him to keep his word.

"My king." Her plea came out as pure seduction, and she dragged her hand down his shaft with agonizingly slow torture, her fingers brushing the pre-cum at his tip as her fist stroked back up. Arthur growled, pulling her hair harder with a shaking arm, but she didn't stop. She wanted him crazed. This man made her wild, and she needed him to understand the pounding in her chest. It had come on like a tidal wave, terrifying her, confusing her, and she couldn't subdue it. She didn't want to. She wanted to drown in this man.

"Take off your clothes," Arthur ordered. When she called him *my king* last night, it had driven him mad, but now that she understood the meaning behind those words, they ruined his control. He didn't care that neither of them slept. That a wound split his side. That she was most likely sore. She had pushed him too far, and he needed to make her his wife.

Guinevere had unlocked the beast he had chained down, and with slow, enticing movements, she stepped out of his reach before removing the stained dress. He sat in awe of her as she bared herself to him, the heat in his gaze molten and fierce. Guinevere knew she was beautiful, but her husband? He studied her as if she was life itself. A divine goddess. The only being worthy of worship, and she never wanted another man to look at her again. Only him.

She stood too far from him to touch, waiting for his command, desperate to submit to him. He had given her freedom to be herself, the permission to not be under his control, but right now, she craved it. Longed for it. Hoped for it.

"Do you wish to please your king?" Arthur asked, and she had to fight the urge to run her fingers against her aching core at his tone.

"Yes."

"Good girl." Arthur pushed his pants off, freeing his thick

and beautiful cock before settling further back onto the table. He spread his powerful thighs wide as an invitation, and Guinevere wasn't sure if she was more aroused by his erection or the pure strength in his legs.

"Get on your knees," he ordered, and for a second, nervous energy flooded Guinevere's muscles. She knew what he wanted from her, but the sudden reality made her hesitant. Her innocence was wildly inexperienced.

"I said on your fucking knees, Guinevere."

As if with a mind of their own, her legs stepped forward and bent until she knelt between his thighs. He was so much larger at this angle, and her mouth watered involuntarily, sending sharp bolts of lust to her core.

"You look so pretty kneeling before your king," Arthur said, placing a firm palm on her head. "You will look even prettier with my cock in your mouth. I'm dying to see your lips wrap around me, to see just how deep you can take me down your throat."

Guinevere's core clenched. She was empty, desperate, hollow. She wanted to stand up and climb into his lap, to push him inside of her and fill the aching void, but she remained on her knees.

"Is this still what you want? To please your king?" His voice was rough, almost cruel, but Guinevere recognized it was his control fighting to wait, resisting to allow her consent. He was giving her a choice, just like he promised, waiting for her to decide, and it made her ache to do every deliciously filthy act he requested.

"Yes, my king."

"Then get to work," he growled. "Put me in your mouth."

Guinevere parted her lips, and he slid inside. He was so thick, so soft, and when he nudged the back of her throat, she moaned, clenching her legs.

"That's it." He withdrew until he almost fell from her lips

before pushing further. He guided her movements, showing her how he liked it, and with each stroke, with each kiss, each lick, she knew she would become addicted to this. She moved faster, welcoming him deeper.

"Guinevere." His hand gripped her hair so tight she felt his muscles shaking. "You are taking me so well. Open your throat, pretty girl. I need to be deeper."

She looked up at him with uncertainty, and he snarled with uncontrolled pleasure.

"Swallow as I fuck your mouth and keep your eyes on me. I want to see your beautiful face as those perfect lips suck my cock." He punctuated his words with rough thrusts, and Guinevere almost gagged from how deep he pushed, but instead of recoiling, she grabbed his thick thighs and accepted all of him. "Eyes on your king, my wife. I wish you could see what a pretty girl you are taking all of me. I will never tire of seeing you wrapped around my cock."

Guinevere gripped the base of his shaft with her fist, stroking him as he fucked her deep. Tears pricked her eyes, but she only grasped him harder as her tongue ran across the vein pulsing beneath his dick, trying to take more and more of him as she gagged slightly. The pure pleasure on his face filled her with so much pride, so much desire, that she ached for him. Ached and ached and ached. It was unbearable. It was everything, and his hand guiding her head as he thrust with wild abandon tightened its grip.

Arthur roared, pulling back until his dick fell from her lips. Guinevere looked up at him in disappointment, concerned she had hurt him, but he reached down and seized her biceps. He hauled her off her knees, brushing the tears and spit from her face, and cemented her to his chest, kissing her until she thought the world was on fire.

"I need to be inside you," he groaned in her mouth. "To make you my wife."

"Please." It was all she could say, her desperation for him rendering her incoherent.

"Bend over and grab the table." Arthur flipped her around and slid his palm between her shoulder blades to grip the back of her neck, gently forcing her forward until she gripped the wood with white knuckles. With hands like worship, he caressed her spine, her ass, her thighs, his fingers running down one side and up the other until they came to rest on her belly.

"Spread your legs for me." His foot kicked the inside of hers with gentle but firm guidance, and she fell open, every inch of her exposed for him. "So fucking gorgeous." He slapped her ass lightly. "Dripping wet and perfect. Do you know how devastating you are?"

She threw a glance over her shoulder. Her cheeks flushed at his words, and he gripped her jaw tight, pulling her to his mouth. She kissed him first before he had the chance to claim her, slipping her tongue against his to show him how she hungered for him. The kiss was raw. Wild. Desperate. She was made for him, meant for him, destined for him. There was no other explanation for how seamlessly their bodies and souls had collided.

"You are mine," he growled in her ear as he slid between her thighs. He rocked back and forth slowly, teasing her. "Say it. Say you are mine."

"Arthur." She was practically crying as she shoved her ass against him, trying to force him into her.

"Say it, Guinevere."

"I am yours," she moaned. "I am yours, my king."

"Good girl." Arthur pushed into her, finally giving her what she craved. She held on to the table with shaking arms as his one hand found her clit and his other, her nipple. The pressure was unbearable, building through her, racing over her sensitive skin. She was so close, and with every thrust, her voice grew louder. She couldn't stop, her whimpers growing into moans evolving into screams. The pleasure was too much, too intense, and she hovered on the edge as he plunged so deep, she would never be the same. He was marking her, claiming her, falling for her, and she wanted it all.

Arthur pinched her nipple harder, and her orgasm exploded, rippling through her with an intensity she didn't think possible. She was screaming, and as the euphoria receded, only to build all over again, Guinevere twisted to stare at her husband's profile. Pride colored his eyes. The whole inn would know who made her scream. The king. Her husband. She captured his mouth in a fierce kiss as her second climax flooded her with burning pleasure, and this time, Arthur followed her over the edge, coming so hard inside her, she felt it leak down her thighs.

"My king," she whispered, not wanting to leave this moment. "Arthur, ruin me."

CHAPTER TEN

5 YEARS LATER

Perspiration clung to Guinevere. The heat bore down on her limbs like a smothering blanket. The summer air was oppressive, and she thought she might crawl out of her skin. It was ungodly hot, and she wanted to both scream and cry in frustration. Her sweat-soaked body was wildly uncomfortable, and Arthur's weight only made it worse.

She scowled at her husband with all the annoyance she could muster. He was sound asleep, sprawled naked across their bed on his stomach. The urge to slap him for being able to ignore this heat tempted her palm, but he looked peaceful. His head tilted toward her, his dark hair falling over his face. He was handsome in sleep, his worry lines fading, his hulking frame curling against hers, but tonight that annoyed her even more. His skin was a furnace, boiling her alive where he pressed against her side, where his powerful arm trapped her stomach. Every time she had inched over to evade his warmth, he expanded until he consumed the entire mattress, forcing her to melt beside him. She felt her scar, as she often referred to it, pressing against her ribs, the thin line still rough despite her care. He lay so close, he almost buried her beneath his weight, and she had to swallow her scream. How could he sleep like this? If she didn't escape, her soul would crawl out of her body and leave her behind in its desperation.

Careful not to wake Arthur, Guinevere peeled his muscled arm from her belly and struggled to slip free. He was so damn heavy, but oblivious to the world, he barely twitched at her movements. She set his limb down atop the damp sheets and felt marginally better as her flushed skin escaped his prison. A pitcher of water sat on the bedside table, and she poured herself a mug as she watched the king sleep. His size enveloped the entire bed. His strong thighs led to a powerful ass and up to broad shoulders. Even at thirty-seven, not a single hair on his head had turned grey, his dark locks long enough for her fingers to grip. His body bore a few more scars since their marriage, but in the low firelight that always burned in their quarters, the shadows hid his imperfections. He looked like sculpted marble in the dimness which made her want to throw her water at him. If she was miserable, he should be too.

She took a sip instead of dumping it on him, though, and grimaced at the tepid liquid. Even the water was hot. She needed to get out of here. To breathe fresh air and dry her skin in the night breeze. Arthur slept, dead to the world. He wouldn't notice her escape. The peace would be her own. No one would be awake at this ungodly hour, only her and her annoyance.

Mind made up, Guinevere pulled on a thin shift. It bared too much flesh, but the thought of anything heavier covering her, suffocating her, made her brain revolt. She wouldn't see anyone, and Arthur was oblivious. Although if he was conscious, she wasn't sure he would stop her. He had made two things explicitly clear when they arrived at Camelot five years ago. First, he did not own her; she was her own woman. And second, no one touched her or they would face his wrath. The scars on his body were proof of what befell those who defied him. He returned, scarred. They never returned at all. No one would bother her as she wandered like a ghost in the night.

Slipping silently out of the room, Guinevere turned her feet toward the garden. She could practically feel the cold spray of the fountain. She wouldn't sit in it, just put her toes in the water, or at least she assumed she wouldn't climb under the fountain's mist. At this point, the heat was so unbearable, her body burning like a soul trapped in hell, that she wasn't sure how dignified she would be outside alone. All she knew was she needed to escape this palace and Arthur's oppressive weight.

Guinevere rounded a slight corner on her bare feet and froze at the low echo of masculine voices; the assumption she was the only one awake on this fever night was obviously misguided. It seemed others found this summer air stifling. She crept closer, curious who else wandered at this hour. The man speaking voiced his words too quietly for her to understand, the tone unrecognizable in its whisper, but just as she closed in on the sound, a second answered the first. Despite the fire and brimstone heat, Guinevere's skin flushed cold.

Lancelot.

His hypnotic voice drifted to her ears, low but clear, his every word circling her with its beautiful caress like a hand coaxing her to respond. It was a song. It was passion. It was sex, and his words dug deep into her soul. Her name froze her muscles. His confession rooted her to the ground. His admissions were not meant for her. She should not have heard them, for his whispers changed everything. His melodic speech was not designed for her ears, yet she stood there listening all the same. She did not know how long she lingered, her lungs heaving, her blood pumping, her mind whirling. Whirling. Whirling. She should run. She should not have eavesdropped, but the moment he uttered her name like honey on his tongue, she had grown roots and planted herself in the shadows. This was impossible. So much of her life had been built on a lie, but now? Now she knew the truth, and it would forever alter the course of her future. Her heart was thundering so loud, she feared Lancelot would notice her, that he would find her hovering in the darkness, witnessing secrets he never intended her to possess. The thought terrified her, uprooting her soles from the stone floor, and on erratic feet, she fled into the dark.

GUINEVERE WASN'T sure how long she hid in the darkness. A breeze whistled through the garden, but her unbearable heat was forgotten. All she could think about were Lancelot's forbidden words, the confession she was never supposed to witness. His voice played on repeat in her memory, welding her to her seat in shock. Her heart raced at the truth. Five years. He had been a knight in Arthur's court for five years. How had he kept this a secret? How had she not known? What would she do with this revelation? She could not return to her oblivious life, pretending his admission had not seared a mark on her brain. She felt panicked and overwhelmed, her muscles refusing to obey her mind's request for even the simplest of tasks. So, she sat alone and hunched. Her body shaking. Her body unnaturally still.

"Guinevere?" The concerned voice embraced her with its warmth, and she jerked as if its melody had slapped her in the face.

"My God, Guinevere." Lancelot raced forward, falling to his knees. He clutched her hands with urgency, a worry that seemed vastly out of place. "What happened? Are you hurt? Are you ill?"

She cocked her head at him, not understanding the panic in his eyes, and then something wet dropped onto her wrist. She looked down in confusion. The sky was clear. How was it raining? A soft hand brushed her cheek, fingers so smooth, so unlike the king's calloused ones, that her mind reeled at the sensation. She watched him as if she no longer inhabited this earthly body, and suddenly, it made sense. She was crying. When had she started to cry?

"My queen?" Lancelot gripped her hands tighter. "Are you well? Should I fetch a physician?"

"No." Her voice croaked, sounding like it belonged to another woman and not her.

"Are you injured?"

"I... No."

"What happened?" He leaned closer until their joined hands pressed against his warm chest, her knees brushing his stomach. She looked at him with a blank stare, unable to answer, and his golden eyes turned dark with a malice that frightened her.

"Did he touch you?" Lancelot spat. "Did he hurt you?"

"What?" The word was barely a breath on her tongue.

"Guinevere, did he put his hands on you?" He was squeezing her finger so tight she couldn't concentrate on his question. When she didn't answer, his demeanor changed, and he flew back as if she was a raging fire, burning him alive where they touched. He stared at her dazed expression, drawing his own conclusions, forming his own story as he assumed her silence was a confirmation of his worst fears. She should stop him. She should tell him she had not been harmed, but his confession blared through her mind, stealing every rational thought.

"Fuck, Guinevere." Lancelot was livid, his body coiled and tense as he began to pace. "Fuck." He whirled around and sat down beside her so quickly, the movement gave her whiplash. "If you were mine, you wouldn't wander the gardens at night to escape me. My presence would never torment you until you fled into the darkness to find solace. Look what he has done to you, forced you from your bed to sob alone. I could kill him for torturing you so."

Guinevere flinched at his statement. She should stop this conversation. Set him straight.

"I have loved you since the day I met you," Lancelot continued, and her vision blurred. His confessions were too much, too confusing. She needed to breathe, to escape.

"You must know that by now." He grabbed her hands again, as if desperate to force his emotions into her skin. "You must realize how truly and ardently I love you. I have kept silent. I tried to bury my feelings and forget you, but I can't, Guinevere, not anymore. Not after I have found you crying in the garden after that brute drove you from your bed."

"I..." she drifted off.

"You must know the depths of my affection. How far I would go for you?"

"I suspected," she whispered. "But you are kind to all the women. I did not believe I was special."

"Guinevere, my love." He drew her knuckles to his mouth, kissing them longingly. The gesture surprised her, his lips too soft, too sweet. "I have to treat the others the same as you. My affection needed to appear harmless. You are wed to the king. What was I to do? I have tried to keep my feelings at bay, but my self-control is slipping. Seeing you in tears, hiding in the middle of the night, has pushed me to my breaking point, and I can hide it no further. I love you and would never make you cry or force you from our bed. Arthur is too old, too boring and brutish for a beautiful creature like you. He's failed to give you a child despite your five-year marriage. He is an incompetent and lacking husband. You belong with me. We belong together."

He leaned forward, and Guinevere realized too late he

intended to kiss her. His lips grazed the corner of her mouth after she turned her head in shock.

"I..." she was going to be sick. Too much was happening too fast.

"You are so beautiful, Guinevere. We are meant for each other."

"I can't." She reeled back, forcing him away from her. "I am married."

"No one would have to know."

"No, please. I'm married in the sight of God. I cannot break my vows and sin." The words poured from her mouth so fast she wasn't sure she was making sense, but Lancelot smiled with pride at her protest. The grin set flutters in her stomach, and he slipped his fingers between hers.

"Your piety makes me love you more." He settled for kissing her hand. "You are a pure woman, and I admire you more than ever. Arthur is not worthy of your perfection. I promise you; I will not cause you to sin."

Guinevere sighed in relief. Despite his declaration, she was still reeling from the night's events. She could barely breathe, let alone contemplate what breaking her wedding vows would mean.

"Answer me this though, my love." A strange look passed over Lancelot's angelic face, almost as if a hidden demon was trying to break free. But then the picture of perfection reclaimed his features, and he pulled her close. "If you were not married? If it were not for Arthur, would you love me? Would you have me?"

Guinevere's voice stuck in her throat, curling and knotting as it choked her.

"If you don't love me, I'll walk away, but you must tell me now that I have no chance."

She said nothing, and Lancelot smiled, her silence all the

confirmation he needed as he parted his gorgeously full lips to speak.

"There is no point imagining that," Guinevere interrupted, gently pulling free from his hopeful grasp. "We cannot change our circumstances. I am married to the king. You are his knight. Why torture ourselves with a fantasy we can never live?"

"My love…"

"No." She stood. "I can't answer your question, because even if I say yes. Even if I tell you what you wish to hear, it will never come to pass. Arthur is my husband. We have no control over our circumstances, nor can we change them, so why make ourselves miserable?"

"Guinevere." Lancelot walked to her with the predatory grace of a panther. He cupped her face, and her eyes went wide as he pulled her close. He noticed her hesitation and smiled as if thrilled with her pious purity, but he simply rested his forehead against her. His mouth hovered so close that when he spoke, his breath whispered against her mouth. "What if things were different? What if we could change our circumstances?"

GUINEVERE SLIPPED SILENTLY into her and Arthur's shared chambers, her mind consumed by fog. She didn't remember how she got there, didn't remember walking through the castle's empty halls, and her hands shook as she closed the door, the latch clicking too loudly in the quiet. Her blood pumped violently through her veins, rushing through her ears like waves whipped by a deadly storm. Everything was too loud. Her breath, her heart, her panic, her steps. And this room was still too damn hot.

She gently sank beside Arthur, her stomach churning with

nausea. Her belly clenched, and her eyes watered. Lying here seemed wrong. Why had she come back? She couldn't sleep next to her husband. Not after everything she knew, after every emotion battling within her.

As if sensing her urge to flee, Arthur groaned. Still on his stomach, his forged and chiseled body bare and on display, he reached a heavily muscled arm out and laid it across her. His broad hand clutched at her belly, his fingers gripping her shift as if it were the bedsheets, and then he froze, fisting her dress in a powerful grip.

Guinevere gasped, struggling to hold the contents of her stomach inside her. She was sweating from both the heat and her secrets, and she wondered if Arthur's arm had always been this crushingly heavy.

"Hmmm," Arthur grunted. His fingers released her dress only to clench again, and then his head twisted toward her, eyes still closed in that unreliable bridge between consciousness and oblivion. "What is this?"

When she didn't answer, his eyelids blinked open. He stared at her chest until his vision cleared, and she saw the moment he realized she was dressed. His peaceful expression disappeared as he tugged at the fabric. Not once in their five years of marriage had either of them worn clothing to bed, opting for body heat and extra blankets when the winter months turned bitter. Guinevere read his thoughts as plainly as if they were carved into his face. He recognized something was amiss.

"Why are you dressed?" He twisted his head off the pillow, and Guinevere almost burst into tears. He was on his knees beside her in a second. "What's wrong?"

"Nothing." The lie unconvincing, and her eyes flicked warily to his erection.

"Ignore that," Arthur said gruffly. "You know I always want you when I wake. Did something happen?" She shook her head, but it failed to convince him. "Guinevere?"

"I couldn't sleep." It was the only confession she would offer him. "I went for a walk."

"That's truly all that bothers you?" Her voice was far from convincing, and Arthur saw right through her.

Guinevere nodded, and Arthur pulled himself closer, pushing his heavy body on top of her until he pressed against her core. He nuzzled his face into her throat and kissed the soft skin as he thrust his hips against her.

"If you couldn't sleep, you should have woken me," he rumbled in her neck. "I would have helped tire you out, my queen."

He thrust again, but Guinevere lay below him, unaffected. He reeled back in concern, staring into the eyes that he loved so deeply, but they were hollow. Fear pricked his skin, and then Guinevere did the unthinkable. She pushed him off her. For the first time since that fateful night at her father's house, she refused his advances.

"What is wrong?" Arthur pulled away quickly and knelt beside her, afraid to touch his wife. "Guin, are you hurt? Talk to me."

"No." Her voice was muted and dead, and his skin pricked with a thousand knives of panic.

"You're scaring me." He wanted to scoop her into his arms and comfort her, but if there was one line Arthur never crossed, it was this one. He had never touched a woman, not even his wife, without her consent, and so he sat there, his heart aching, his fingers clenching to keep from grabbing her.

"I…" She looked at him, her features softening marginally. "I feel ill, that is all."

"Should I fetch a physician? Merlin?" He should have been relieved at her explanation, but something dark still nagged at his mind.

"No." Her answer came too fast. "I just need to rest. I'm

uncomfortable, that's all. Go back to sleep. Don't let me disturb you."

She said it so nonchalantly that Arthur wanted to shake her. How could he not worry? But as if to signal the end of the conversation, Guinevere rolled to her side, her clothed back to him, and Arthur's heart dropped from his chest. She never turned her back on him.

"All right," he sighed, his voice struggling to remain even. "Get some rest. I love you." Unable to stop himself, he reached out and brushed a hand comfortingly down her side to her hip. His fingers lingered for only a few seconds before he pulled away, keeping the caress innocent and soft. He wanted her to know he was there, that his comfort was hers for the taking, but she never once turned around.

THE NEXT MORNING, Guinevere secretly gathered herbs for a tea that would make her feverish and nauseous. A maid had taught her how to brew it when she was too young for marriage, yet a suiter had come calling, anyway. The maid showed her how to blend it properly, and Guinevere had thrown up all over the nobleman. He never returned.

It had the same effect this time, rendering her violently ill. She told Arthur she would move into another room while the sickness brutalized her. He argued and begged, but in the end, it was no use. For two weeks, she drank the tea in secret, and for two weeks she slept alone in her illness. When she finally recovered, Arthur was overjoyed. He had barely seen her in days, and he missed her voice, her laugh, her scent, her touch, but Guinevere never returned to his bed.

CHAPTER ELEVEN

The sun felt glorious on her skin after two weeks of incapacitating nausea. The sickness had been her own doing. Nevertheless, the violent spasms and clammy sweats had left her used up and thrown out like a rung-out dishrag. Her hair had grown stringy with grease. She had lost a significant amount of weight, her bones protruding more than before, and she vaguely wondered if Arthur would find her appealing now that she was too boney. She hoped not. Not with what she planned.

Guinevere brewed the tea every few days partially to convince Arthur of her lie and partially to escape him. He was always there, always worried, and she needed space to think. He checked on her every day, but her maids repeatedly denied him access to her room. As a warrior and king, he could have forced the issue, but she was thankful he had refrained. She needed to be free of him while she thought, while Lancelot's confession played over and over in her memory, haunting her dreams with fever. *We are meant for each other. If it were not for Arthur, would you love me? What if we could change our circumstances?* After two weeks, she could no longer bear the vomiting, and she stopped drinking the tea. She could not hide forever; she knew what she must do. What she wanted to do.

It took another two days for the tea's effects to vacate her body, and that morning she bathed and ate her first full meal. The four walls of this sick-room were suddenly claustrophobic, and she announced she would walk through the gardens. She heard through the gossip mill that some wondered if she was with child, but as she passed servants and court officials on her escape outside, she knew the rumors would die with a vengeance. She was too thin, too gaunt to be carrying the heir to the throne. Arthur's disgrace continued.

But Guinevere paid little attention to the whispers. All she cared about was escaping her isolation with a clear head. She needed to find him, to see him. Two weeks of restless nights and endlessly circling thoughts only confirmed what she wanted. Deep down, she knew where her heart's longing would lead. Her mind could no longer fight it.

The ring of clashing metal drew her gaze to the training grounds, and Lancelot used his weight to knock his sparring partner to the ground, their swords ringing with each blow. The ladies of the court often gathered to observe the knights of Camelot train. They were men unmatched in battle, unparalleled in strength and stamina, and with sweat coating their gleaming muscles, they were veritable Greek Gods as they fought. Biceps curled, thighs lunged, chests heaved. They were brutal and efficient. They were sex incarnated, and Lancelot's beauty was nearly blinding. He had shed his shirt, his chiseled abs flexing with every movement as if he was carved marble made into flesh. Every woman studied him with rapt attention, lust crackling over their skin to pool in their bellies. Normally Guinevere kept her eyes from his golden skin and alluring face.

He was shorter and leaner than Arthur, his power vastly inferior to the hulking king, but no scars marred his perfection, not a single hair strayed out of place, and in Arthur's absence, Guinevere's eyes lingered on every inch of exposed muscle.

Lancelot paused when he noticed her stare. How it drifted up his body as if it were her tongue tasting him and not her eyes, and he swallowed hard. He met her gaze, and instead of looking away, she held it. Bold. Brazen. Heated. Lust flickered between them, and Lancelot broke the connection first. He returned to the task at hand, but her vision never left his skin. It consumed him, a fire raging against his flesh, a flood drowning his lungs. He could barely focus on training, for every time he glanced over at the spectators, he found her unwavering gaze. It aroused him realizing she watched him, wanted him, and so with each swing of the blade, blow of his fist, curl of his muscles, he showed her just how formidable he was, how different from the brute king he was. He won each match, pride rippling through him, knowing she saw his every move. He hated that they had an audience, but perhaps it was for the best. Their watchful presence was the only reason he didn't charge across the field and take Guinevere right there where she sat. He controlled himself though, and as the training session came to a close, he peered at her one last time. Her expression changed, something dark and seductive playing over her lips. She stared at him as if trying to convey a message, and then she left, aiming for the extensive gardens.

GUINEVERE'S HEART was in her throat. She prayed she looked calm because she felt anything but. Her nerves were live with excruciating currents, her stomach roiled, and her brain whirled. She should go back inside. She should not be here. This was wrong. Wrong. Wrong.

"Did you enjoy the entertainment?" Lancelot's seductive voice danced on the breeze, and Guinevere froze. It was too late to flee now. He had accepted her invitation, and regardless of her anxiety, this was what she wanted. She had hoped he would follow her, and every part of her body was keenly aware of his presence.

"Immensely," she whispered, turning to face him. Gone was her panic as she looked into his gold eyes, his gravity pulling her close, and she unconsciously took a step forward.

"Your attention was most welcome," he purred, following her lead and stepping closer. "I've never fought as well as I did today, and it was all because I was blessed with my queen as my spectator." He surveyed her body, not bothering to hide his blatant desire, and gooseflesh pricked Guinevere's skin.

"Are you well?" he asked, gazing too long at the neckline of her dress. She wore a modest garment, but her weight loss caused it to gap slightly. "I was afraid after my confession that you were hiding from me. Your maids made it known you were gravely ill, and I see the truth now. You are still the most exquisite creature, but I hope my words were not the cause."

Guinevere said nothing, but she held his gaze with a sweet smile playing across her lips. Lancelot took another step, closing the distance between them, brushing her cheek with his knuckles. His touch seared her skin, burning even once his hand fell to his side.

"So, it was not my love," he continued with a grin, filling in her silence with his own answer. "It was him then? He drove you to illness?" Lancelot's eyes darkened, the demon hiding behind his irises flickering to life for a fraction of a second.

"I feel better now." Her eyelids blinked with her double meaning, but Lancelot stepped away from her.

"That night in the garden, you were alarmed, so ready to

flee. Why the sudden attention?" He looked at her warily. "I realize my confession may have been desperate, but I am sure you understand. The thought of Arthur putting his hands all over your body, making you cry, requiring you to submit to him makes me sick with rage. I spoke too passionately, but it was out of love. Your attention is all I dream of, but I'm left to wonder what has changed after five years. After two weeks?"

"One can only resist for so long." Guinevere stepped forward until her chest almost brushed his, and Lancelot's sharp inhale was all she needed to confirm he was under her spell. She kept her body just far enough away that they did not touch, only the heat of their bodies colliding, and she gazed up into his golden eyes, wondering when his control would snap.

"A woman can only pretend for so long." She moaned her whisper, breathy and desperate, and a visible shiver ran up Lancelot's spine.

"Be careful," Lancelot groaned. "Those words are dangerous."

"I know," she purred, her voice hypnotic. "For five years, I thought you cared nothing for me besides a passing infatuation. You treated me as you treat all the women at court, but now I know the truth. I cannot stop hearing them in my memory." It was the truth. The confession she was never supposed to hear was all she thought about. It invaded her every waking moment. It ruled her sleepless nights. "Now that I know your heart, I cannot hide. I cannot pretend. If I try, I will break into a thousand pieces. I've endured so much, but I can do it no longer. I knew Arthur only a day before he wed me, and I met you hours after my marriage. If the king had not been hasty in claiming me, I would've been free to choose when I arrived in Camelot. I would have found you in time to change my fate."

"Of course, he forced you to marry him quickly," Lancelot sneered, and Guinevere had to force her features to remain neutral at his outburst. "He knows a woman like you will never love him. He is a brute, an ugly and boring man. How you have weathered your marriage to his gruffness and emerged with such grace is a testament to your strength. I do not understand how you let him bed you without growing ill more often. I cannot stomach the thought of his hands on you, his mouth on yours. I want to kill him for defiling your beauty." He took a steadying breath, and Guinevere was thankful he could not see her heart. It thundered violently against her chest at his every word, and she clenched her fists until her fingernails bit into her palms, the pain grounding her.

"If only we had met first," Lancelot groaned, and unable to control himself, he leaned forward to kiss her.

Guinevere anticipated his movements and ducked, slipping under his arms and out of his grasp, Lancelot's lips landing on the air. He whirled around in confusion, and when their gazes collided, Guinevere's eyes twinkled with mischief.

"Yes," she agreed with a seductive smile. "If only we had met first." And then she vanished into the garden, heart racing, and stomach nauseous again.

ARTHUR SKIPPED TRAINING. He hadn't laid eyes on his wife for a week. Dread gnawed at his gut, and he had spent every night tossing and turning with exhaustion. How he ever slept without her was beyond him. He would be no good with a sword today. She was ill, but he didn't understand her sudden need to hide. Whenever he was wounded, he never hid from her. She usually insisted on tending to his wounds, regardless of how gruesome and disturbing they were. She was never shy about sharing every aspect of her life with him. How many times had her blood come, dashing their hopes of a child? She cried with him, telling him everything while he held her, and he never backed down from her confessions. He wanted to know her—body, mind, and soul—and she never shied away from the difficult. It was one of the things he loved about her. She was honest, taking her marriage vows seriously. Nothing would ever stop him from loving her, especially not an illness.

Two winters ago, she found it amusing to tackle him outside in a snowstorm. He was almost impossible to sneak up on, but the first time she tried was an innocent attempt to kiss his hair while he leaned over his desk. He had captured her and pulled her onto his lap before she even registered his movements. Ever since, she vowed that one day, she would catch him unaware. Despite her constant attempts, she had never been successful until that night. She had lain in wait for him, and her small body flying at him in the darkness startled him more than he cared to admit. He pinned her on her back in the snow before he recognized her, and she laughed infectiously at his anger. He was terrified. Not of her harmless attack, but of how he might have accidentally hurt her. But she wrapped her arms around his neck and kissed him with triumph, telling him she wasn't afraid because she knew he would never harm her. Deep down he realized it was her, and then she kissed him until both of them felt the raw bite of the cold on their reddened skin. He pretended to be mad as he carried her inside, but her laughter warmed his soul. They fought occasionally and disagreed often, but remaining angry with her was impossible. She had so thoroughly woven herself into every fiber of his being that her smile was sometimes the only thing that anchored him when the demands of his kingdom pushed him to his breaking point.

The next day she caught a mild fever, and while not as devastating as her illness these past two weeks, she never stopped him from seeing her. He had laid beside her, changing the cooling cloths on her forehead and forcing her to stay hydrated until it broke. He refused to allow anyone to care for her save himself. In sickness and in health. He took that vow seriously.

Rumors she might be pregnant worked their way through the castle's whispers, and while none of the maids confirmed their truth, the prospect sent Arthur into a tailspin. If she had lost the child, that would explain her need to hide, but he couldn't bear the thought of her braving that alone. He promised to make her happy. To love her with every inch of his soul. He remembered with crystal clarity the first time she told him she loved him. Six months after their wedding, they had fallen asleep wrapped around each other. Hours later, a shaking woke him, and he bolted upright, afraid something was wrong, but Guinevere simply knelt in the darkness at the edge of the bed. Her voice was soft and hesitant, but her words were an arrow to his heart. *I love you.* And how he worshiped her back. She shouldn't be alone if she was enduring horror and heart-break. If the gossip proved true, he didn't want the love of his life to suffer in solitude. He wanted to, no, needed to be at her side. To tell her he loved her forever, no matter what this life threw at them, but she had shut him out, and suddenly his world was unstable. The one person who grounded him had been ripped from his chest, and he never realized how much he relied on her honesty and conversation to guide him through his day. She was young, only twenty-five, but she was wise beyond her years, and her youthful abandon allowed him glorious freedom. He needed to find her. To make this right between them and help her. He wouldn't let her bleed out in sorrow without his support.

Arthur stepped outside and crossed his arms over his chest, surveying the cluster of women. When he visited her room this morning, the maid told him Guinevere had ventured into the gardens. The knowledge that she had recovered and not found him was a knife to the gut, and his already surly temper soured.

He prayed she possessed a rational explanation as he searched the women's faces, but Guinevere was absent. He grunted low and angry and turned to leave when he saw her. Like being drawn to the moon on a starless night, his eyes collided with her, and his heartbeat quickened to the point of pain. She had lost weight, but she was whole and well. She was beautiful and safe and healthy, and before he realized he was moving, his feet pulled him toward her.

A second figure in the distance emerged shortly after her. He exited from the same direction as his wife, both slipping unnoticed into the crowd. No one noticed their emergence, their staggered entrances enough to be inconspicuous, but from his vantage point? He saw everything, and he had witnessed Guinevere exit the gardens with Lancelot.

Arthur's world spun. His feet were suddenly unsteady on the earth. He thought he was going to vomit his breakfast or pass out. And his heart? It was breaking. Breaking. Breaking. It was being ripped from his chest. It was a bloody, beaten pulp. He understood Guinevere's absence. Her dismissal of his attention. His greatest fear played out before his eyes. The wife he loved beyond compare could no longer stomach him. She had finally caved to the beauty of Lancelot.

For the first time in two weeks, Arthur didn't inquire after her before going to sleep.

Days passed as Arthur ignored his wife. He wanted to kill Lancelot, to use his bare hands so that he could feel the knight's heart as he broke open the man's chest and crushed it in his fist.

He wanted to use his bloodied knuckles to break every tooth in his mouth, every bone in his face, but instead, he hid like a coward. Lancelot was beautiful. He admitted that without shame, and while it initially concerned him, he had come to trust and rely on the man. They were friends, allies, confidants, and he loved Lancelot. Over the years, the knight had flirted with Guinevere, but he flirted with anything that walked, so Arthur assumed his fears were merely his insecurities. Guinevere sometimes returned his stares, and at the beginning of their marriage, it intimidated him. But she never gave him a reason to doubt their love, and if he was honest, he didn't blame her for looking. They were always quick, innocent glances, and he understood the appeal of beauty. God help him, he stared at his wife way too much. It was almost embarrassing how often people caught him watching her. Yes, he understood the pull of beauty well, and so he humored her occasional glimpses. Compared to his appearance, Lancelot was a god. But he was also his friend. Could he truly stoop this low? Be this underhanded? And while Arthur burned with the overwhelming urge to kill him, he couldn't murder someone he cared about without definitive proof.

As the days progressed, Arthur wondered if he had misjudged the situation. There were other reasons that might explain what he witnessed. Perhaps he was a fool, letting his own self-doubt fill in the blanks. He had avoided Guinevere, afraid to discover that every trace of love for him had vanished, but perhaps there was a reasonable explanation.

Resolved to uncover the truth instead of drawing imaginary conclusions, Arthur set out to confront his wife. She would explain. He was sure of it. This was a misunderstanding they would one day laugh about, but in the days that followed, no matter how hard he tried, Guinevere evaded him. Any time she caught sight of him, she fled. Anytime he asked after her, no one knew where she hid. He visited her new room, only to discover she had moved, and not even her maids were privy to where she slept. She simply vanished one night, abandoning them all, and rumors crept through the castle about their marriage. Another week passed without his wife in his bed, and as he lay alone, he knew. Guinevere was having an affair with Lancelot.

CHAPTER TWELVE

Arthur's entire body hummed with awareness, his mind unable to concentrate on the wedding. Tristan and his beautiful bride stood before God and their families, pledging their lives and souls to one another, but Arthur only thought about how Guinevere hovered inches from him, this celebration forcing her to act like the queen at his side. She refused to meet his gaze as they entered the ceremony together, and even though her fingers hung by her thighs, achingly close to his clenched fist, their skin never touched. Arthur felt dizzy at their proximity, sick from their lack of contact. Tristan smiled, promising love and eternity to his new wife, but all Arthur saw was his own wedding. Guinevere hadn't even waited for the priest to pronounce them *man and wife* before she was in his arms, but now her closeness meant nothing. She might as well have been across the room.

He hated how nausea stormed in his stomach, drawing sweat from his skin and insanity from his mind. He longed to reach out and lace his fingers with hers, to smile at her as they welcomed their friends to the wonderful adventure called marriage. This was supposed to be a joyous occasion, but as Tristan kissed his bride, Arthur noticed Lancelot's gaze slip to Guinevere. She did not move, her stance rigid beside him, but her eyes flicked to meet the knight's. As the priest blessed the union, Guinevere experienced that tender moment with Lancelot and not her husband, and it took all of his willpower not to draw Excalibur from his back and cleave Lancelot's head from his neck. That brutal reality was all Arthur needed to confirm he had lost her. The only thing that stayed his hand was his love for Tristan. His knight deserved his wedding to be pure and absent bloodshed, and Arthur's focus fought to hold on to that fact.

Arthur had given Guinevere everything. His heart, his mind, his body, his soul. He bared his secrets and his darkness to her, his hopes and his pain. He had never sacrificed so much for another person, and he had prayed it was enough. Hoped she could look past his scars and his discomfort in crowds, his blunt mannerisms, and sometimes harsh demeanor to see the man who craved nothing but her happiness and equality. Arthur's fists clenched as the crowd applauded. He disliked large gatherings, Guinevere the balm his spirit required to endure small talk and ass-kissing, but without her, his anxiety bloomed into a feral monster. He was an embarrassment, and the thought coiled violence through his muscles. He wanted to hurt someone. He longed to feel the crack of bones beneath his knuckles, the spray of blood against his skin. To hear a gurgling voice beg for mercy as it choked, and with every dark fantasy, the imagined voice morphed from an abstract sound to Lancelot's beautiful tone. Gods, he would love to break that melody, to witness it turn vile as he skinned him alive for daring to touch his wife.

Suddenly, the crowd was moving. Exiting the chapel to begin the marriage feast, and her wifely duties fulfilled, Guinevere slipped free without a single glance. Arthur wanted to grab her fleeing hand, to force her to stay by his side, but he would not cause a scene. It was not the time nor the place, and he already disliked the overwhelming attention he received on a regular basis. He would not survive the entire court watching him beg a wife who no longer cared.

That thought cleared the bloodlust as she vanished into the crowd. Despite his pain, he told her on their first meeting he wouldn't force her to want him. He loved her to ruin, to destruction, to agony, but if this was her choice, her desire, he knew Lancelot was not fully to blame. Yes, he was guilty, and Arthur wanted revenge, but Guinevere chose the knight. Arthur had failed in his promise to her. Perhaps it should be him strapped to the table, being gutted like a fish. He hadn't been able to give her what she longed for, and maybe he should be the one to pay the bloody price.

GUINEVERE SAT BESIDE ARTHUR, doing everything in her power not to look up at him and to eat the entire contents of her plate instead, but his seething anger burned the food to ash on her tongue. She stood with him for the wedding, but it made her want to crawl out of her skin. She felt like she might go insane, and she grabbed her goblet, washing down the bite clogging her throat. The king made no attempt to hide his frustration, but she forced every forkful past her lips. She couldn't speak if her mouth was full, and she refused to talk to Arthur. She would rather sit anywhere than next to him, but unless she wished to alert the court to her actions, she had to act like the queen. Rumors of their separate sleeping arrangements had already begun growing like vines suffocating a tree, but that was all they were. Petty rumors. As long as she played the part, she would be safe. She knew her husband would never cause a public scene. He would sit with her and seethe, but he would make no move until they were alone. She had no intentions of waiting around till then. Soon the wine would flow freely, and the edges of reality would blur. Then she would be free. No one would notice who she danced with, who she spoke to, who she touched.

She took another sip of wine and caught Lancelot staring at her. She could tell by the unbridled lust in his gaze that he, too, longed for the party guests to grow drunk enough to slip through unnoticed. His longing had burned throughout the wedding, the marriage conjuring images in his own mind, and she knew by his expression it was not just images of pledged love and eternal fidelity but also of tangled bodies, thrusting hips, and wet kisses. Guinevere blushed wildly, lowering her eyes to her food, but Lancelot had already noticed her stained cheeks, and she was glad. She wanted him to see it.

It wasn't long before intoxication ran rampant. Clearly unable to stomach being close to her, Arthur left with a goblet of wine to congratulate Tristan and his wife. His departure made breathing easier. She could not bear his vicious glares and huffed breaths. She needed him gone from her side, to leave her alone, and she had gotten her wish.

Lancelot wasted no time in making use of Arthur's absence as he approached her. No one paid him any mind. He was the king's knight, his beloved friend. The guests would never question an innocent dance with the queen.

"May I?" He extended long and agile fingers, and she took them graciously, her skin burning with hellfire where they touched. It was a simple hold, barely their fingertips, but there was no innocence in their connection. Lancelot's breathing changed at their contact, his mind picturing everywhere else he wanted to drag his fingers.

"I thought of you during the ceremony," he whispered as

they joined the other dancing couples. "You had a hasty and pathetic wedding, and all I pictured was us standing there, you in glorious white as I gave you the wedding you deserve."

"Women would hate me for taking you for myself." Guinevere blushed as his fingertips lightly grazed her hips as they passed each other in a dance.

"No." Lancelot's gaze burned into her so fiercely, she swore it swept against her skin, coaxing her closer. "I would be the hated one for stealing such a perfect being for myself. Your beauty is blinding, and you would be mine."

"If only that were true." Guinevere lowered her face, and Lancelot brushed against her as if by accident. "But I am not yours. I cannot be yours. He would kill you if he learned about us." She looked up at him with a suddenly serious expression. "He would kill me."

Lancelot bristled, pulling back from her with a jerk as he scanned the room for Arthur. The king stood beside Tristan, but his cold, emotionless eyes watched their every move.

"I will never let him hurt you." Lancelot twirled her, as if they were merely friends. "I won't let him have you either."

"What do you mean?" Guinevere gazed up at him innocently.

"Nothing," he grunted, as if realizing his misstep.

"Lancelot?" She threaded a soft whine into her voice, sweet and begging in the hopes he would melt.

"Forget I said anything." He smiled brighter than the sun. "Do not worry, my love. I will take care of you, of everything."

The song finished, and Guinevere stepped away, her fingers trailing down his biceps. "We should find new partners," she said, but when his irises darkened, she added, "only for now, sweet Lancelot. Eyes are everywhere. I won't let Arthur hurt you because we were not cautious."

"Your care for me is admirable." The knight bowed as if in respect, but as he hunched forward, his fingers brushed over her skirt, hidden from sight by his frame. He lingered for a moment, and then he disappeared into the crowd.

THE HOUR WAS LATE. The crowd was drunk, and while they had not danced together again, Lancelot and Guinevere's gazes never parted. Every look promised passion and pleasure. Each stare spoke of brazen lust and bold longing. If the wedding party had not been so intoxicated, they would have noted Lancelot's eyes didn't watch the queen as a knight's should. Guinevere noticed, though. With every sip of wine he took, his gaze became more and more feral, hungry, dangerous, and she struggled to breathe in the stifling room. Before she lost her nerve, she threw a glance at Arthur, who was looking down as he poured himself more wine. Now was her chance, and with a blatant stare at Lancelot, she fled.

Guinevere burst out onto an empty balcony, the warm night air cool against her flushed skin. Gripping the railing with white knuckles, she leaned over the edge and stared at the stars, begging them to steady her. Her breath was ragged and rushed, but before her heart rate could slow, the atmosphere changed. The hair at the nape of her neck bristled, and she knew who had come.

"I love you, Guinevere." Seduction and song, the words were too melodic, an aphrodisiac on the breeze. "I want you so badly that my control is slipping. You shouldn't be with him. You should be with me, and I can no longer stop myself. I cannot hold back."

Guinevere swallowed at his insistence as she turned around, forcing her heart to slow as she gazed into his perfect face. "Then do not stop yourself." It was a whisper. It was all her voice could manage, the command too dangerous to be spoken aloud.

But the whisper was all Lancelot needed, and he crossed the balcony in seconds, capturing her in a fierce embrace. He slammed his lips against her, and Guinevere was shocked at how soft they were, how gently they pressed against her. This was not like her first kiss with Arthur, which had been all tongue and teeth and intensity. Despite his arms caging her in, his lips devouring her mouth, she felt nothing compared to what she did with Arthur. The realization thrilled her. She wanted this to be wholly different from the king. She preferred nothing to be the same.

Lancelot's hands ran down her back to her ass, but before he could grip her, Guinevere bucked against him. The shock of her sudden movement broke their kiss, and Guinevere escaped his embrace, putting a respectable distance between them. The hunger in Lancelot's eyes, in his tensely coiled frame, made it obvious she had seconds before he reclaimed her.

"I am married," her words rushed out, and they were like ice water being thrown on the flames. The lust in Lancelot's features lessened slightly, and Guinevere continued. "The king will notice I'm missing, and I'm afraid of what he will do to you, what he might do to me if he caught us. And even if he doesn't, the kingdom knows I am wed. This will bring me shame. Is that what you wish for?"

"Of course not, my love." His eyes told a different story as they dragged over every inch of her curves.

"Then we must return." Guinevere turned, but Lancelot grabbed her wrist, pulling her back to him.

"I am a better man than Arthur. Give me a chance. Give in to this passion between us."

"How can I, when it could get me killed?" She flung the words at him in frustration. "I am not a free woman."

"And if you were free?" He echoed his question from that

night in the garden.

"But I am not."

"Yes, my love, but if you were?"

"Why do you ask?" she pushed. "Is your goal to torture me with the impossible?" Lancelot remained silent, and she jerked her wrist from his grip with annoyance. "I see." Her voice overflowed with disappointment. "This is all a game to you. To see if you can convince the queen to give you her virtue, but this isn't a game to me. I don't want yet another man to torment me and offer me nothing but sleepless nights."

"Guinevere?"

"No." She turned toward the castle. "What is the point if I cannot be with you?"

"But you can!" he blurted so fast she wasn't sure she heard him right. "You can," he repeated, striding up behind her until his chest only just brushed against her shoulder blades. His voice pitched low and sultry as he whispered in her ear. She smiled as he spoke, his confession only for her, but it was what she wanted to hear. What she longed to know and dreamed of hearing. Lancelot had given her what her heart truly desired.

ARTHUR STOOD BESIDE MERLIN, his goblet of wine almost empty. He rarely drank at feasts, preferring to remain in absolute control when in public, but after watching Lancelot stalk his wife, he couldn't stop himself. He barely felt his extremities, he was so drunk, yet the pain in his chest refused to wane, especially since he realized both Guinevere and the knight were missing.

"Have you noticed anything uncharacteristic about Lancelot?" he slurred. He longed to ask Merlin what he truly thought, to share his secrets with his friend like he used to, but he was afraid if he spoke it out loud, it would be true. There would be no going back. Guinevere no longer wanted him, choosing to be unfaithful rather than spend one more minute alone with him. Over the past five years, she had become his most trusted confidant, and while he was still close with Percival and Gawain, something had changed between Merlin and him. He couldn't put his finger on it, but he worried that if he divulged too much, it would cause his beloved wife to be burned at the stake.

"How so, my king?" Merlin asked, and Arthur recoiled. The mage rarely called him by his title, preferring to use his name, and he wasn't sure if it was the alcohol or his neglect of his friend in favor of his wife's company that had wrought this change.

"He..." Arthur couldn't say it. "Seems distracted, that's all."

"No, I have not noticed."

Arthur glanced at Merlin, and the mage's eyes seemed glassy. Did they always look like that, or had they both drank more than he realized?

"Oh..." Arthur's cheeks flushed. He should have kept his mouth shut. Gods, he was drunk. "Probably nothing," he back-tracked, hoping Merlin wouldn't detect his jealousy.

"You worry about your friends. You are a good king." Merlin smiled, and Arthur blinked. No, his eyes were glassy and dazed. His senses were impaired, but Arthur knew his friend's eyes. There was something off about them tonight.

"Thank you, my friend." He pounded the mage's shoulder, and Merlin grinned before disappearing into the throng.

Arthur collapsed in his chair as Guinevere slipped back into the room. Lancelot followed a minute later, and Arthur drained the last of his wine. He should kill the man, and then take his wife over his knee and spank her for her behavior. He should go to bed before he made a fool of himself. He was intoxicated and heartbroken, but he couldn't allow this to continue. If Guinevere didn't want him, he wouldn't make her stay. He told her he would never force her. He meant it.

But instead of putting himself to bed, he grabbed the pitcher of wine, only to find it empty. Reeling with disappointment, he spotted Guinevere's mostly full goblet. He captured it before he could stop himself. Her lips had touched this, and if he could not kiss the woman he loved, he would drink from the cup that had graced her lips. Sorrow filled his chest as he raised the goblet. This was undoubtedly the last time his mouth would touch any part of her. He wouldn't hurt her, and an affair would ruin her. No, he would confront her, and then he would let her go. With that bitter thought, he drank deep.

Arthur gagged, immediately spitting the mouthful out, and he stared in shock at the red liquid. It was tea. Fucking tea. A small amount of wine was mixed in to give it the color and perfume of alcohol, but it was predominantly a floral brew. Arthur's mind swam, and his head scanned the room for Guinevere. He found her with the other women, and through his drunken haze, he fought to see her clearly. Everyone was drunk, Lancelot beyond intoxicated, but as he studied his wife, he realized she was sober. He knew her body language intimately, and the woman before him was in full command of her senses. The rest of the wedding party assumed she was just as delirious as them, the drops of wine in her tea enough to scent her breath, but she wasn't drunk.

Arthur's wine-soaked brain tried to decipher the reason behind her drink of choice, but he was far too intoxicated to attach meaning to her actions. He desperately wanted to know why she felt it necessary to trick the guests, to fake her mental state at a wedding celebration, but the room was spinning. Spinning. Spinning. He might be sick. No, he would definitely be sick, and so Arthur left to suffer alone, the puzzle unsolved and forgotten.

Chapter Thirteen

Arthur's mood was foul, his headache crippling. He was so fucking hungover that every inch of him ached. His mouth was dry, and his eyeballs itched. He wasn't aware that was possible, yet here he stood, miserable and nauseous. This was why he rarely drank. He lost all sense of control, and his body revolted. When they were younger, he and Gawain would drink excessive amounts of ale, sleep outside under the stars on the unforgiving ground, and then fight the next morning like they were invincible. Gods, he felt old, and what's worse, he vaguely recalled discovering something potentially significant, but for the life of him, he could not remember. He had spent half the night hunched in sickness, but even at midday, he still felt like shit. At least now, his body matched his spirit. He may not recall much from the wedding, but he remembered with vivid clarity the image of Guinevere reentering the feast with Lancelot, looking flushed. Her clothes appeared untouched, but it didn't make the situation better.

Arthur watched Gawain spar with Percival, wishing he could

tell his friends about it. They were the only family he had after Guinevere, and while he was more open and honest with her, he desperately needed someone to talk to. His confidant and best friend of five years had disappeared from his side overnight, and while he missed her body, her kisses, her love, he was surprised how greatly he missed her friendship. He hadn't realized just how much he relied on her. He wasn't even sure when it had happened. They were essentially strangers when they married, their raw sexual connection making them inseparable, but somewhere along the line, he had opened up to her. Insignificant conversations became a nightly routine as they lay entwined, struggling to catch their breaths. Somehow, small talk had turned into deep confessions, and before he knew it, his wife was the person he trusted most. He stopped flinching when she touched his scars. It had taken over a year for the involuntary recoil to disappear when she brushed against them, but with the trust of his body came the trust of his emotions. She was incredibly smart for her age, and it angered him that she had grown up in a household that only saw her for her beauty. She would have been magnificent if someone had cultivated her mind beyond what she had managed herself, and Arthur pushed her to excel.

She learned everything she could from him, and as a result, he often trusted her judgment over his advisors. Their connection had become so much more than sex. It was a marriage, true to its core, and most nights when he came to bed, no matter the time, he would fuck her until she was breathless, and then he would fold her in his arms and talk to her until neither of them could stay awake.

And how he missed her. She would know how to comfort him, how to ease his throbbing hangover. Teasing would accompany her care, but he even missed that. How her eyes sparkled, how her voice pitched with mischief, but she was gone. He longed to speak to Gawain. To ask his friend for advice, but the moment he admitted to anyone that she had been unfaithful, everything would change, and goddamn it. He loved her. The thought of the kingdom calling for her head made him ill.

"Watch it!" Gawain yelled, his voice laughing despite the warning.

"Fuck, sorry," Percival groaned as he lowered his sword. "I think I'm still drunk."

"I'll say." Gawain rubbed his knuckles from where Percival caught him.

"I'm definitely still drunk," another knight added, and the group of men broke into exhausted laughter. Arthur's gut swirled in relief at their confession. If his knights were this intoxicated, there was a good chance that none of them had detected Guinevere's indiscretions or his own struggles this morning.

"I hope Tristan didn't drink this much," Percival grunted, "or his new wife is going to be disappointed."

"Oh, he drank plenty," Lancelot teased, tapping his blade against Percival's. "But not everyone is as sloppy as you." He waggled his eyebrows in a challenge. "Come on, old man. Think you can take me?"

"I may be a few years older than you." Percival raised his sword, the formidable warrior assuming control. The same age as Arthur at thirty-seven, most of the knights had at least half a decade on Lancelot, but the teasing that normally rolled off Arthur's shoulders struck a nerve.

"But I will spank you until you cry for your mother," Percival continued, and with a resounding blow, he lunged.

"Stop," Arthur's voice boomed. He needed to hit something, someone, and he hoisted a practice weapon in his broad grip. "You want a fight? I'll give you a fight."

Lancelot raised his eyebrows, and a strange expression

passed over his face like a combination of disgust and annoyance before his normally jovial smile replaced it.

"As you wish, my king." He bent in a mock bow and raised his weapon.

No sooner did his sword level before him, did Arthur strike. Taller and broader than the knights, the king always held back during training. He was a gifted warrior, a death dealer, a savage. He was power and grace on the battlefield, the sword in his hand, God's vengeance, but today his patience had snapped. All he could see was Guinevere watching Lancelot during the wedding vows. All he could hear was her laugh aimed at the knight, and his control broke apart like a dam pushed too far.

The second his sword slammed into Lancelot's, the knight's eyes widened as he stumbled to regain his footing. Even hungover, Arthur was deadly, and with a swift lunge, he brought his blade down again hard. Lancelot grunted as he nearly lost his grip, and Arthur used his shoulder to knock him aside.

"My king?" Gawain leaned forward. He knew the king well enough to realize he was not monitoring his blows.

Arthur ignored his friend. His vision was red, every dark fantasy playing before his eyes, and he punched Lancelot in the face. The man spat blood, understanding this was no longer a bet between friends. He lashed out, but Arthur's footsteps were a well-choreographed dance, despite the seething mass in his brain. He spun and dodged, retaliating blow after blow, and the crowd grew uncomfortably silent as they watched in horror. Lancelot was no match for the king, and if someone didn't stop him, he could kill the knight with even the practice blades.

"My king?" Gawain stepped forward, only to leap back to avoid being smashed in the face. "Arthur!"

Gone was Lancelot's smugness. Gone was his disdain, replaced by gritted teeth and alarm. He threw glances at the others for help, but no one dared challenge Arthur when he was like this. He was a man possessed, the devil in the flesh.

Lancelot's footing slipped, and the king slammed into him, forcing blood from his beautiful mouth. The knight tried to escape the second blow, but he was too slow, and Arthur's blade came down hard on his side. Lancelot screamed as crimson soaked his white shirt, the blunt edge driving into his torso with enough force to break skin and bruise bone.

"What the fuck, Arthur!" Gawain was yelling, and seeing the blood, Arthur stumbled back as if woken from a trance.

He looked at his knights, who stared in apprehension, and his stomach coiled with regret. With an unceremonious toss, he threw his practice blade on the ground and stormed off. The men crowded the injured Lancelot, but Arthur didn't care to see if he was all right. Let him bleed out. He should have used Excalibur and skewered him like a hunted boar. He should have never fought in the first place.

"Lancelot?" Guinevere slipped into his room, slamming the door behind her as she leaned against it for support.

"What are you doing here?" Lancelot hissed as he jerked in surprise, but his pain forced him to recoil. "Someone could have seen you?"

"When I heard Arthur attacked you, I nearly went out of my mind with worry." She rushed to where he sat shirtless on the edge of his bed and knelt before him. "God have mercy, Lancelot." She rested her elbow on his knees and slowly reached her fingers toward his ribs. The massive bruise forming over his sculpted torso was already purple and grotesque, a thin slice of flesh scoring the center. It had stopped bleeding and was far less severe than the wounds she stitched closed on Arthur, but somehow it looked worse on Lancelot's unmarred skin. An ugly stain on his impeccably carved physique.

"He did this to you?" Tears formed in her eyes as if she couldn't fathom the cruelty. "How could he do this to you?"

Lancelot brushed the wetness from her cheek with a gentle caress, and Guinevere leaned her head into his touch.

"He is a madman, my love," he soothed. She should voice her agreement, but her gut clenched painfully at the words, and she stood abruptly.

"Let me bandage you." She seized the linen strips he had gathered.

"Guinevere." Lancelot grabbed her shaking hands, stilling them in his grip. "I am not Arthur. I will not force you to clean my wounds like a common maid. Come sit with me and ease my pain. I can fetch the physician for this."

"No, this is my fault. I should do it. I want to." She dipped a linen in the bowl of water as she returned to the floor and wiped the dried blood from his side.

"This is not your fault." Disgust curled around Lancelot's words. "The king is to blame. You did not wield the sword; you did not force him to cave to his dark nature."

"But I still hold the guilt." Her fingers brushed his ribs, and he flinched at the contact. She peered up through tear-soaked eyelashes to stare into his golden eyes, and Lancelot suddenly forgot the pain in his side at the sight of the queen on her knees before him.

"I am married, but I want another," Guinevere continued, seemingly oblivious to his arousal as she worked. "Of course, this is my fault. Arthur knows… he knows, and now he'll kill you."

"He won't—"

"Look what he did to you." She exploded in quiet anger, her eyes blazing with fury as she glared at him. "And with a mere practice blade. I wouldn't be surprised if you have fractured ribs. If this is what he did to you with witnesses during training, imagine what he'll do to you with Excalibur. Lancelot..." Her voice broke, and she cupped his face with desperation. "I am to blame. I am his wife, and he will kill you for trying to take me. Lancelot, as much as it shatters me to say this, we need to stop. I want you with every fiber of my being, but I cannot cause your death."

"Guinevere—"

"It is for the best. After today, we must act as if nothing between us has ever transpired, even if it desiccates our souls."

"Guinevere." Lancelot gripped her wrists and pulled them from his face with such force, she flinched at the pain. She wanted to cry out, to pull away, but instead, she let him hold her close as the devil flickered in his eyes.

"I will never let that unfit excuse for a king touch you again. It disgusts me he had five years to defile you and this kingdom, but I won't allow him to take you back to his bed. Is that what you want? His disfiguration hovering over you, panting and sweating as he violates you." Darkness consumed his voice, and Guinevere had to force the fear down into her gut. She had never seen Lancelot so unhinged. He was always the picture of grace and refinement. Something had cracked, and as much as it unnerved her, it also excited her. She intimately understood the lengths one would go to for love.

"No, I don't," she whispered, and he released her wrists, red marks already burning on her skin from his roughness.

"Of course, you don't, my love," he soothed, the angel firmly back in control, and she grabbed the bandages to wrap his ribs. "I'm sorry if I startled you," he continued lovingly as he brushed her black hair behind her ear. "It is just that the thought of you with him makes me physically ill. I've spent five years in agony, watching the way he touches you, kisses you, stares at you. And if that isn't vile enough, he also sits on the throne, controlling all our lives with his brutish ways. It sickens me."

"What are we going to do?" She looked up at him with innocent eyes as she wrapped the bindings. Her hair brushed his bare skin as she leaned dangerously close, and Lancelot shivered. "We cannot live like this. In fear, in separation. If we don't stop, he'll execute you. Arthur may even kill me. We cannot continue in secret forever, and the moment he has proof, he will destroy us."

"What would you do?" Lancelot asked, and Guinevere sensed the weight of his question. A test. How far would she go for him? How much was she prepared to sacrifice?

"Anything." She gave him what he desperately longed to hear and brushed her cheek against his jaw as she fastened his bandage. "I would do everything for you. Whatever you ask, I will do it if it means we don't have to hide."

"What if I told you I had a plan? A way for us to be together?"

"I meant anything, Lancelot." She leaned closer, almost falling into his lap.

"I want to trust you, Guinevere." Lust consumed his body as he talked, and she pushed him, brushing her nose just over the corner of his mouth, hinting at what he could take if she tilted back. "I want to tell you my plans, my desires. Promise me I can trust you."

"You can," she moaned, the sound almost an orgasm on her lips. "I love you and only you. Confide in me, Lancelot. I'll follow you to the ends of the earth if you tell me what you need."

"Guinevere," he groaned, grabbing her face and pulling her in roughly for a kiss. She flinched in surprise at the contact, and after a moment, she jerked away.

"We could be caught." She fiddled with his bandage.

"I don't care." He grabbed her chin again, too rough this time.

"I only came to bandage you," she protested. "If anyone walks in, it would appear innocent, but this? Lancelot, please be patient. Don't make me sin."

"I'm dying, Guinevere. You tease me with your every look, your every move. I cannot wait."

"You must." She stood up, forcing his hands to fall from her face. "But it will be that much sweeter in the end. Please, we must do something, and I beg you not to leave me in the dark. Let me help you do what's needed."

"I love you, Guinevere."

"And I, you." Her eyes were wide, her skin flushed, her breath panting. "Handsome Lancelot, tell me what to do before it's too late."

"You'll do anything?" His darkness flickered back to life.

"And everything." Her darkness burned to match.

"Good." He shifted on the bed and patted the seat beside him. She obeyed, taking his hand in hers to solidify their connection, and then Lancelot told her. He spoke in a hushed voice, all of his secrets pouring off his tongue as she held him close, and when he finished, Guinevere blessed him with a chaste kiss. She knew everything. She memorized his plans. They were finally in this together.

GUINEVERE SAT WITH LANCELOT—HIS head in her lap as he slept—for as long as she dared, but as the sun set, she knew her maid would be looking for her. Getting caught in Lancelot's bed would be disastrous after today, even if it was only to stroke his hair. They had a plan now. She only needed to endure a little longer, and then she would be free.

Cracking the door to scan the halls, she slipped silently into the night. Luck was on her side. The corridors were blessedly empty.

Guinevere heaved an audible sigh of relief as she entered the unused hallways on the outskirts of the castle. Reserved for visiting dignitaries, these rooms sat idle most of the year, and she had moved here after she stopped drinking the tea. They were secluded, no one even cleaning here unless guests were announced. She was gloriously alone, if not surprised that Arthur hadn't thought to search them. She had chosen the most inconspicuous chambers, though, and only a single maid held her secret. It was a girl the king had never met, the queen's normal entourage suddenly dismissed, and she was thankful he hadn't had the foresight to locate her. She couldn't bear the look in his eyes. Guinevere needed him as far away from her as—

A rough hand clamped around her mouth, smothering her scream. A second seized her stomach, welding her to the giant chest at her back, and she was helpless to fight against the raw power containing her.

With undeniable force, the man shoved her into an abandoned moonlit bedroom, slamming the door and locking it behind them. She couldn't see him clearly in the sudden darkness, but she didn't need sight to recognize who it was. The callouses that brushed firmly against her lips, the mountain of muscles manhandling her. She already knew who it was. The king had found her.

"What the fuck are you doing, Guinevere?" Arthur hissed as he whirled to face her, his mass looming threateningly. He didn't touch her as he lunged forward, but fear still roiled in her gut. He was livid. Feral. Distraught. His anger and hurt played clearly across his features, and even in the dimness, she saw how haggard he looked.

"Wasn't I a good husband?" Arthur continued without waiting for her response. "Didn't I treat you well? Didn't I give you everything and love you unconditionally?" With every sentence, his voice grew louder, his body vibrating with rage, and Guinevere stepped away from him. "I thought we were happy, Guinevere. I may not be the man you dreamed of marrying, but I would burn the world for you. I respect you, adore you, treasure you. You are my best friend, and I would have given you the world, but I guess I wasn't enough. We were a lie, and I was a fool for trusting that beauty wasn't all you craved."

He stepped forward again, closing the distance she had put between them. He needed her to see the fire in his eyes, to read the pain she had driven through his heart.

"I told you the night we met, I never wanted my wife to be forced into this marriage. I tried to send you away, but you chose me, even though I gave you an out at our wedding. You came to me, Guinevere, and I spent these past years adoring you. I don't deserve this. I do not deserve to be humiliated and mistreated. I have feelings too. People don't think I do. They assume I'm the introverted brute king who is brilliant at running a kingdom but void of everything that makes me human, but they are mistaken. I feel more than I care to, and you have devastated me. What did I do wrong?"

"Arthur." Guinevere struggled to hold back her tears.

"Please, tell me what I did to warrant this," he barreled on as if he hadn't heard her. "Was I so horrible a husband? What did I do to make you embarrass me, to break my heart and my spirit? I desperately want to believe you are better than this, that you wouldn't be so callous, but I guess when everyone warned me against marrying such a young wife, my defense of your character was useless. You broke me."

"Arthur." The tears were streaming as she croaked out his name.

"I want to kill Lancelot." The king's voice turned bitter, its edges jagged and sharp as he snarled. "I want his death to be slow. I need him to intimately experience glorious pain before he leaves this world, my face the last thing he sees before I deliver him to Hell. I promised you at our wedding that I would kill anyone who touched you, but then every time I fantasize about peeling his flesh from his bones or forcing him to swallow his own teeth, I see your face. I remember how desperately I love you. I love you so fucking much, Guinevere, that if you had told me you were unhappy, I would have let you go. It would kill me, but watching you suffer is worse. If I had realized I made you this miserable, if I had known you loved someone else, and not me, I would have released you. I don't own you. Never have. Never will. You are only mine as long as you agree to be, and it seems I lost the right to call you that."

Arthur seemed to realize how close they stood, how afraid she looked as she sobbed, and he stepped back in horror. It killed him to step away from her. He hadn't touched her in weeks, and he knew he never would again. Standing close to her was all he would ever have, and even that had vanished.

"I didn't deserve this betrayal. It is taking all my self-control not to finish what I started with Lancelot during training today, but I won't because I am weak. I love you too much to make you stay and suffer, and if I kill him, it'll only solidify your hatred of me. So, against every fiber of my being, I'm telling you to leave and never come back. I won't stop you. You can both live happily together, just not here. If you return, I can't promise I won't harm him, but if you go now, I will grant you safety."

"Arthur?" Guinevere stepped forward in shock.

"Now, Guinevere." She recognized that tone. It was the one he used when his mind was made up. When he could not be swayed.

"You can't—"

"Get the fuck out of my home." She flinched at the cruelty in his voice. He had never spoken to her so viciously before, and panic bubbled in her chest.

"I said, get out," Arthur repeated, slow and menacing. "Leave before I change my mind and do or say something I'll regret."

"No." He couldn't do this. He couldn't send her away.

"We are done." His words were the nail in their coffin. Her world imploded, and before she could stop herself, Guinevere launched herself at the king.

FOURTEEN

Guinevere's reaction was visceral. Alarmingly instinctual, and in a desperate flash, her chest smacked his before either of them registered the movement. Arthur stared down at her in shock, and she seized his temporary paralysis to clutch the back of his neck with both her hands. With all her strength, she heaved herself up his muscled frame and crashed her lips against his.

Arthur grunted in surprise and grabbed her hips, trying to drag her off, but Guinevere slid her fingers into his hair and held on. Pain lanced his scalp, and he growled as he tried for a second time to push her away, but his movements only hoisted her into the air. With graceful legs, she swung her thighs forward until they locked around his waist, and then with every ounce of strength, she cemented herself to his chest.

Her kisses were wild and rough, all teeth and tongue and hunger as she lost control. Her soul was screaming. Her mind was screaming. Her body was screaming. A ravenous monster seethed in her gut, pushing its way out of the box she had desperately tried to lock it away in, and all she saw, smelled, tasted, touched, was him. Her skin sealed against his, and still, he was too far. With a desperate cry his mouth swallowed, she pushed further against him, kissing him with such ferocity she worried she might draw blood. She didn't care. She cared about nothing but this moment, his scent, his lust thick between her legs. Unable to stop herself, she drove her hips down, dragging her core over the hard length pressed against his belly, and both of them moaned at the contact.

The instant Arthur's mouth parted, Guinevere pushed her tongue inside, claiming every part of him for herself. Wrapping her arms tighter around his neck, she ground down on him and practically came just from the friction. Her body was all thunder and lightning. Fire burning beyond control. Ice cracking in a freeze. The contact wasn't enough, and with a snarl, she bit his lip and captured the back of his shirt.

Guinevere yanked hard, and Arthur didn't resist. He was as lost in her as she was in him, and within seconds, his shirt lay in a heap on the floor. Guinevere pressed her body against his scarred chest, her fingers running over his muscles as she devoured his mouth. His hands slipped under her dress to cup her ass, and she grabbed his hair in her fist, jerking his head backward to gain better access to his mouth. Normally, he took charge, but not today. Not now. She needed him more than she had ever needed anything in her life, and she slipped her free hand down between them to stroke him.

Arthur roared and dropped her to the ground. He stepped away in a daze, confusion warring with lust in his glazed eyes. But Guinevere closed the gap between them, peeling her dress from her body as she moved.

"Arthur," she moaned as she grabbed his pants' laces, ripping them open with a hunger that scared her. She was afraid. Terrified. Frantic. She needed to feel him, to have him thrust inside her and claim all of her, and his name on her tongue severed the last thread of control Arthur had been desperately clinging to.

He pushed his pants down, his thick cock springing free, and he grabbed his wife. He hoisted her into the air and strode for the wall, slamming her back into it with a soft slap. The pressure forced her legs wider as he met her gaze. Her expression shoved him over the edge. *Challenge.* There was no hesitation in her eyes, no alarm at his roughness. Just pure unbridled desire, challenging him to rise to the occasion.

Arthur hoisted her higher, pressing her further into the wall, and with a searing kiss, he impaled her. Guinevere's groan was obscene as she took him deep, and Arthur drank her pleasure down as he reclaimed her mouth. This would not be slow or beautiful. This would not be kind. No, this would be rough and hard, but by the way her legs wrapped around his waist, it was exactly how she wanted it.

Arthur slammed into her, his pace brutal, and Guinevere's spine banged against the wall. Her skin stung, but she liked it. She needed him harder, faster, deeper, and she bit his lip. He had no words for her as he normally did, no praise, no tenderness. He only had her body, but that was all she required to tell him what she craved. Her teeth sank into his lip, and he roared into her mouth as his thrusts picked up speed. She was so wet that she felt it dripping between them, and her stomach clenched as her orgasm built with delicious intensity. She knew it would ruin her, ravage her, undo her. She wanted to scream at how exquisitely deep he thrust inside her, at the friction of his scars rubbing against her swollen nipples. He hated them, but she loved every inch of his uneven skin.

"Come for me," Arthur growled in her ear. It was rough and low, barely audible through his grunts, but his broken silence was all it took to destroy her. Her climax exploded, rolling through her unlike anything she had ever experienced, and desperate not to scream and give their hideout away, she threw herself forward and bit the soft flesh between his neck and shoulder. She screamed into his skin as she bit hard, vaguely aware that she tasted blood, but she couldn't concentrate on anything but the pleasure devouring her body. It was Heaven and Hell. Bliss and fire, and her voice was uncontrollable as her thighs shook around her husband's waist.

Her pussy gripped Arthur's cock as waves of pleasure barreled through her, but it was her teeth latched onto his skin, her screams muffled in his flesh that pushed Arthur to follow her. He thrust hard as he came, his cum hot and thick as he emptied himself into the woman he loved. He should have felt guilty about taking her ruthlessly against the wall, and he knew the pace would bruise her back, but all he cared about was filling her with every last drop and her teeth sinking into him. It hurt. Gods, did it hurt, and he liked it. He wanted this pain. Not the heartache. Guinevere had never been shy in their years together, always pushing him to test her limits, and by the sharp sting in his shoulder, he desperately longed to believe that nothing had changed between them, that she was his. That she loved him.

But as their breathing slowed, the ugliness of their situation came flooding back, and sickness festered in his stomach. He shouldn't have done this. He should have left the room. She didn't love him anymore. One last fuck wouldn't change that.

"I don't understand," Arthur said flatly as he lowered her to the floor, stepping backward, and his heart broke at the look of disappointment on her face.

"We are so good together." He gestured between them, noticing his cum slowly running down her thighs. He loved that sight. He worshiped the way she looked freshly fucked, his cum covering her skin. Any other day, he would have asked her to stand before him so he might revel in how perfectly destroyed he had left her, but with a knife of pain in his chest, he forced his eyes to her face. "And not just the sex. Everything. We are good together. I don't understand, Guinevere. I thought we were happy."

He turned and walked to the bed, putting more distance between them. If he stayed closer, he would touch her again, and he couldn't. He was already in so much pain. He had never had her without folding her into his arms after, and his body was screaming for him to capture her, to clean her up and soothe her bruises. To tell her he loved her. But he couldn't, so he simply sat like a dejected animal at the edge of the mattress.

"If this was an attempt to convince me to let you stay, it won't work." The air rushed out of him in defeat, the sound breaking Guinevere's heart into a million pieces. She had never heard defeat in his voice, and it terrified her.

"I don't want you to stay if you don't love me," he continued, "and if this was goodbye, then please get out. I need you to leave. I don't want you to witness this."

She knew what he meant with sudden clarity. Arthur, the warrior king, was about to cry, and Guinevere closed the distance between them until she stood bare and honest before him.

"This wasn't goodbye," she said with as much strength as she could muster. This wasn't part of the plan. She hadn't intended for this to happen yet, but the dam in her soul broke at Arthur's heartbreak, and she couldn't do it anymore. It would kill her if she kept the secrets bottled up any longer. "It wasn't an attempt to manipulate you, either." She reached out to touch him, wanting so badly to feel his skin against hers for this next confession, but she pulled back, unsure. "I love you, Arthur. That's what this was about."

"Then what the fuck are you doing?" His gaze snapped to

hers, white-hot anger replacing the despair. "If you love me, why are you doing this? Why are you having an affair with Lancelot right in front of my eyes?"

"Because." She took a deep breath, steadying herself for the bile she was about to speak. "Lancelot is planning to kill you."

CHAPTER FIFTEEN

"This isn't funny, Guinevere." Arthur reeled back in disgust. As if flaunting her infidelity wasn't enough, now she had the gall to insult his intelligence.

"I know, it's not funny." Guinevere seized his jaw, forcing her legs between his spread thighs until she stood inches from him. She needed him to see her eyes, to read her truth. "I am doing this because Lancelot plans to kill you, and I am trying to stop him."

Neither spoke as Arthur grabbed her wrists, attempting to peel her hands from his face, but she latched on tight, refusing to budge. For a moment, husband and wife warred in silence. They glared at each other in the darkness, Arthur seething beneath her touch, but she did not yield, her stare boring into his soul. And then it struck him like an arrow on the battlefield. He knew his wife, her tells, her expressions. How often had they spoken with only their eyes, and his disgust morphed to horror?

"Shit," he swore, gripping her wrists tighter, but this time it was not to pull her away but to ground himself. "You're telling the truth?"

"Yes."

He barely heard her voice, his head spinning. How quickly his life had changed, and while part of his brain whispered her declaration was the rantings of a desperate queen trying to hold her position, his gut recognized she spoke the truth. He released her wrists as if they were burning coals and backed up onto the mattress. He needed space. He caved too easily under her touch.

"The night before I got sick." Her explanation tumbled from her mouth in desperation. She had been hesitant to tell him, but now that she had begun, she couldn't contain the confession. "It was so damn hot, and I was annoyed that you were peacefully hogging the bed while I was miserable. You were smothering me, which normally delivers me to sleep, but that night, something about the heat drove me mad. I only intended to get some fresh air, but then I heard something not meant for my ears. Lancelot was talking to someone I didn't recognize, and while they spoke with vague words, two things stuck out to me. One was that he worried about involving me because he was convinced you forced me into this marriage. The second was you were in danger." Guinevere slipped onto the edge of the mattress, kneeling far from her husband as if not to spook him.

"I panicked and ran into the garden," she continued. "I only meant to hide until it was safe to return to you, but Lancelot found me. He mistook my distress as evidence of your cruelty, and he declared his love for me. I always assumed he loved you, Arthur, but the way he spoke about you when he admitted he wanted me was terrifying. It was at that moment I realized I had overheard an assassination plot. When I came back to bed, I considered telling you, but what bothered me was there was someone else there. Someone else plotting your death in this castle, and if I told you about Lancelot, whoever it was would continue their plan. I faked the illness so I could think. If I stayed with you, I would confess everything, but then every night I closed my eyes and saw the second, faceless man murder you.

"Lancelot's confession gave me an idea. I've always known he had an infatuation with me, but he was your friend. I never guessed he would cross that line. The moment he did, I wondered how much of his plot he would reveal if I played his game. He arrogantly walked right into my trap. He hates you with such a passion that all it took was a few longing gazes, a few well-spoken words, and he believed I loved him and not you. His arrogance is disgusting, and he is convinced that there is no reality where I choose you over him. Your incident this morning only furthered his conviction." Guinevere crawled across the bed to kneel before her husband. "It's worse than I expected. He isn't just planning on killing you. He wants the throne, and he will not stop until you are dead and Camelot is his."

Arthur sat in a daze, staring at her as if she was a stranger, and panic boiled over in her chest, spilling from her lips. She had to make him understand the danger, make him recognize just how far into Hell she would descend to save him.

"I am sorry." She wanted to reach out and hug him, to comfort him as his vacant eyes haunted her, but she forced them to clench her bare thighs instead. "I hate myself. Hate that I hurt you, but I would rather ruin my life than watch you die. I won't let them kill you. I won't let a man like Lancelot take your throne and destroy your legacy. I love you too much to stand by helplessly while they murder you, and if I have to suffer to save you, so be it.

"And it worked, Arthur. His hatred made it easy for him to believe my lies. Lancelot shared part of his plan with me today, and this goes beyond an assassination. There are traitors in this castle, and they are transporting an army into the kingdom. Soldiers travel to Camelot under the guise of trading, but they disappear upon arrival. We are welcoming them into our borders, but they never leave. Your enemies are gathering right under your nose, and no one has any idea. I tried to force him to divulge more, to reveal who his co-conspirators are, but he is keeping that close to the chest. I'm afraid to push him too hard. If he is willing to kill you, I am terrified of what he might do to me if he discovers where my true loyalties lie."

"Why didn't you tell me this was your plan? Why didn't you trust me enough to explain what you were doing?" Arthur's voice was numb, and Guinevere couldn't stop the tears from falling. She was losing him, losing the only man she had ever truly loved.

"Because you love me so much, you were about to let me leave to ensure my happiness." Guinevere felt sick. The prospect of leaving Arthur lodged an excruciating scream in her throat, and that he had been willing to let her walk out made her hands ache to shake him. She knew it was because he would never force himself on her. He believed she no longer cared, but her soul was screaming for him to forbid her from ever leaving his side. "The only way Lancelot would trust me enough to divulge his secrets was if he thought I hated you. If you knew I was manipulating Lancelot to save your life, he might not accept we were over. I love you too much to regard you with hatred. The only reason I was able to play this game was because your despair drove me to sickness, made me afraid to look at you. Our unity shattered, and your anger convinced him. But if you knew the truth, I wasn't sure you would be able to suppress your love. It lives in your eyes, as obvious as the stars on a cloudless night. I needed him to believe we despised each other. It was why I moved to a room you couldn't find. If you kept showing up, I would have caved. I would have begged you to visit me, and Lancelot is undoubtedly watching me. He would have seen my betrayal, and it would have sealed your fate."

"Then I have failed you as a husband." Arthur's voice was

flat, and Guinevere wanted him to scream. To yell and fight with her. At least that meant he still cared.

"You could never fail me. How is loving me a failure?" She sobbed uncontrollably. There was always a possibility he wouldn't understand. She understood that and told herself that her misery was a small price to pay to save his life and his throne, but kneeling before him with his voice hollow convinced her she had been wrong. Living without Arthur and his love would destroy her.

"You didn't trust me to keep you safe," Arthur spat. "You didn't trust me to play a part, so you lied. Guinevere, do you really think me so foolish that I would purposely put you in harm's way? Do you think I can't control myself to stay away from you while you do something incredibly stupid and dangerous to save my life? I have failed you if you assume I would ever jeopardize your safety."

"I'm sorry." She collapsed in on herself in defeat. Breathing was impossible, and she wanted the earth to swallow her whole. "I didn't know what to do. He needed to be convinced of my loyalty before he shared his secrets. I love you so much that all I obsessed about was saving you. I am just a naive girl, and I've destroyed everything." She could barely speak. Her sobs were too great. At least Arthur had learned part of Lancelot's plan before he exiled her. He was a man of unmatched intelligence. He would find a way out from under this threat. "I have ruined us, haven't I?"

Arthur didn't answer.

"I'm sorry. I'm a fool, and I ruined us."

"Stop talking." His words were so harsh she recoiled as if he had slapped her. This was the end of their marriage, and she shifted, readying to leave. She couldn't stay here anymore and watch how her actions wrecked the one person in her life that truly loved her, but before she moved, an excruciating sob ripped from Arthur's mouth. Guinevere froze in horror as the almost emotionless king bent forward and sobbed. Tears cascaded down his cheeks, trailing down his uneven nose, and his shoulders shook violently. It was the most heartbreaking sight she had ever witnessed. The warrior reduced to tears. It was also the most beautiful show of strength she had ever seen from her husband. His raw emotion emanated from his body, and while she hated herself for breaking him, she felt awe at his vulnerability. He was beauty and power as he cried.

For long seconds, she knelt transfixed by the massive man wracked by sobs, and before she could escape the gravity of his sorrow, he leaned forward. He wrapped a heavy forearm around her waist and pulled her against his heart until he cradled her in his lap. His powerful arms ensnared her back and legs, and he buried his face in her hair. She was so small compared to him that as he drew her closer, she almost ceased to exist in his consuming embrace.

His sobs intensified as he hugged her. The emotions wracking his chest were brutally raw. They cried together, and with every second, his grip grew stronger, harder, tighter. His heart pounded beneath her cheek. Her neck flooded with his tears. His ribs struggled to breathe. His movements were so familiar, yet so foreign, as he wept. And then, to her surprise, his nose nudged her head, forcing her to look up at him. He claimed her mouth with a kiss, wet and rough, his tears melding with hers, and then with a ragged breath, he pulled back.

"If you are telling me the truth," he heaved against her lips, "if this is happening under my nose, then you have ruined nothing. You saved my life."

Chapter Sixteen

The sob that exploded from Guinevere was wet and unattractive as she clutched Arthur's chest.

"I am, I swear." Her words tripped over one another. "I promise, I will do everything in my power to prove I'm telling the truth, that I am trying to save you."

"Guin." Arthur kissed her silent, and her lips met his with overwhelming relief. "This never happens again," he said as they pulled apart, tears still streaming down his face. "We don't lie, we don't hide things from one another. Do you understand me? Of course, I have to forgive you now. Lord knows what I would do if your life was threatened. I understand why you felt your actions were justified, but this is the last time you withhold a secret this damning from me. I am your husband, and if you can't trust me with the truth, then something between us is broken."

"Never again, I promise." She kissed him softly, her fingers digging into a scar on his chest. "As long as you're still my husband?"

"I should bend you over my knee," his voice was angry as he studied her. "Gods, do I want to teach you a lesson. You almost killed me, Guinevere, but yes, I am still your husband. I've always been and always will be yours. Even if you left, I would remain yours."

"I am never leaving you," she swore, and he saw the truth in her eyes, the ferocity. "I am yours, and you are mine. Never say you'll let me go because you're wrong. You do own me. My heart is yours. It has been since the moment I caught sight of you."

"If what you are telling me is true, you just signed Lancelot's death sentence." He looked at her to gauge her reaction to his threat, but all he saw was desire. It warmed his chest that it was what she wanted, that she wasn't trying to protect the knight. "I will fucking kill him for this."

"And I will help." The challenge in her eyes returned, and even though her actions had driven a dagger through his heart, Arthur loved her to the point of ruin. However irresponsible her actions had been, she had thrown herself at a wolf to save his life. It was a brilliant plan, despite driving him to madness, but without her, he would have been oblivious. Oh, foolish Lancelot, how he had underestimated Guinevere.

"So, I haven't lost you?" Arthur hoisted her further into his lap, refusing to let her go. He had underestimated her, too.

"You will never lose me." She kissed his chest. "People sometimes fear you because of your size. Women recoil at your scars and your gruff demeanor, and you worry you aren't enough. Arthur, I realize I made you doubt my love, but I need you to listen to me. I don't want anyone else, and you never frightened me. I never told you, but the moment I laid my eyes on you, I knew you were it for me. Everything about you was what I wanted. You are the only man I have ever found attractive, and I've spent five years falling deeper in love with you. I don't see the scars or your introverted nature, but a jawline so powerful and alluring it drives me to distraction. I see a husband so handsome, I can't control myself. Can't you see how viscerally you affect me? You are beautiful to me.

"You treat me like a human being, respecting both my mind and my body. You consider me your equal, your partner, your queen and friend. No one, not even my father, has ever held me in such high regard. I was always an object flaunted to attract wealth and power, but to you, I am a person. A mind. A soul. There is freedom in loving you. Safety. Dignity. Honor. I could never love anyone after you. If you die, I die."

Arthur grunted uncomfortably at her words, and she shifted to seize his face. "I'm serious. If you die, I die. I won't allow a man to treat me like property after I've experienced a genuine marriage. Lancelot only sees my beauty and status, and if he kills you, if he steals you from me, I will kill myself before I marry him. I promised you till death do us part, but that isn't true. Death won't separate us because if you perish, I will follow you. I am sorry I didn't fully convey how much you mean to me over these past years, but Arthur, there is more to you than your crooked nose and one-word answers. Few women are fortunate enough to find a husband with your honor, and I'll never trade you for beauty or youth. I choose you until the day I die, and then I want to lie in the dirt beside you for eternity."

"I should have never doubted you." Another tear trailed down his cheek, and Guinevere wiped it away with gentle fingers. "I should've known that other forces were at play. At Tristan's wedding, I think I discovered something that made me question that there might be more to your behavior than what met the eye, but I was too drunk to remember."

"The tea? I saw you take a sip and then spit it out."

"Yes, that sounds familiar." He smiled at her.

"I wanted Lancelot intoxicated so I could manipulate him, but I needed to maintain full control of myself."

"Smart girl." He brushed her hair back from her red and

blotchy face. Gods, she was beautiful, even when she cried. "I should have paid better attention and trusted our marriage. You were unbearably convincing, though, and then I remembered the look you gave him the night we met Lancelot. How handsome you thought he was, and it drove me to doubt."

"His attractive features are impossible not to notice, but my thoughts never dwelled on his beauty." Guinevere shifted in his lap to glare at him. She needed him to understand this so thoroughly that her words burrowed into the very cells of his body. "When I first saw him, I felt something evil, and it frightened me. I couldn't explain it, but just like when I met you and recognized my future, I met him and experienced dread. I hoped I was wrong. He saved your life and became one of your closest friends. After all this time, I assumed I'd been mistaken, so I kept quiet. It kills me, but I read a wrongness in him that night, and I should have warned you. I could've cut this off at the roots. I never once wanted him. Ever. You told me you would ruin me for other men. Arthur, you don't realize how true that is. In every aspect, you ruined me, and Lancelot terrifies me. I can't stand to be near him, but then I picture you, cold and dead, and I force myself to face my fear so I might save you."

"You seemed afraid of me just a few minutes ago." Shame colored Arthur's cheeks, and Guinevere kissed him, whispering against his mouth.

"I have never been afraid of you. I was worried I had ruined us and lost you, but I never once feared you. Lancelot? He terrifies me every day, and I am glad you found me and forced me to confess. Arthur, I'm so scared that he will find out I love you and strangle me. I am frightened that despite my efforts, he will still kill you."

"I am sending you to your father's," Arthur said, "Because if he harms one hair on your head, I won't be able to stop myself. I won't allow you to see that. It is not a side of me I want you to witness, and I can't have you anywhere near Lancelot anymore."

"No." The small word was so forceful that Arthur glared at her in surprise. "I'm not leaving you."

"Guin—"

"No." Her face turned savage. "If I leave, he'll realize something is wrong. I won't abandon you when you need me the most. We still don't know who else is working with him or his exact plans. His timeline. You need me to figure those out."

"Absolutely not." Arthur squinted at his wife as if she was insane. "You really think I'm going to let you anywhere near that lunatic? I'll take it from here and investigate the vanishing traders. See if I can discover where they are hiding if they never left Camelot."

"But—"

"No, Guin." He gripped her biceps in his fists and held her out before him. "Do not fight me on this. You promised to always defer to my judgment in times of danger. Please, I'm begging you. I need you to keep that promise."

"No!" She squirmed against his hold, but it was no use. His grip was iron, so she collapsed and glared at him. Sleeping alone in the same castle as him was too great a distance. She would never survive the miles of separation, worrying if she had said goodbye to her beloved husband for the last time. "It's a good plan, and you know it. I'm the perfect spy for you. Lancelot has been careful. No one suspected him for five years, and the men he polluted against you will never return to your service. I'm all you have, and I can do it. Arthur, let me find out who he is working with and their plans. Then I promise to go to my father's, but I want to help. I need to."

"This is not up for discussion."

"If I were Gawain, would you let me do this?" She was a raging fire in his grip, all sparks and heat and vengeance.

"That's—"

"What if I was a maid? Would you let me spy for you if I were a soldier? A servant?"

"Guinevere, this is different," he growled, matching her intensity. "You are my wife."

"It's because I'm your wife that I need to do this. Arthur, I am the one person sworn by an oath of God and body to love and protect you. You are more than my husband. You are my other half, my best friend, my reason for living. If anyone should face the depths of Hell for you, it should be me."

"I can't let you." Arthur's breathing turned ragged as his chest heaved, and still unable to escape his grip, Guinevere leaned forward and placed her forehead lovingly against his.

"You injured him, and he will suffer for the next few days," she whispered soothingly. "He won't be mobile, which buys us time. Your outburst during training will help me portray the fearful wife who doesn't wish to be caught. I won't be with him for more than a few minutes, and you'll keep me from danger. Please, let me attempt to pull more secrets from him before we give up. You know it's a good plan. I am in the perfect position to destroy him."

"I know." Arthur kissed her softly, the touch of her lips easing his panic slightly. "If you were anyone but my wife, I would agree. You hold his loyalty but offer none back, and I need that. I need someone on the inside, but I can't stop thinking about him touching you, about your fear that he might strangle you, and I feel ill." He paused and then jerked his head up to meet her gaze. "You two haven't?"

"No," Guinevere practically screamed, recoiling in disgust at the thought of anyone other than her husband stripping her bare, kissing her, making love to her. "You're the only man I've been with… will ever be with."

"Oh, thank God." Arthur blew out a relieved breath and folded her back into his lap.

"I told Lancelot I'm married in the eyes of God and the law, and it would be a sin to break my vows. That was my explanation for why I abandoned your bed. I was keeping myself pure for him, but I also needed to wait to become his wife and queen so I could remain holy. It was the only excuse I could think of to keep him from touching me." Guinevere blushed remembering just how little she cared about remaining pure before her marriage to Arthur, how she had thrown herself into his arms and never once looked back.

"And he believed that?"

"For now."

Arthur grunted and pulled her naked body further against his. It had felt like a lifetime since his skin had touched hers, and he was afraid if he blinked, he would find it had all been a dream.

"First, you do nothing stupid," he said through gritted teeth. "I am deadly serious, Guin. I don't care if you think it might push him to reveal something. You do nothing risky or foolish. Second, you do not go anywhere alone with him. Stay in public. Tell him whatever you need to about me to ensure he meets you with witnesses present. Third, if anything happens that scares you, and I mean anything, you tell me. I refuse to risk your life. The minute concern pricks your conscience, tell me, and I'll send you to your father's until it is safe to return." He grabbed her jaw and pulled her gaze to his. "Do you understand me?"

She nodded.

"Use your words, pretty girl," he growled. "These are my terms, and I'll only stand by and let you try your plan if you agree to them. Don't worry, I will play my part. Lancelot will believe we are over, but I can't protect you if I don't know where you are."

"I swear it." And she sealed her vow with a kiss.

CHAPTER SEVENTEEN

Guinevere lay on her stomach, her shoulder pressed into Arthur's chest as he stretched out on his side. His fingers traced lazy circles over her bare back, his skin unable to part from hers. He thought he would never again feel her warmth, and now that he knew the truth, he never wished to be parted from her. The spell would break in the morning. He would return to being the jilted husband, but right now, he was the love of her life. With Lancelot injured and this section of the castle unoccupied, he had begged her to stay, and she had agreed with such relief and enthusiasm he almost cried again. He had tucked her against his body, meaning to sleep beside her, but he couldn't close his eyes. I wanted to drink up every moment.

"I missed this," Guinevere said into his chest, her head tilted so that her lips brushed his skin as she spoke. "I forgot how to sleep alone. Every night without you was misery."

"When this ends, we never sleep apart." He kissed her shoulder. "I will drag you everywhere I go. These past weeks have been horrible."

"I don't know how I convinced him I don't love you." She smirked against him, her mouth tickling his ribs as the expression moved her lips. "We have been inseparable since we married. How could anyone think we don't love each other?"

"I may talk to you a lot," he huffed as he tangled his fingers in her dark hair, "but I share little outside of our bed. I am not tender or emotional. You are the only person I trust with my secrets, my hopes, my darkness. We see a different version of our marriage than the world does."

"I guess." She slid her leg sideways until her knee brushed his thighs. Instinctually, he parted his legs to let her softness slide between his, her thigh brushing his already hard cock, and he groaned.

"These were the moments that bound us together." Arthur kissed her head, sweeping his lips seductively over her ear as he spoke, and she shivered against him. "I always wanted a marriage where our bed was sacred and safe, and you gave that to me. You became my best friend during those nights. I found more than a wife in you. You are my soulmate. Your presence became so integral to my existence that removing you is like carving off my limbs. I've shared more with you in a single evening than I've shared with others over my entire life, but the world doesn't see that. They don't see the man who bares his soul to the person he trusts most. They don't see the way I hold you when your body shakes, unable to come anymore. All they see is who I am in public. I reveal little of what lingers within me when we are not alone, and it's easier for them to assume what we present when they don't know the truth."

"But your eyes when you watch me." Guinevere slid her hand down his abs and gripped the head of his cock. Arthur groaned at the soft contact, and he captured her ear between his lips. "They are full of love. Not obsession. How anyone could ignore that is beyond me."

"People expect love to be gentle and romantic." Arthur's breathing hitched as she slowly stroked every delicious inch of his length, her thumb wiping away his pre-cum. "They see how I touch you, yet don't know you like I do. They only notice how different I am from other men. How different we behave compared to other couples."

Guinevere tilted her eyes to his, and her heated gaze almost made him come in her hand.

"Fuck, Guinevere," he grunted, struggling to keep from spilling into her palm. "You bit me earlier. You fucking bit me, and while it hurt, that was not what I thought about when your teeth drew blood. It made me come so hard, and all I could think was, I wish you had bitten me harder. I have scars from men who tried to kill me, but I want one from the woman I love. I want you to mark me. To make me yours. Most kings lay with their wives until she produces an heir and then find whores to warm their bed, but not me. I demand it all with you, and only you. I crave your love and your fire. I need every delicious and depraved thing you have to offer. People don't understand us. They assume it means I don't love you, but you and I are the same. I see it in your eyes. You want it all."

"My king." She drew closer so he might read the feral hunger in her gaze.

Arthur heaved a ragged breath, tightening the reins on his control. He was right. She was exactly like him, and he adored her. Fuck what anyone else thought. He dragged his gaze down her bare body and slid his fingers against the back of her thigh, tracing them slowly over her soft skin until they reached the swell of her ass. He cupped her roughly, and she gasped, rearing backward into his hand. Her fist tightened around him, desire curling through her strokes, but he pulled away from her. He wouldn't spill in her palm. No, he had other plans. He wanted it deep inside her, reminding her who she belonged to, and as he knelt behind his wife, he saw how her arousal glistened between her legs, dripping and glorious and all for him. Before he could stop them, his knuckles swiped teasingly at her opening.

"My king," she moaned, bucking back against his fingers, desperate for release, but Arthur wasn't ready. He was going to take his time. She had made him suffer. Now it was her turn.

"Not yet, pretty girl." He pressed a palm against her hips and pushed her gently into the bed so she couldn't move. "Be patient for your king. Maybe if you're a good girl, I'll give you my cock."

"Please." Her begging was breathless and needy, and his fingertips dragged along her leg so close to where she craved him, yet impossibly far. Guinevere jerked sideways, trying to force his hand where she wanted, but Arthur tsked under his breath, holding her still.

"So greedy, my pretty girl." His fingers trailed up her ass, drifting farther from her aching core. "Look at your perfect cunt, dripping wet for me. You are so beautiful when you are desperate."

"Arthur," she groaned, reaching her hand around to force him between her thighs, but he shoved it gently aside.

"Be a good girl, Guinevere," he commanded as his fingers continued over her ass and down the inside of her thigh. "If you want my cock, then you will be patient. I want to hear you beg first. I want to hear how badly you crave your husband, the man who loves you."

"Arthur" Her voice came out in such a hungry whine, she felt embarrassed.

"Arthur?" he questioned, gripping her ass harder.

"My king." She bucked in his hand, reveling in the sensation of his calloused palm against her skin. "I need you, my king."

"Beg, Guinevere." He dragged his knuckles toward her center but stopped just short of her entrance, and she practically screamed at him. She was wild and out of her mind, grinding on the blankets as she searched for friction. Arthur laughed when he noticed what she was doing and gripped her hips tighter in his massive fists.

"I didn't say you could come." He yanked her back until she knelt before him, and she almost sobbed at the loss of contact. "If you can't be a good girl for your king, then you don't get rewarded. Now I told you to beg, my beautiful wife. Tell me how much you want your husband."

"Every night while I was alone, I would lie naked in bed, pushing my fingers deep inside me, imagining it was you," she gasped as he cupped her ass with one hand, his other holding her hip still. His body heat radiated behind her, and she thought she might pass out from desire if he didn't touch her soon.

"Continue." Arthur's voice was tight at her confession, his control slipping as he pictured her fingering her wet and gorgeous cunt to thoughts of him.

"I would close my eyes and imagine you gripping my throat as you thrust, choking me with just the right amount of pressure. Owning me. Ruining me. I would pinch my nipples hard until I came, imagining they were your teeth. I bit the pillows to keep from screaming as I twisted them until they were pink, fantasizing about how rough your fingers are. Please, I need you inside me, filling me, making me yours."

"Good girl." He stroked her ass softly, and his words bathed her soul. "I love you, Guinevere. I will always love my queen."

"I love every part of you, Arthur. I never knew true happiness until I married you."

"Fuck, Guin." He lost all control and raised his hand high. He paused for a moment, savoring how pale her soft ass looked, and then with brutal speed, he brought his palm down hard. Guinevere gasped at the spank, her skin stinging, and he gently caressed the pink flesh.

"That was for making me doubt your love," he said as he pulled his arm back. Her ass was pink, but he wanted it red.

He waited for a moment, watching her for signs of discomfort or a signal that she didn't want him to continue, but he observed nothing but her squirming anticipation. Arousal dripped down to coat her thighs, and he smiled as he slapped her again.

"That was for lying to me," Arthur growled as she moaned, and unable to stop himself, he took aim for a third time. He unleashed on her, the sound of his palm smacking her, echoing around the room, and she bucked backward as if searching for him as she gasped.

"And that." He gently brushed the gloriously red flesh. "That was because you fucking liked it."

Guinevere looked over her shoulder at him with a wicked grin. "Yes, my king." Her words were slow and drawn out. She knew exactly what she was doing to him, and Arthur reached forward and grabbed her hair. He wrapped it around his fists and reared her back, thrusting into her as her ass slammed against his thigh.

"Arthur!" She was almost incoherent from the bliss, the sting from his slaps mixing deliciously with the intense pleasure building in her core.

"You feel so good, Guin," Arthur growled, as he pulled her hair tighter. Her head tilted back, displaying her long and beautiful throat to him. The throat he had plans for, and he reached forward with his free hand to pinch her nipple. She moaned at the pressure, thrusting against him in wild moves until he was deeper than he had ever been.

"Is this what you pictured?" He grunted in her ear as she bucked against him. She was so lost in her pleasure, she didn't answer, and Arthur tugged her hair gently as a reminder. "Use your words, pretty girl."

"Yes, my king... harder."

"Tell me how much better my cock is than your fingers," he ordered, as he twisted her nipples slightly.

"You're so deep, Arthur." She could barely form coherent thoughts. "You fuck exactly how I like… oh God."

"Not God, Guin. Your husband," de reminded her. "If you are going to call out anyone's name while I'm inside you, it had better be mine."

"Yes, my king." She was panting, heaving, spinning. Her orgasm was so close she tasted its sweetness. "Yes… Don't stop. Please don't—"

Her orgasm cut her off, and Arthur's hand flew from her taut nipple to her mouth, capturing her scream, hiding it from all and keeping it for only himself. He held his palm against her lips, letting her ride out her climax as he fought to keep from joining her. She tightened deliciously around him, but he didn't want to come. Not yet. He wanted to feel her again. Knowing he brought her this much pleasure was his favorite thing in the world.

Arthur removed his palm from her mouth and lowered it to her throat. He wanted to grant her every fantasy, and he knelt upright, pulling her up by her neck until she knelt before him, her back cemented to his chest, her thighs pressed to his powerful ones. His fingers squeezed the sides of her throat, careful not to crush her airway, and his other hand dragged erotically down her breast to her clit. He held her tight against him as he stroked her exactly how she liked, and within seconds, her breath quickened.

She leaned further against him, riding him gloriously hard, and she tilted her head, kissing him with desperate hunger. As their lips touched, she moaned into his mouth, "I love you."

Arthur picked up his pace. His fingers coaxed her orgasm to the surface, his tongue plundering her mouth. He was utterly lost in this woman, hopelessly obsessed, and while the pain of her actions still lingered, he knew he had already forgiven her.

"I love you, my queen," he groaned, his hand gently choking her. "You are mine. Tell me you are mine."

"I am yours. Always yours." Her breaths were faster, ragged, intense, and he felt her tighten around him, and this time he could not fight his own orgasm.

"Come for me, pretty girl. Come on your husband's cock."

"Come with me," she begged, reaching her hand back to grip his hair, and she kissed him. "I want it all."

"Fuck, Guin," he roared, claiming her mouth as he lost all control. His climax barreled through him like thunder and lightning, powerful and electric and jaw-dropping. She tightened around him, pulling every drop from his body as she exploded in ecstasy. He swallowed her cries as she breathed in his moans, and together they came in perfect harmony.

Chapter Eighteen

"I can't stay long," Guinevere whispered as she slipped unseen into Lancelot's room. "Arthur is in a mood, and I think he has the maids tailing me." She glided across the floor and perched on the edge of the bed, capturing his hands. She knew for a fact Arthur had instructed the maids to watch her. He hadn't told them why, only that he wanted her watched. It had been one of his demands when he agreed to her plan. If he couldn't keep an eye on her, he needed someone else to ensure her safety, and when Lancelot's brows pinch, she knew it would also aid her cause. He wouldn't harm her or push her to break her marriage vows if he thought they were being hunted by nosey servants. He was well aware of how gossip ran through the castle's underbelly, and she hoped it would be enough to create a sense of urgency.

"Of course, he is," Lancelot spat, and Guinevere wondered how she ever believed the two were friends. His unbridled disgust made her skin crawl, but she shoved down the bile burning her throat.

"I had to visit you, though," she continued in an enticingly low voice, pressing a quick kiss to his knuckles to distract him. "Even if only for a second."

"I am glad, my love." He leaned forward to cup her face, his lips moving toward hers. Her body braced for impact, but a grimace broke over his features, and with a groan, Lancelot fell to the bed. Guinevere's soul heaved a sigh of relief. She was prepared to do whatever it took to drag the name of the second traitor out of him, but after kissing Arthur goodbye in the dark morning hours, even Lancelot's slightest touch felt wrong. Her skin crawled. She wanted to flee, but she forced herself to look at him as if he were her entire universe. Her ass still stung slightly from Arthur's palm, and she concentrated on the discomfort. She was thankful he had been so rough. Not only because she enjoyed it, but because it, combined with the bruises on her spine and the ache between her legs, was a constant reminder of the man she truly loved. Every time Lancelot touched her, her mind went to her husband's lingering reminders. They would help her endure.

"Lancelot?" Concern laced her voice as she peeled back his shirt to reveal the gruesome purple consuming his side. The less he could move, the less she would have to interact with him. It would also inflame his anger, and maybe if she pushed him, it would cause him to break.

"I hate to see your beautiful skin marred," she soothed.

"He will pay for this." Lancelot's voice was ice as he grabbed her hands and pulled them away from his pain.

"He should," she agreed. "I can't bear the thought of you looking like him. He is so deformed, and I loathe how he has tried to steal your beauty. Lancelot, it makes me sick to think of you suffering, of how scars remind me of his body, and what he would..." She dissolved into convincing but fake tears, collapsing to rest her head on his biceps. She needed to hide her face as she spoke the words furthest from the truth, but she knew it would anger the knight, and by the way his muscles tensed beneath her, she had driven the blade home.

"I will never look as vile as him," he spat, grabbing her chin and yanking her up. "Do not cry, my love. What you've endured sickens me, but when I am king, you will never again have to suffer at his hands."

"When, Lancelot?" She leaned forward desperately, purposely putting pressure on his injured ribs, and he flinched, pushing her away. "I am sorry." She recoiled, removing her hands from him in mock concern. "I just don't know how much I can bear. He is having me followed. He hurt you. How long before his actions turn deadly? I'm afraid, Lancelot. When? Please tell me when I no longer have to suffer?"

"Soon, my love. Can you hold out a while longer?"

"For you, I would do anything." She glanced at the door nervously. "You need your rest. I shouldn't even be here, but I couldn't stay away. Sleep and heal, so you may return to me."

She shot forward and kissed him on the cheek before he could protest and then fled the room. She crept as fast as she dared down the corridors, her body bristling with annoyance. Soon wasn't an answer, and she was desperate to help Arthur stop the oncoming evil. Last night hadn't been enough. It only made missing him worse.

A deep voice rumbled ahead of her, and her heart thudded in her throat. She had avoided her husband since seeing him only enhanced her suffering, but now that he knew the truth, she walked faster. She craved even just the sight of him, and despite her carefully arranged features of indifference, her body screamed with excitement.

Arthur and Percival rounded the corner, and the king peered at her in surprise. His shock quickly soured into a glare, and Guinevere's heart almost stopped at its disdain. Anger and disgust wafted off him in waves, making Percival uncomfortable. The scowl was so stunningly harsh, she felt like an insect crushed beneath his boot. He did not stop as he strode toward her, but just as their shoulders passed, the angle hiding their gazes from Percival, the king's gaze softened. His frown was still plastered to his face, his sneer brutal and unforgiving, and to anyone else, he held only hatred for his wife, but Guinevere knew him well. How many conversations had they spoken with only their eyes? The momentary change was for her. A love letter, a caress, a gift. Guinevere's heart stuttered, and she had to force her own features to remain indifferent.

Arthur ripped his gaze from hers and strode away, the perfect picture of a jilted husband, and Guinevere clenched her lips to keep from calling after him. She should have never doubted his ability to act. He was flawless. Terrifyingly convincing, and yet still he let her witness the love in his eyes.

ARTHUR FOUGHT the urge to turn around and kiss his wife. He saw her surprise at how fierce he looked, but then watched her soften when he spoke with only his gaze. She understood, and the frown faltering on her lips swelled his chest with pride. He hadn't needed to take this hallway back to his private study. It was out of his way, but he knew she was returning from Lancelot's room. They avoided each other before, but now he refused to remain far from her. His heart couldn't survive the separation, and he was terrified of leaving her unprotected. He needed to be close in the event of an emergency. So help him if Lancelot harmed her. God have mercy on his soul, for he would not.

"Is everything…?" Percival started with a confused glance backward at the departing Queen.

"Yes." Arthur cut him off, his dark tone a warning to drop the subject.

"As I was saying." Percival shook his head in confusion, but heeded the warning. "Strange rumors have traveled from Grishem Monastery. None are clear about the specifics, but something doesn't sit right with me. Many of Camelot's orphans live there, and I don't like the idea of a disturbance with children involved. It could be nothing, but I felt I should make you aware."

"If the reports are concerning you, then I trust your judgment."

The men turned toward Arthur's private study, and Percival paused. It was the only place no one, not even his wife or Merlin, was allowed.

"Check it out," Arthur continued. "Be discreet and report your findings back to me and only me."

"Yes, my king." Percival bowed before turning on his heels to leave, and Arthur hiked up to his study. Once locked away, he settled at his desk, staring contemplatively at the wall before grabbing his ink quill. He had an idea.

THE NEXT TWO days passed uneventfully, and Guinevere was thankful for the reprieve. She still visited Lancelot, hoping that the privacy and her care would push him to reveal more of his plan, but it was to no avail. On the last visit, she begged her maid to knock on the door while she was in his room so she could blame her sudden distance on almost being caught.

Frustration coiled through Guinevere, and each night, she drowned under the urge to crawl into Arthur's bed, but she forced herself to pace the floor alone instead. Beyond the basics of his plans and the timeframe of soon, Lancelot offered her nothing, and she had fallen asleep to the truth that Lancelot was not like her husband. He didn't view her as his equal or his partner. She was a prize to be won, a jewel to be exhibited. Maybe she should visit her father and let Arthur discover the rest of the treachery. Her father could feign an illness. Not even Lancelot could refuse her departure for such an urgent reason.

Morning did nothing to ease her agitation. Arthur would have been on his feet before she had finished knotting the bandages, but thankfully, the knight was not her king. His pain had given her three days of peace without worrying when he would appear behind her, and at least now she could walk past Arthur without warranting his anger. She tried not to taunt her husband, not wanting to arouse more suspicion than was already weaving through the gossip mill, but her body settled whenever she saw him. His scowl stayed firmly in place, his muscles rigid and unforgiving, but the subtle changes in his eyes reminded her of her purpose. She refused to imagine a life where those eyes ceased to track her movements.

Guinevere stood from the bed and crossed to her wardrobe. Her hand reached for a light blue garment, but paused as her red wedding dress in the wardrobe's corner caught her attention. She yanked it down and pulled it on, the garment gifting her strength. No one knew the importance of this gown beside her and her husband, and it felt like armor as she fastened it in place. Arthur would be with her. He would understand her unspoken message.

A soft knock interrupted her thoughts, and her maid entered with breakfast.

"Thank you." Guinevere sat before the tray, and the girl curtseyed before she left. The queen lifted the tea to her lips, and the moment the cup moved, she saw it. A folded piece of paper hid below the saucer, invisible while the cup had been in place. Guinevere's heart thudded as she peeled it free from the plate, hoping it was from both Arthur and Lancelot for different reasons, but when she unfolded it, the ink that greeted her was the last thing she had expected.

The note was a crudely drawn sketch. It was rough and blocky, and Guinevere flipped the paper upside down, but its significance still escaped her. She leaned back in confusion, tracing every line with her eyes as she ate before turning it clockwise. She hoped viewing the drawing at a new angle would spark some recognition, but all she saw were shapes. Clearly, someone had worried this might be intercepted and had opted for an innocent sketch instead of words. If her maid found it, she would have assumed it was the product of idle hands, and that thought made Guinevere bolt upright in her chair. This was from Arthur. Only he would send her something this cryptic, trusting she would decipher the meaning.

Guinevere shut her eyes and pictured her handsome husband bending over this paper, the quill trailing roughly through the ink as he tried to speak to her. She imaged his movements, his strokes, but after a long moment, her eyelids snapped open in frustration. She had no idea what he was trying to say.

GUINEVERE IGNORED the small crowd lounging in the garden. Her public shaming had begun. Their eyes soured with disgust, and the condescending glares set her teeth on edge. She should be thankful her plan was working. Rumors of the queen's infidelity would bombard Lancelot, which would hopefully ignite a sense of urgency in him. She hoped it forced him to reveal more of his plans, but right now, the shame was a thousand bees stinging her spirit. Camelot had regarded her with suspicion when she first arrived. A much younger bride, she was a stranger to the king, and unsavory speculations about her and her intentions spread like wildfire. Arthur ruthlessly shut them down, but she was on her own now. She had made this bed, and she would lie in it until her husband was safe. It was a small price to pay if it meant she never had to build him a funeral pyre.

A shrill laugh grated over her skin like coarse sand, and Guinevere held her breath, forcing herself not to meet the woman's gaze. She knew the lady was mocking her, and she forced herself to concentrate on the sketch instead. She had tucked it into her bodice, carrying the paper Arthur had once touched close to her heart and surveyed the garden for the tenth time. The rough image drew her subconscious to the gardens, but now that she sat there, all she could picture was the woman's sneer.

With an exasperated sigh, Guinevere stood abruptly and stalked away from the small gathering. She needed space to think, to hope something out here would spark a memory. She was missing something, something obvious. It teased her mind, begging to be captured, but each time she reached for it, it evaporated like smoke.

"My queen," a deep voice interrupted the silence, and Guinevere jerked. She'd been convinced she walked alone, and the reality that someone had silently followed frightened her. She twisted, coming face to face with Gawain, and he smiled. It was not a welcoming expression. It was a threat masked as a pleasantry, and she involuntarily stepped backward.

"Lovely afternoon, is it not?" he continued as they fell into step, and she forced herself not to run.

"Indeed." She was thankful her voice slipped from her lips without a tremor.

"And are you well, my queen?" The unnatural smile remained plastered on his face.

"Yes, thank you." She could barely manage more than a few words as he strode steadily beside her.

"And the king?" He looked pointedly at her. "How is he?"

"He is well."

"Is he?"

"Of course." She forced herself not to shake. The tone of his voice was wrong, and with a sickening dread, she wondered if Gawain, loyal and loving Gawain, was Lancelot's conspirator. Guinevere swallowed, but her throat had gone desert dry. She should not have wandered off alone.

"That is good to hear," he continued, his gaze and smile still trained on her, the picture of politeness. "I would hate for the king to be unwell. He is my friend and lord. He is this kingdom's salvation. Camelot needs him, and if he were unwell, I would be terribly unhappy."

Guinevere almost tripped as she met his stare.

"As his wife," he emphasized the word, "I am sure you understand. We wouldn't want anything unfortunate to happen to Arthur, would we? It would be terrible if I had to fix things for him. I want what is best for Arthur. You appreciate that, of course?"

Guinevere's mind flashed to her wedding night when Gawain made his judgment of her clear, where he claimed she would either be Arthur's salvation or his ruin and what he would do if she were the latter. Relieved that a traitor didn't stalk her, she met his eyes with all the dignity of a ruthless queen.

"Absolutely."

"I am glad we understand one another." His smile broadened, and her fear doubled. His expression was terrifying to behold, and she knew Gawain would kill her if he found any legitimacy to the rumors sparking into flames.

"I'm pleased we spoke, aren't you?" He bowed irreverently and turned on his heels. "I shall see you soon, my queen." It was not a promise nor a fond farewell. It was a threat. One he would carry out with brutal efficiency if needed.

The moment he disappeared from sight, Guinevere hiked up her skirt and ran. She raced blindly, aimlessly scrambling over the grass. She had no destination in mind, nor did she care where she ended up. All she knew was if she stood still, she would explode. Fear radiated from her every pore, soaking her in sweat, and she did not stop until her lungs burned in agony. She should be thankful Arthur had at least one faithful knight, but the fear was ugly and cruel, a savage in her gut. Tears burst from her eyes, and shame at her own weakness scorched her cheeks, but the encounter terrified her. She was loyal to the king, but now Gawain's suspicions would drive him to stalk her. One perceived misstep, and he might kill her, leaving Arthur unprotected before the wolves.

Guinevere doubled over and heaved, tears coating her skin as she coughed, and it took long minutes before she could stand upright, her side cramping from her brutal pace. She was blissfully alone, no one nearby to witness her shame, and she sighed in relief as she surveyed her surroundings. She stood in a small section of the garden no one ever ventured to. It was wild and unkept, its beauty raw and untouched, unlike the pruned and controlled hedges where most of the court spent their afternoons. It was peaceful here, the small untamed patch of land hugging the castle wall, and a prick of familiarity rang through her.

Guinevere snatched the folded paper from her breast, her memory sparking to life, and held it before her as she slowly turned. She had been here before. Once, when she first moved to Camelot. It was right after she admitted she loved Arthur. They had been married for six months, and she had tried to wait for him to voice it first, but containing the confession threatened her sanity. She remembered vividly the look on his face when he woke in the night. He had been concerned by her behavior until the words tumbled from her mouth of their own accord. He said nothing, but she knew by his eyes he felt the same. A few days later, they attended a celebration in the gardens, and Guinevere spent the entire evening teasing her husband. She realized that with every comment, with every glance, every touch, she was digging herself in too deep, but watching his control slip made her feel alive. After the guests grew drunk and oblivious, Arthur simply looked at her and said, "Run." It was the only warning he gave her as she raced into the darkness. If he caught her, there would be the devil to pay.

He let her pretend she could escape him for a while, but when they reached this wild section of the garden, his mercy ended. He captured her and made her his, over and over, until she was boneless and exhausted. Afterward, he carried her to bed because her legs were deliciously weak, her body drunk on his love, but before he scooped her from the grass, he whispered he loved her. She had been peering into his dark eyes when he said it, her heart ready to explode from happiness, but something hovered behind him. Something unique and—

Guinevere froze, the pieces clicking together in harmony. She held up the sketch, staring at what lay before her, and Arthur's meaning was painfully obvious. Running from Gawain must have triggered her subconscious, leading her to the place where Arthur told her he loved her for the first time. Leading her to a section of the castle wall that matched her husband's sketch exactly.

CHAPTER NINETEEN

Guinevere's eyes searched for Arthur, but the stillness told her she was alone. He had clearly led her here, but she was still missing something. Most never ventured here, but its openness offered little privacy. No, he wanted something else from her, so she held the sketch closer to the wall.

This section of the castle rose to a protruding tower that housed Arthur's private study. Perhaps he could see her from his room, and Guinevere craned her neck heavenward, but no window loomed above. He wasn't watching her, which meant this ivy-covered wall was the reason he called her here. She brushed the vines aside to reveal more of the patterns carved into the stone. This tower was all that remained of the original castle before war ravaged Camelot. Arthur had rebuilt stronger, but this part stood wholly unchanged, and he had claimed it for himself. This worn wall still bore the remnants of an ancient carving, although its image was almost impossible to distinguish after decades of weather. The lines were abstract, but an archaic beauty remained, which is why Arthur never altered them.

Guinevere ran her hands over the faint carvings and glanced down at the paper. A section on the rightmost corner of the sketch was darker than the rest. She had assumed her husband had traced those lines first to get his bearings before finishing, but staring at it now, she wondered if he emphasized them on purpose.

Her eyes snapped to the correlating lines on the wall. There was something odd about them. Something you would only notice if you knew where to look. And with hesitant fingers, she reached out and pressed them.

With a groan that sent her reeling backward in surprise, the stone gave way. Understanding gripped her brain. That was why Arthur had never removed the faint carvings. Their uneven lines hid the creases of a door.

She pushed against it, and it slid wide with ease. Expertly designed to appear solid, the opening yielded gracefully beneath her hands, and Guinevere stepped inside. She stood in a tunnel that led deep into the darkness, and while she guessed Arthur meant her to follow it, the idea unsettled her. She couldn't leave the door open, but the prospect of locking herself under the tower filled her with uncomfortable claustrophobia. What if Gawain followed her? What if Lancelot searched for her? The cryptic sketch was proof enough that Arthur intended this for her eyes alone.

Guinevere heaved a soft sigh of relief when she spotted a lever on the interior of the stone. Concealed on the outside by the carvings, the inside mechanism was obvious. At least she could escape, and with slightly more faith, she sealed herself beneath the tower.

She expected to be plunged into consuming darkness, but to her surprise, a faint light glowed in the distance. She hadn't noticed it with the sunlight pouring through, and afraid to overthink her decision, Guinevere drifted toward it. The tunnel was mercifully straight and singular. No side corridors to lose herself within, but she barely walked more than a few minutes, when a hulking mass lunged from the shadows.

She should have screamed. She should have been terrified, but with a thundering heart, she threw herself at the form. Its warm body caught her in its powerful embrace, lifting her feet off the floor, and she almost choked him as she hugged his neck. She would recognize this presence anywhere.

"You are wearing my dress," Arthur groaned into her hair as he buried his face against her throat.

"I needed you with me today." She tightened her arms around him, half expecting him to cough from lack of air, but he only kissed her throat.

"Thank God, I had already sent you the sketch. If I saw you like this but couldn't touch you, people might think I was rabid."

"Have you been waiting here all morning?" Guinevere laughed, and it was the most beautiful sound Arthur had ever heard.

"I couldn't miss you. I knew you would come." He set her down and captured her throat in his massive hand, pulling her to his mouth. He kissed passionately, his other arm wrapping around her small waist as she clutched his chest.

"I'm sorry it took me so long to figure it out," she moaned as they broke apart. She hadn't realized just how much she needed to be in her husband's arms, and while their lips separated, their bodies did not.

"It's all right. I was prepared to wait all day," he smiled. Guinevere loved when he smiled. The expression rarely graced his face, but when it did, it was breathtaking, and only for her. "I knew you would figure it out, my smart girl. Come." He shifted her to his side, draping his heavy arm over her shoulders as they began to walk. "I want to show you something."

"What is this place?" Guinevere asked as she wrapped both

her arms around his waist. The tight embrace slowed their movements, but neither of them cared. "I wasn't aware the castle had secret tunnels."

"It didn't. I made this." Guinevere's gaze shot up to his, and he waggled his eyebrows at her. Her heart almost exploded at the teasing gesture. This was Arthur, her Arthur. The man no one else knew, and after weeks of pain in his eyes, she had to fight back tears at seeing him happy again.

"I was too overwhelmed to consider everything the other night," he continued as the ground started an easy but steady incline. "We hadn't made a plan to meet, and while the empty rooms are comfortable, they are risky. I distracted your maid before slipping the sketch under your tea. This tunnel has two entrances, and as long as you and I exit from opposite ends, no one will suspect us."

"How come you never mention this?" she asked.

"Some habits are impossible to kill." His voice darkened, and she almost regretted asking when he continued, "living on the streets taught me to always have a backup plan, always have an exit strategy and keep it secret, because there may be a day when your survival depends on it. Growing up, we all had contingency plans. When the guards raided the slums, those escape routes were the only reason I lived to become king. I never forgot that lesson, so when we rebuilt Camelot, I built this." The sloping floor gave way to a winding staircase, and Guinevere realized that the dim light came from the sparsely lit torches Arthur had ignited.

"The original tower sustained minor damage in the war, and its bones were good. I designed this and then swapped the builders out every day, changing the plans they received." Arthur tightened his grip on her as the walls narrowed. "In the end, none of them realized what they helped me build."

They stopped before a similar lever to the one below, and Arthur pulled it with a flourish. A door swung wide silently, and the couple emerged into his private study. Guinevere released her husband and stepped further into the room. She had never been inside his study. No one had, but this sparse room wasn't what she expected. She assumed it was private because it was his sanctuary, but seeing its cold functionality, she realized the gaping door at her back was the reason it was forbidden.

"I'm sorry I never told you about it. If something ever happened, I would die getting you to safety, so I figured telling you was irrelevant. I would never leave you behind to save myself."

"I know." She turned and patted his muscled chest, her fingers absentmindedly rubbing a scar. He rested a palm over hers, and she smiled up at him. He used to flinch every time she touched those raised marks, but now it brought him peace. Her acceptance of him and her adoration of the things he disliked about himself had changed his life irrevocably.

"You are the king." She pulled her hand away. "You are allowed your secrets." She threw him a mischievous glance over her shoulder as she drifted toward his desk. "Although, now that you've let me in here, I'm going to snoop."

"Be my guest," Arthur chuckled as he leaned against the desk, his arms folding over his chest. "You'll be bored in seconds. This room is private because of the tunnel." She quirked a disbelieving eyebrow, and he rolled his eyes before grunting, "And because I need an escape from people."

"There it is." Guinevere patted his biceps before moving to a small bookshelf against the wall.

"The only reason it's private from you is because I don't want to spend our time together locked in here," he continued. "I wouldn't have refused your company if you followed me here, but when I'm with you, I prefer to be far from work."

"You like your space." Her fingers brushed over the book's spines. "It never bothered me that you didn't ask me up here."

"Although, I am thankful everyone knows this place is off-limits, even to you. It means I can have my wife again."

Like the moon trapped by the earth's gravity, Guinevere drifted back to him, standing against his leaning frame. He unfurled his arms, and she stepped into his embrace, resting her head on his chest to listen to his strong heart.

"As long as you enter and exit from the garden, no one will suspect you are here," Arthur murmured into her hair. "We can meet in peace. If you feel the study is still unsafe, we'll remain in the tunnel. Those doors are thick. No one will hear us in there. I just wanted you to see where it led."

"I never thought a tunnel and a nearly barren study would make me so happy," she whispered into his chest, and without warning, tears burst from her eyes to soak his shirt.

"Guin?" His broad hand cupped the back of her head, pulling her close as if he meant to swallow her body whole. The intense affection only made her cry harder. "Talk to me, my queen."

"I—" She snorted unattractively, the sound coaxing a laugh from her lips. Her tears slowed, but she kept her chest cemented against his. "Lancelot won't offer any more information. All he says is, 'soon, Guinevere.' But that isn't an answer." Arthur stiffened, but he remained silent.

"He responded to a threat that came from you, but nothing I do loosens his tongue. I feel like I've failed you. I want to help, but I can't let him take more from me. It is bad enough that I let him get between us."

"Stop." The gruffness in Arthur's voice was almost a slap. "Don't go there. You've helped me immensely. I had your claims of traders entering Camelot investigated. I was discreet, but you were right, Guin. Many have entered our borders only to disappear, and I don't understand how they went unnoticed. Something is drawing them here, and we don't know how many potential enemies we have in our midst. You aren't a failure. He has already laid claim on too much of you, and he can't take anymore. As it is, I am going to kill him painfully slowly for what he has done to you."

Guinevere nodded against his chest, squeezing him tight.

"Are you considering visiting your father now?" he asked

"Lancelot would be suspicious if I left, but I could blame my departure on an illness. What daughter wouldn't visit a sick parent?"

"That's a smart idea."

"But I can't leave you, Arthur." She pulled away so she could look him in the eyes, their hips pressed together as she leaned against him, his thumb absentmindedly stroking the small of her back. "When we got married, I told you you couldn't leave without me, no matter the danger. Well, I won't abandon you now. If I could convince Lancelot to trust me completely, he might admit more, but he isn't you. You see me as your equal partner and have never hesitated to tell me your plans. To him, I am a trophy. The prize he wins for destroying you. I've manipulated him to a point, but I'm missing something. My affection isn't enough."

"You don't think he suspects your true loyalty?" Concern marred Arthur's handsome face, and Guinevere kissed him until it faded.

"You've been in a tunnel all day, but I should warn you, the rumors have started." She brushed a dark curl behind his ear, twirling the lock lovingly between her fingers. "You need to be prepared when you leave here. Those at court are already spewing venom about me. It hasn't spiraled out of control yet, but it won't be long before everyone hates me. Trust me, Lancelot knows I am loyal to him. The hatred I'm walking into will prove it."

"If anyone so much as touches a single hair on your head—"

"It's just gossip. I'm fine... although Gawain threatened me, so I guess I officially staked my loyalty in Lancelot's corner if your friend believes me guilty. If Gawain believes it, Lancelot will be convinced."

"He what?" Arthur grabbed her arms, icy terror crackling on his skin.

"He didn't threaten me outright," she tripped over her words as she rushed to explain. She recognized that expression. It meant death. "He said it would be a shame if anything happened to you. He suspects I've been unfaithful, and he made it clear that if that is the truth, then I am your enemy."

"Guin, why didn't you tell me this sooner?" Gods, Arthur wanted to shake her. Fear coursed through his veins. He knew what Gawain was capable of. If he was threatening his wife, if he laid one finger on her...

"I'm fine," she protested. "It's a good thing. It proved he isn't working with Lancelot."

"Yes, but..."

"I am fine." She cupped his cheeks. "You ordered the maids to watch me. I won't go anywhere alone or do anything stupid. I am all right."

"You are going to be the death of me, Guin," he teased.

"Don't say that." Her voice ran cold. "Don't fucking say that."

"I was—"

"I know, but don't."

"I'm sorry." He shoved off the desk, pushing her with him until they both stood. She nodded, accepting his apology, and he bent to kiss her gently. "If you are being threatened, go to your father's."

She shook her head and pressed her lips against his. "Where you go, I go. Stop trying to get rid of me."

He laughed and pulled her to his chest. "Pretty girl, I miss you so much that when this is over, I'm dragging you everywhere with me. You better get used to this room. I'm going to make you sit here every time I work because I refuse to let you out of my sight ever again."

"Can I decorate, then? It's depressing in here."

"You can do whatever you want, my queen. Whatever the fuck you want, as long as I have you for the rest of my life."

ARTHUR KISSED Guinevere in the tunnel's darkness before watching her retreat into the garden. She left with the promise to wear a necklace when she needed to meet him. As a man who wore nothing but dark clothes and his signet ring, she asked him to turn its seal toward his palm as a signal. To anyone else, the ring would merely look twisted, but she would understand.

Arthur's world felt empty the moment his wife disappeared, wearing that dress he loved too much. She didn't wear it often, but the fact she had it on today filled him with a joy he hadn't experienced in weeks. The entire castle might question her loyalty, but he knew who she fought for. The plot she had uncovered shook him to his core, and while he didn't want his fear leaking from his pores to frighten Guinevere, he wished they had more information. Putting her in harm's way nauseated him, and every time he saw her, the predatory urge to throw her over his shoulder and lock her safely away shredded his mind. He wanted to chain her to his bed to keep her from harm, but their souls were so intertwined, he understood her as if she was a part of his own flesh and blood. If she needed to stay by his side, he had to let her. He only hoped he wasn't making a mistake. If she was injured trying to save him, he would die in agony. He would never survive losing her.

Arthur left his study, wandering about the halls, absent purpose. He merely wanted people to see him somewhere his wife was not to deter suspicion. He passed a few servants and nobles, and Guinevere had not been lying. By their faces, word of her indiscretions was spreading. His hands clenched into fists as he endured every pitying expression. He wanted to rage at them, to defend his queen, but he made her a promise. He swore to keep her safe by keeping her secret, and so he wore the defeated mask of a jilted husband.

"My king," Gawain slipped silently beside him, appearing from nowhere, and while it unsettled most men, Arthur simply glanced at him in greeting. "I need to speak with you."

"So, speak."

"It's about..." Gawain looked around. "Can we talk somewhere private?"

Arthur rolled his eyes and grabbed his friend's biceps, pushing him into an empty room. The knight was a mountain of a man, but no one matched Arthur's severe size.

"What?" Arthur grunted as the door slammed behind them. He had used up all his words on Guinevere, and after seeing everyone's apologetic expressions, he felt irritable. His soul grated raw.

"Something has to be done about your wife," Gawain said. He knew Arthur well, arriving right at the point like an arrow.

"What did you just say?" Arthur stepped forward, looming over the knight. Fear rippled through him even though his face was stone. He recalled his wife's words. Gawain had threatened her, and if he had done something...

"I know you've seen it," Gawain answered, not backing down. Only three people possessed the tenacity to challenge Arthur. Tristan and Percival were among his closest friends, but the only ones brave enough to go toe to toe with the king were Guinevere, Merlin, and Gawain. "I've been watching her, and this is no longer harmless flirting. Arthur, she is going to destroy you, and I won't let that happen. You can't do anything about it. You love her, but that is why I am here. I refuse to let her ruin you."

"Gawain, you need to watch the next words that come out of

your mouth." Arthur was rage and menace, the king gone, replaced by the warrior.

"My king?"

"I love you, Gawain, I do, but if you so much as touch a single hair on her head, I will kill you."

"How can you not see it? She'll destroy you. Let me help."

"Gawain." Arthur gripped the back of his friend's neck, and the knight stilled as the king drew him close with a growl. "I need you to listen to me very carefully."

Chapter Twenty

Guinevere sat apart from the group, watching Lancelot spar. He had finally resurfaced, his charming mask fully in place, and he had wasted no time garnering sympathy for his suffering. Outwardly, she was pleased he had the favor and compassion of the others. After all, it was her husband who could not control his temper, but inwardly, her stomach churned with acid. While she was morphing into a social pariah, the knight had emerged from hiding as a friend and victim. The scowls she received weren't related to Lancelot, only a few observant eyes picking up the clues. No, her scorn was because she had publicly fled the king's bed and refused to play her role of both wife and queen. Before long, someone would confirm the rumors of the affair, but for now, she was simply the bitch queen, too young to adhere to her duty.

She still blamed Lancelot, though. Her current predicament had been her doing, but it was his fault, and she channeled all her annoyance into her longing gazes of lust. She would break him. She would force his hand, and when he yielded, Arthur would peel his flesh from his bones. It was that thought that kept her acting as his secret lover. Maybe Arthur's gruffness had worn off on her more than she realized. Picturing all the ways her king would end this traitor fueled her act, and her performance was flawless. Lancelot devoured her every look, her every movement. He thoroughly believed in her desire, and she wanted to be there when Arthur started cutting. She longed to watch the man who had betrayed his king and friend realize she never loved him. That she had used him and then fed him to a ravenous lion. She hoped he screamed like the little bitch he was as he died. No one touched her husband and escaped to see another day.

Training ended, Arthur mercifully absent, and Lancelot threw her a glance. She poured every ounce of strength into her carefully constructed act, her desire oozing out in thick, warm waves, and she saw him almost buckle under her gaze. Perhaps if she tortured him with the promise of her body only never to concede, he would lose his control and cave to her questions. Denying a man what he so desperately craved might drive him insane, and she was wholly committed to this course of action.

Lancelot wiped his brow and started for her. Guinevere stood with an eager smile when glowering anger suddenly filled her vision. Instinct had her reeling back, but a firm hand gripped her biceps and pulled her close so only she could hear his snarl.

"Walk with me, my queen." Gawain jerked her toward the garden, and fear bloomed in her gut. All pretenses of his politeness were gone, replaced by hostility, and Guinevere swallowed hard. Her mind screamed for her to fight against his hold, to cry for help. He had threatened her yesterday. She had not expected him to carry through so soon, but as he pulled her away from the crowd, her heart sank into her stomach. Would he drag her to the dungeons before he started, or would he simply strangle her in the bushes, leaving her for someone to find? Guinevere threw a panicked look at Lancelot. Their eyes locked, and the knight surged forward.

"Tell him to stand down," Gawain whispered, his grip tightening to the point of pain, and with a soft yelp, she pitched her gaze over her shoulder. She shook her head, but Lancelot ignored her, rushing to catch them.

"I'm serious, my queen." Gawain glared at her. "Make him stand down."

There was a reason Gawain was Arthur's second. Lancelot would pay the price if he attacked, especially with his ribs still sore, and Guinevere's eyes screamed at him as she mouthed, "*Please, don't.*"

He seemed to register the urgency in her plea and halted with a sharp jolt, letting Gawain carry her away. Arthur would have never stopped. Gawain would have been dead already if it was Arthur.

They walked deeper into the expansive gardens, and when they were hopelessly alone, the knight released her. For a fraction of a second, Guinevere contemplated running, but she would barely make it five seconds before he caught her. It would do little good. This deep into the foliage, no one would hear her scream.

"I'm sorry." He settled before her, and to her surprise, every drop of malice had evaporated from his face. "I needed Lancelot to buy it."

"What is happening?" Guinevere looked around wildly.

"I know."

She squinted at him.

"I know everything. About you and Lancelot. About the plot against the king. Arthur told me."

Guinevere sagged in relief, and her legs almost buckled beneath her. With quick and gentle hands, Gawain steadied her.

"I'm sorry I scared you. Lancelot knows I am loyal to the

king, which means you and I cannot be on pleasant terms. For him to believe your lie, I had to be harsh. I needed to get you away from him so we could talk."

"Oh, thank God." Guinevere flung her arms around Gawain's neck, and the knight stiffened before awkwardly patting her back. "After you threatened me yesterday, I realized you were loyal to Arthur. He needs someone on his side, and I am glad we have at least one person in this castle who knows the truth."

"About that." Gawain looked uncomfortable as she released him. "I threatened you to Arthur. That's why he told me."

"You what?" Guinevere snorted a laugh and then clapped a hand over her mouth. "How did that go for you?" she asked teasingly through her fingers.

"Fuck off." His comment was harsh, but his smile was large, and relief warmed every inch of her body. The knight's demeanor was similar to her husband's, and while his words would have disgusted most women—herself included until recently—she found herself at home with his humor. She had missed the camaraderie she had with these men, with her husband.

"I am glad you're not a traitor. Someone else in this castle is working against him, but thank God, it's not you. It would have killed Arthur."

"It practically killed him when he thought it was you."

"I…" Shame colored her cheeks. "I can't let Lancelot kill him. I won't."

"I know." Gawain cupped her cheek with brotherly affection. "That's why I'm here to help. Arthur can't be around you while upholding your narrative, but I can. Lancelot will believe your loyalty to him, especially in the face of my hostility. I'll protect you and act as your go-between."

"I would rather it be Arthur, but if I can't have him, you are the only other person I trust to keep me safe," Guinevere agreed.

"Even though I threatened you?"

"Gawain." The seriousness in her young eyes unsettled him. "If the roles were reversed, and I thought you had betrayed him, I would not stop until you drowned in a pool of your own piss, blood, and vomit. Do not mistake my plan with Lancelot for weakness. I am playing him, leaning into his obsession, but mark my words, his fate does not differ from what I would have done to you. He will suffer when this is over, and he will know it was at my hands."

"I never noticed this about you, but you are terrifying." Admiration colored his expression.

"On my wedding day, you told me I would either be Arthur's downfall or his salvation, and my answer is the same today as it was then. I will never be his demise."

WHEN GUINEVERE and Gawain emerged from the garden, their hostility had returned, firmly in place on their features. Gawain made an obvious show of storming back toward the castle, and the moment Guinevere's eyes found Lancelot's, she all but flew to him. He caught her panicked escape and pulled her into his arms as he hauled her behind a row of carefully pruned bushes.

"Did he hurt you?" He grabbed her jaw, searching for signs of harm, but all he found was fear and blotchy cheeks.

"I'm scared, Lancelot." Guinevere clutched his shirt, pulling him close. "Gawain is suspicious. He doesn't know about you, or at least he doesn't have proof, but he knows something is wrong. He threatened me." She threw her face against his chest with an emphasizing sob. "Lancelot, I can't keep this up. I avoid and deny Arthur at every chance, saving myself for you, but how long before he forces me? How much longer must I wait to be yours?"

"If he forces you, I will skin him alive from the balcony so that his precious Camelot can watch what happens when a man touches what's mine."

"I know." Guinevere sent a silent apology to her husband. Arthur took nothing she didn't willingly give, and while these words were meant to trap Lancelot, she felt the overwhelming urge to scrub her tongue and teeth clean from such a heinous blasphemy.

"And we don't have to wait." Lancelot's breathing changed as his palms drifted down her back, and Guinevere stiffened. "You have been so loyal, so pure, for me. God will surely forgive you. How could this pleasure be wrong?"

"Lancelot..."

"I love you, Guinevere. You are mine, and I can bring you—"

"Lancelot, please." She shoved him away before his hands could find their mark. "I can't do this. I am afraid all the time. Scared we'll get caught and hung. When will this be over?"

"My love," he sighed placatingly, as if she were an unreasonable child, his fingers reaching for her waist.

"Let me help you."

"Guinevere, stop." His voice snapped, and the darkness behind his eyes flickered before the soft gold resumed control. Guinevere flinched at his tone. Had she finally made him suspicious of her motives? She readied her legs to run. Hopefully, Gawain had not abandoned her. Maybe he would hear her scream.

"I'm sorry." Lancelot reached for her, but she pulled back nervously. His eyes softened, and his seductive voice dripped from his lips like nectar. "Forgive me, my love. I'm as frustrated as you are. I want you by my side and in my bed."

"I want that too." Her confession was barely audible.

"I am not trying to hide my plans from you." He gripped her shoulders. "I can't have you involved. Please understand. If you are to be my future queen, I must protect you. You are holy and beautiful. I won't taint you with my sins. They are necessary sins, but my love, I beg you to trust me. Can you do that?"

"Yes." She nodded submissively, barely restraining the urge to launch herself at him and claw his fucking eyes out.

"Now tell me you love me before we part. I don't want to leave you sad."

"I love you, Lancelot. I'm sorry I am desperate." The words were acrid bile on her tongue, but her face was the picture of unadulterated devotion, bringing Lancelot's too perfect smile to his lips. He leaned in to kiss her, but she turned her head at the last moment, letting his mouth fall against her cheek. To avoid suspicion, she flung her arms around his neck as if the movement had not been an act of avoidance but merely a miscommunication as she sought his embrace.

A soft footfall broke the silence, and they ripped apart in surprise. She hoped it was Gawain coming to save her, but whoever it was, she was thankful for their timing.

"I will go to the chapel to pray for your safety and victory." She smiled sweetly; the mention of the chapel intended to maintain her pious image.

"Yes, pray for me, my love." Pride beamed across Lancelot's features. "It won't be long now."

"I would do anything for you." She turned with a meek smile. "I will get on my knees and pray with passion."

Heat flared in Lancelot's eyes at the vision, and Guinevere sauntered away, leaving him frustrated. It took every ounce of willpower for her to force her steps to remain slow and calm. If she had to be submissive to him for one more second, she might scream. She and Arthur had argued their fair share of disagreements over the years, but he never demanded her blind obedience. The only time she was ever submissive to her husband was so deep inside her, she saw heaven. Her skin flushed, begging her to march up to Arthur's study and demand he bend her over his desk. She wanted him to fuck the thoughts out of her mind until she was nothing but firing nerves, his fingers gripping her hips so tight they left bruises. She wanted him to fold her in his embrace and protect her from the world, but he couldn't protect her if he was dead, so she stormed toward the chapel.

As she rounded a bend in the greenery, Guinevere almost slammed into a solid wall of flesh. She flew back, half expecting Gawain, but her relief morphed to horror as she came face to face with Merlin. They were his footfalls, which meant—

Guinevere's blood turned to ice, her mouth into a desert. Merlin, the mage of Camelot and Arthur's close friend, had heard her with Lancelot, heard her declarations of love and devotion. Bile burned her throat, threatening to heave itself on the mage's chest, but she forced down the sickness.

She smiled at him with childlike innocence, but the look he gave her stopped her heart. His eyes weren't right. They hovered hauntingly in their sockets, and all the air rushed from Guinevere's lungs. She couldn't breathe. Her heart had no pulse. Her heart was too loud. Too loud. Too loud. He would hear. She was scared and not because she had been caught, but because his sight was unnerving. He looked through her, into her, past her. He saw her every sin. He saw nothing.

And then, as suddenly as he arrived, he blinked at her and left. The air came rushing back, and Guinevere almost choked as it filled her lungs. She had never seen such an expression on Merlin's face before. It was indescribable. Was he angry? Indifferent? Had he even registered her presence? Had Arthur told him the truth? Perhaps he was tailing Lancelot, but she didn't care to stay and find out.

Hiking up her skirts, Guinevere ran as fast as her legs would carry her to the chapel, flinging herself inside its blessed solitude. The second the doors slammed behind her, she burst into tears. She longed to hug her husband and tell him she was afraid. She had never gone this long without talking to him, and the separation felt like a rusted knife carving her chest open. She hated waking every day with the fear it might be his last. That despite her efforts, Lancelot still stole him from her. She despised Lancelot. Arthur had accepted him, loved him, trusted him, and this is how he repaid his kindness. The king was rough around the edges, sometimes awkward and silent, but he was the best of them. Camelot flourished under him. She flourished.

When her mother passed away, Guinevere lost the only person who truly cared about her. She lost her friend and mentor, her protector. She had been so excruciatingly lonely and hollow, but then Arthur stormed into her life with a scowl, rewriting everything. He would never replace her mother, but he filled the void the woman left. He treasured Guinevere, giving her purpose and hope. She fell in love with him long before she admitted it, but she had been too nervous to speak the truth. The moment she did, he gained the power to ruin her, but he took her gift and multiplied it. In his own rough way, he loved her and his knights and his kingdom. Everyone was better because of him, and she sank to the floor in sobs, her worst fears being realized. She adored him, and he possessed the power to shatter her. If he died, if she failed to save him, she wouldn't survive. Losing her mother had been devastating, but losing Arthur? It would end her.

The chapel door creaked open, and Guinevere froze, slapping a hand over her mouth to stifle her cries. She shrank further behind the pews, hoping whoever it was would leave, and a second later, the door closed. Silence returned, and she exhaled in relief.

"My queen?" Gawain's soft voice reached her ears, and she jerked in surprise. "I saw you run in here. Are you hurt?" He paused, but when she didn't answer, he continued, "You don't have to talk to me. Just tell me you are unharmed?"

Guinevere leaned sideways so he could see her, and relief

washed over his tense muscles. He tiptoed hesitantly toward her and crouched down, his eyes full of tenderness.

"I stayed close in case you needed me, but then I saw you run here. Did he hurt you?"

She shook her head and wiped the dampness from her cheeks.

"Good." He reached out, patting her shoulder awkwardly, and she smiled at the gesture. She had never seen him so gentle. "I just wanted to make sure you were well."

"I don't know what to do," Guinevere blurted as he rose to leave, and he halted, returning to his crouch. "I don't want to do this anymore. I miss my husband, but then I think about Lancelot's plot. He can't kill Arthur."

"I know." Gawain shifted until he sat next to her and wrapped a muscled arm around her shoulders, pulling her close. Guinevere sighed at the embrace and leaned her head against the knight's shoulder. "I understand how you feel. That man is my brother. I have fought at his side for years, and I love him so much I threatened you to his face." Guinevere huffed at his words, and he pulled her closer with a smile. "I appreciate how badly you want to help. Trust me, knowing this traitor slept among us for five years makes me sick. None of us suspected him. Don't be hard on yourself. We would be blind without you. Arthur would be in grave danger. You did a brave thing. A stupid thing, but a brave thing."

"You won't let him die, right?" She looked at him with pleading eyes. "If I fail to discover who else is working with Lancelot, if I can't learn of his plans, you won't let him die? Promise me."

"I promise, my queen, Arthur dies over my dead body."

She nodded and leaned her head back down. The two sat on the floor for long moments in comfortable silence, and Gawain absentmindedly rubbed her arm with his thumb.

"Come to think of it." Guinevere reared backward to stare at him. "The first time Lancelot revealed his intentions was the night he thought Arthur drove me from bed. The second was after training when Arthur injured him." Excitement filled her eyes. "I don't intimidate him. He doesn't consider me his equal, so he sees no need to include me, but Arthur's threats loosen his lips. He hates Arthur and wants him dead, but deep down, he still fears the king."

"We all have at least a little fear of the king running through us." He paused and offered her a teasing grin. "All save you, that is."

"I'm being serious." She shoved him, and he smiled at the hope in her eyes. He didn't like the defeated Guinevere. He hadn't realized how close they'd grown over the years, and if he had learned anything about Arthur's young wife, it was that she was his match in every way. She was opinionated and strong, daring and brave, caring and determined, and her soft edges mellowed out his harsh ones. Seeing her on the chapel floor scared him more than he liked to admit. Threatening her shamed him more than he liked to admit.

"Lancelot fears Arthur, and then he unloads his rage on me. No matter how much I tease or prod or seduce, I learn little. But a threat from Arthur? Gawain." She clutched his hand. "I need you to bring Arthur a message from me. I have an idea."

TWENTY-ONE

Arthur tilted whiskey into his mouth and swished it before spitting it out. He swallowed a small amount to ensure the alcohol stained his breath. He needed to appear drunk, but he couldn't be intoxicated. Not for this.

Looking at the cold, empty spot in his bed where his wife should be, he poured whiskey onto his fingers and wiped them on his collar for good measure. He inhaled deeply and grimaced. He reeked for so early in the morning.

Arthur mussed his hair as he walked to the door and untucked a corner of his shirt, worrying he was overdoing it. He rarely let himself get annihilated, and if he did, he tried his hardest to mask the alcohol's effects, but hopefully, his audience would be more concerned with his actions than his exaggerated appearance.

Arthur drifted on silent steps to the dining hall. Ever since their dramatic split, Guinevere had not set foot in the room, but as he peered inside, his heart both pounded uncontrollably and stopped at the sight of her. She was there, and she was stunning.

She hovered on the outskirts, talking to some of the other women, her overly friendly presence an attempt to regain favor.

Arthur collected himself, but before he could move, Lancelot filled his view. The angelic man drifted closer to Guinevere, his gaze predatory, and Arthur's stomach pitched. This had better work. And with a violent curse under his breath, he stumbled into the room.

The diners jerked at his abrupt entrance, and Arthur dramatically staggered to the closest chair to steady himself. Every pair of eyes fell on him in burning shock, and Guinevere met his gaze with disgust. He had to give it to her. She looked appalled, but maybe the emotion was easy to portray. This was a degrading vision of himself he never allowed her to see.

"I need more whiskey," he slurred, but when no one moved he barked, "I said I need more whiskey. Don't just fucking stand there."

The servants leaped into action, desperate to escape the room, and Arthur hiccupped before turning his sights on Lancelot. Guinevere told him the man frightened her, and the knight's face explained in appalling detail how well-founded her fear was. Always the picture of grace and beauty, perfection and angelic purity, Lancelot's gorgeous façade slipped. There was a darkness in his eyes, a demon peering out behind his golden irises, and Arthur struggled to stop a scowl from marring his features. He had seen that expression before, but not on Lancelot. He had seen it on someone else. Someone long dead.

"My king," Gawain interrupted, gripping Arthur's thick biceps. "I think you've had enough. Perhaps you should lie down."

"Don't tell me when I've had enough," Arthur snarled. "I am the king. I decide when I am done." He yanked his arm from Gawain's gentle grasp and stumbled before catching himself. "Why are they taking so damn long with my whiskey?" He cringed internally at his outburst. He had never spoken like that, a fact not lost on the room's inhabitants.

Guinevere shifted, her movement capturing his eyes, and his sight zeroed in on her terrified face.

"You," he snarled. *You?* Since when did he address his wife so disrespectfully? He hated this. "I've had enough of your games. Come here."

"Arthur," she whispered placatingly.

"Do not disobey me, woman," he slurred so loud that even Gawain flinched in disgust that seemed genuine. Lancelot moved toward her, but Guinevere obeyed the king, forcing the knight to halt.

"Enough is enough," Arthur drawled, towering over her. "You are my wife. This nonsense has gone on too long." He grabbed her wrist, and she reared back in surprise. "You have a duty to me, and if I have to drag you kicking and screaming to my bed, so be it."

"Arthur!" Guinevere yanked hard, causing his fist to involuntarily tighten around her wrist.

"My king!" Gawain leaped forward at the same time as Lancelot, the beautiful knight's devil tearing through his facade.

"I'll punish anyone who dares to interfere." Arthur aimed the threat at Lancelot. Gawain was acting, but the king wanted to see if Guinevere's assumption was correct. If he still frightened Lancelot. "This is a matter between husband and wife. No one interferes. Do you understand?"

Lancelot froze, his body tense and primed for action, but he didn't move, and Arthur smiled internally. If it had been him, he would have not stopped. If Guinevere was in danger, only death would stop him from getting to her.

"Come, woman," Arthur tugged gently on her arm, putting more show than force into it, but she threw herself backward, tightening his grip again. He cursed under his breath. If she didn't stop moving, he was going to leave an accidental mark.

"Arthur, stop," she sobbed as she grabbed his fist, trying to peel his fingers back. "Please." Her begging was terrified, desperate, angry. Everyone in the room felt sick at her cries.

"Let me go." She bucked against him.

"Do not fight me," he growled, yanking her to his chest. "If you're going to be a whore," he whispered loud enough so their bystanders heard, "you should have no problem spreading your legs for me."

Guinevere's eyes went wide, and she gripped his fist tighter. As she fought to free herself from his grasp, he felt her tugging at his finger, but he didn't want to look down and lose his focus. Those had been her words. This entire speech had been hers, but agreeing to this plan, and acting it out, were two different things. He wanted to vomit at the vile hate spewing from his mouth, and the sheer terror she wore didn't help.

"Let me go," she screamed, fat tears rolling down her face. "Please stop. Let me go." Her voice turned dangerously frightened, and she parted her beautiful lips and yelled, "You are hurting me!"

Everything within Arthur froze as he noticed how tight his fist claimed her small wrist, and he released her as if she was a blazing fire eating at his skin. He was supposed to come in here, rave like a lunatic, scare Lancelot in the hopes he might spill his accomplice, and then leave. But he had done the unthinkable. He hurt his wife, reading fear in the way her chest heaved. He should have never agreed to this stupid plan.

"Leave me alone." Guinevere pulled her arm to her breast, cradling it like an injured bird. For a second, she stood before him, gently tapping her ring finger against her collar bone, and he stared at the movement with squinted eyes. Was it a nervous tick, or was she trying to tell him something? His gaze drifted from her hand to her face, searching for what he might have missed, and holding his stare, she spoke impossibly slow and clear. "My king."

Arthur felt like someone had punched him in the stomach as she tapped her ring finger one more time before fleeing the room in hysterical sobs, a swarm of maids chasing her with panicked footfalls. Arthur backed up in surprise, meeting Lancelot's gaze. For a second, he thought the knight might attack, but the man rearranged his features back into their angelic visage and chased after Guinevere.

Arthur stared at the horrified diners, but when he saw Gawain's concern, he turned on his heels and strode out of the room. He raced through the halls, unable to stop until he reached his study, and locked himself inside. He leaned heavily on the door in relief, and only once he was alone did he laugh. That perfect and beautiful woman. Gods, she had scared him, but that name. To everyone, it was a sign of respect. A title that held little warmth in her mouth compared to his name, but not to her. She only spoke it when he was between her thighs, when she wanted him to know how wet she was. She used it privately often, but it was always their code in public for when she was desperate to leave a social gathering, aching for him to slide his tongue over her clit until she was begging for his cock. Over the past five years, *My King* had morphed from a respectful term to an aphrodisiac, and she knew it. All she needed to do was speak that phrase, and he would grant her every desire.

She realized how worried he was and reassured him he was performing perfectly. To the crowd, she was terrified, but with that single title, he knew. He had not taken it too far. Her acting was impeccable, but she would not leave him unsure. With two words, she settled his spirit, and he adored her for it. She was always surprising him, and while she was a strong woman, mature and capable, it didn't stop him from wanting to protect her, shield her, cherish her, even from her own schemes.

When his laughter died, he pictured her face as she said *my king*, and her twitching finger spiked his memory. She did something to his hands when they struggled, her subtle parting gesture a clue, and he looked down. The seal of his ring faced his palm, the sign they needed to meet, and Arthur groaned.

"Guinevere," he chuckled to himself, "I love you."

HER MAIDS WERE A HURRICANE, panicked and chaotic as they yelled after her, and it took every ounce of her restraint not to scream. Guinevere hated the insults escaping their lips about their king, her king, and she wanted to rage at their disrespect, but she couldn't. This was part of the plan, and Arthur had played his role so beautifully, she was almost convinced he despised her. It was their last shot to get Lancelot to confess, and everyone had to believe she would never return to her husband. He didn't deserve this hate, and she loved how selflessly he had thrown his image to the wind to help her. Arthur made it increasingly impossible to pretend to love Lancelot. The knight made her jump through hoops just to gain a sliver of truth, yet Arthur humiliated himself simply because she had asked for help. Gods, she loved that man, and she had to bite her lip to keep from defending him. It killed her to hear his name tarnished, but if this deception worked, if Lancelot fell for their trap, it would be worth it.

Sobbing as she fled, Guinevere listened carefully to the commotion behind her, and just as she had hoped, a heavier set of footfalls joined the thunder. She smiled to herself and then inhaled a fortifying breath. If there was a time to be convincing, it was now.

"Leave us," Lancelot roared, the demon speaking through him, and the maids balked at his command. "Get out now!" They didn't disobey when his tone was a bloodthirsty blade.

"Guinevere?" She didn't stop. "Guinevere." He seized her arm, and she whirled on him so violently, he jumped back.

"He is insane." She screamed through gritted teeth as her fists slammed against his chest. "Do you see what he did to me? What he said? And you let him! Lancelot, you let him put his hands on me." She was practically foaming at the mouth as she beat his body. "He was going to take me, hurt me, defile me, and you didn't stop him. Screw you, Lancelot. I can't do this anymore." She spun on her heels but barely made it two steps before he caught her.

"Guinevere, please."

"Let me go." She pulled against his gentle hold. "This will get me killed. I thought you loved me. Is this what you want? Is this your plan? To get me killed."

"How could you say that?" Disgust laced his voice. "I love you, Guinevere, and I will kill him for what he just did."

"You keep saying that." Her tears grew inconsolable. "But I'm terrified. You leave me in the dark. Refuse to tell me your plans, yet you expect me to risk my life and dignity. He tried to take me, Lancelot. He hurt me, and all you say is soon. How soon? Or does something worse have to happen before you trust me? Surely you must realize how devoted I am. Wasn't that proof of what I'm risking to be with you?"

"I would never forgive myself if harm came to you." Lancelot pulled her into his arms, and she collapsed against his chest. "I love you, Guinevere, and I know how much you are sacrificing. I promise you, this will be over soon."

"There you go again." She tried to escape his hold. "Always soon, yet you leave me vulnerable for Arthur to abuse. I am on your side. I need to help, otherwise, I'm left out in the open like a carcass for the crows."

"Everything is finally in place." Lancelot seized her face, cupping it gently to force her gaze to his. "My entire army is lying in wait within Camelot's borders, awaiting my signal. Arthur's defenses will be useless. We are already inside."

"But the king also has an army." Guinevere pushed. "He is a legendary warrior. It will be a bloodbath."

"Not after what Arthur will do." Lancelot's angelic eyes gleamed demonically.

"After Arthur will do what?" She was almost too afraid to ask.

"Something so horrible, so unforgivable, that not even his own army will fight for him. Camelot will turn against him in a heartbeat, welcoming me to the throne. The kingdom will be so appalled by his treachery that there will be no battle, no bloodshed. Then together, we'll cleanse this land of his rot."

"What will Arthur do?" she repeated, her stomach seething.

"Don't bother yourself with that, my love." He stroked her cheeks affectionately, her skin crawling at the contact. "I'll carry this dark burden for our cause, but I don't want that on your shoulders. You are a woman; it would give you nightmares. Just know, my beautiful Guinevere, that everything is finally in place, and when Camelot witnesses Arthur's unforgivable sins, not a single soul will follow his leadership. I can't tell you the details because they'll bring you sorrow, but consider the bigger picture. Think about how many lives I'll save this way. So much blood would be shed if we fought this war, sword to sword. Do not worry. I shall bear the horrors for you."

"And this will happen soon?" She cried, her tears no longer faked as Lancelot's words terrified her.

"You don't have to fear that brute anymore." He released her face and seized her hands, kissing each of them reverently, and it was all she could do not to slap him. "In a few days, you'll be my bride, my queen, my wife. Can you hold on, my love?"

"Yes," she whispered, and he smiled, pulling her into a suffocating hug.

"You are so brave, Guinevere. We'll be together soon, I

promise. My most important player is ready. My five years of hard work have finally paid off."

"Who?" She kept her voice level, but her heart was racing. *The other traitor.*

"Someone of great importance has finally come to see things my way, and I think it will please you to discover who it is."

Guinevere opened her mouth to ask again, even though she knew he wouldn't tell her, but he pressed his fingers against her lips before she could utter a syllable.

"All in good time, my love." He kissed her forehead. "For now, I need you to stay safe. Can you do that for me? I don't want you going anywhere near the king until this is over."

She nodded. "We should keep our distance too, just in case."

"Remain in your room. I will find you when it's time." He smiled, and it baffled her how someone so perfectly beautiful could be so treacherously evil. "This is it, Guinevere. Do not cry, Arthur's reign is finally at an end."

Chapter Twenty-Two

Guinevere waited as long as she could physically bear. The sun had set, Earth's inhabitants joining her in her slumber, and with every passing second, she thought she might crawl out of her skin. It was too hot, too tight, caging her inside her own body. And this room? It was claustrophobic. She had paced it until she was dizzy and finally it was dark enough.

Guinevere fled out into the garden. Careful not to make a sound, she moved along the tower walls until she came to Arthur's secret. She made sure no one had followed her before pressing the lever. The door slid quietly open, and she sealed herself inside before descending into the darkness. Nothingness lit her way, but she remembered how direct the tunnel was, and her hands against the wall guided her steps. Before long, she was at the stairs, praying he was up there. She knew he understood her words, and she had drawn attention to his ring, but that had been this morning. Would he still be locked in his study so many hours later?

Guinevere reached the study door and rapped her knuckles against it in hope, but her fist barely sounded against the stone when it swung open. Its speed took her by surprise, and she teetered on the stairs. Arthur's powerful hand instantly caught the back of her neck, yanking her into the room as if he had been hovering on the opposite side of the wall. She barely had time to register the door shutting behind her before his mouth was on hers, his chest pressed firmly against her skin, and all the tension in her body evaporated as he pulled her into his arms.

"Did it work?" he moaned against her lips. "Tell me it worked?"

"Yes," she bit his lip, reveling in the way it made him grow hard, and suddenly she was desperate for him. All her anxiety and fear and hatred had been brewing a vicious storm in her soul, and as his mouth devoured hers, tasted hers, worshiped hers, she knew she needed him with a longing so fierce she almost cried.

"What—"

"I need you," she cut him off, silencing him as her hands flew to the hem of his shirt. "Please, my king." She tore the fabric over his head, knowing what those words did to him, and with a growl of pure desire, Arthur gripped her throat and tilted her gaze to his.

"Say it again." His whiskey smooth voice was rough and low.

"I need you now, my king," she moaned, trying to recapture his lips, but he held her throat tight, staring at her with dark and dangerous eyes. He loved it when she begged, and her fingers shot to his pants, working them down his hips as she gave him what he wanted.

"Please." She slid her fist over his thickness, and his muscles twitched at the contact. "Please, Arthur. I need you inside of me."

"Fuck, Guinevere." He pushed her back until she hit his desk before bending to capture her thighs. He hoisted her onto it, sliding his calloused hands up her body as he ripped her dress off. Arthur paused for a moment, his eyes drinking in every inch of her beauty, and then his head dipped to her breast. His lips sucked a peaked nipple into his mouth, and she arched off the desk from the aching pleasure, clenching her legs together in search of relief.

"Spread your thighs, Guinevere," he ordered as he trailed kisses over her breasts.

"Arthur." She reached desperate fingers for him, but he caught her hand and pushed it away.

"I said spread your thighs," he growled around her nipple, and she reluctantly obeyed him.

"Good girl. This pussy is mine. It comes only for me, so keep your legs open. You don't get to cheat me out of your pleasure." He placed his palms on either side of her, caging her in, and leaned close until his face was inches from hers. "Do you understand?" She nodded, and he smirked, kissing her softly only to part with a bite to her lower lip. "Use your words, pretty girl."

"Yes, my king." She almost climaxed from the sheer hunger in his eyes.

"You are beautiful." Arthur straightened, kicking his pants off to bare his chiseled body, and then he knelt slowly, reverently, before her. "Tell me, my queen, do you like the sight of your king on his knees before you?"

"Yes," she gasped as he grabbed her thighs and yanked her to the edge of his desk.

"Would you like your king to worship you on his knees to apologize for the horrible things he said earlier?"

"Yes, my king." If he didn't touch her, she was going to scream.

"Good, because I am going to atone for my sins between your thighs."

Guinevere's back arched in exhilaration as her husband's

tongue dragged across her opening, but his powerful arms kept her tight against his face. He knew exactly how she liked to be licked, to be sucked, to be fucked, and he wasted no time pulling her clit into his mouth. She stifled a moan as her body ignited in pleasure, and her pussy vibrated as Arthur chuckled against her.

"Don't hide your voice, my queen." He licked her slowly, pushing his tongue deep inside her. "No one can hear you up here." He trailed his fingers down to her ankle and lifted her leg until her knee hung over his shoulder. Her heels brushed his back as he tugged her closer against his face. Devouring her. Claiming her. Owning her. Her legs wrapped around his head were the most beautiful form of ownership, and she never knew if it was she who owned him as he worshiped on his knees, or if he owned her as he pulled her thighs higher over his shoulder.

The dam inside her broke, and Guinevere threw her head back, her orgasm building. It was strong and insistent, her skin on fire, and the coiling in her core tightened. Her voice grew louder. Her mind grew quiet. All she could see, hear, feel was his tongue, his hands, his love.

"Arthur." His name was a whimpering scream as her release hovered on the edge, teasing her with its beauty, with its pleasure. "Arthur, please."

Her body tensed, every nerve firing as her orgasm crested, but then suddenly his mouth was no longer on her. She gasped at the loss of contact, her words preparing their protest, but as her head snapped forward, her husband pushed off his knees, his cock gloriously hard. He stepped swiftly between her spread legs and fisted his shaft. He gave it a few erotic pumps as she watched, and she knew he did that for her. She loved to watch him. Sometimes she would sit at the table in their bedroom and ask him to fist himself while he stared at her until he spilled into his hands. She loved everything about the raw sexuality of this man. Her stomach clenched at the sight of him stroking himself, base to tip, but before he lost himself in the pleasure, he lined himself up with her and thrust.

"Guinevere." He grabbed her throat as he seated himself deep, and she instinctively wrapped her legs around his waist. "I'm sorry," he panted as he pulled her forward, kissing her rough as he bottomed out inside her. "I had to be inside you."

He gripped her hip with his free hand, guiding her pace, and her hands tangled in his hair as her head fell back. She was seconds away. Her breath panting, her body screaming.

"That's my girl," he groaned, thrusting faster. "Come on my cock."

"Arthur, please."

"Look at me, pretty girl. Look at me when you come. I want to watch how beautiful you are when you unravel."

Guinevere's eyes snapped to his, and she held his gaze as he took her. Her lips parted, and he smiled in awe of how gorgeous she was, how her pleasure consumed her entire being, and how she trusted him to be the one to push her over the edge.

"You're so wet." He slammed into her, his control slipping, his fingers tightening around the slender column of her throat. "Come for me, Guinevere. Now."

Like coils snapping and lightning striking twice, Guinevere's entire body lit up. Her scream so sweet and loud, Arthur's chest swelled with pride.

"You are so beautiful." He fucked her through her orgasm, holding her gaze and her heart. Her wide eyes held nothing but desire as they stared back at him.

"I love you," she moaned when her breathing steadied.

"I love you so fucking much." Arthur let go of her throat and wrapped his arms around her, pulling her against his chest as he thrust deeper. He loved how her sweaty body heaved in pleasure against his, and he groaned as his tongue pushed inside to claim her mouth.

"I hated having to say those things to you. I felt disgusting, but then you called me my king, and it took everything not to bend you over the table and take you right there in front of everyone."

Her grip on him tightened, and she spasmed as her breathing changed. Arthur tilted his head back to study her eyes and saw her staring at him with the challenge he loved so much.

"You like that idea?" he asked hesitantly as she lowered her hands to his ass. She grabbed him tight, her nails scraping his skin, and she used her grip to guide him harder, deeper. "Do you like imagining me fucking you for everyone to see?"

"Yes, god, yes." He could hear her orgasm on her voice. "Don't stop. Please, tell me… tell me how you would do it."

He fisted her hair in his hand and yanked her head back, devouring her mouth in a desperate kiss. He would never allow anyone to look at her, touch her, taste her. She was his, and he was hers. No one else was allowed to enter their marriage bed, but fuck did he like this game.

"I would have tugged down the top of your pretty little dress until your gorgeous nipples spilled out, and then I would have bent you over the table, food and guests still at it."

"Please." She buried her face in his neck, and he secretly hoped she would bite him again.

"Then I would push your skirt over your hips and find you wet and bare for me, waiting for my cock. I wouldn't let anyone leave. I would make them sit and eat and watch as I grabbed your hair and fucked you so magnificently from behind that you saw stars."

Her teeth gently grazed his skin, and he almost came from the contact.

"Then," he growled so low, she felt the vibrations in his chest, "I would come so hard inside you that you would be dripping and ruined. Everyone would see my cum fill your cunt, and you would love every minute, your pretty bare nipples dragging against the cold table as I filled you."

"Arthur," Guinevere screamed, her teeth biting down on his shoulder as she came, convulsing in his arms, and Arthur held her close as her heart raced against his.

She didn't respond for long seconds as she rode the crashing waves, but eventually, she pulled back and smiled at him. He caressed her face and then pressed a kiss to her forehead. She was the most precious thing in this world to him, and he gazed lovingly at her as he chased his own release.

"Get on your knees," he broke the silence, pulling out of her. He was so close, his vision was almost black, and he hoisted her up and placed her on the floor. She dropped to a kneel without hesitation, and with an alluring heat in her eyes, she opened her mouth. Arthur thrust passed her lips until it hit the back of her throat and grabbed her hair with a roar.

He tasted like her, and Guinevere seized his thighs, using his strength as leverage as she deep-throated him. Breathing became difficult, and a tear escaped her eye, but she didn't stop. She loved the way he felt in her mouth, how thick he was, how strong. And he was hers. Only hers.

"You look stunning with your mouth wrapped around my cock," Arthur praised, his voice rough as his balls drew tight. "You choke on me so well." Guinevere moaned as he shoved deeper. "Be a good girl and don't swallow. I want you to show me how hard you made me come."

Guinevere didn't speak as she dragged her tongue over his head, her hand joining the frenzy. She stroked and sucked him in a torturous rhythm, and Arthur lost all control. His fingers tangled in her hair as he exploded in her mouth. He thought his legs would collapse at the intensity, and it made him almost blind when he saw his wife had listened to him, not swallowing a single drop.

"Open your mouth." He dragged himself from her warmth and leaned back against his desk, folding his arms across his heaving chest.

Guinevere looked up at him through teasing lashes, and then slowly parted her lips. His cum coated her mouth, filling it to the brim before some of it spilled over her tongue. It landed on her breast, and when she saw the heat flair in her husband's eyes, she leaned back and tilted her head down. The rest slid from her tongue and dripped down her nipples in erotic paths over her skin.

"Perfect. Utterly and undeniably perfect. I will never stop worshiping you and your body." Arthur leaned down and kissed her roughly, not caring that he had just been in her mouth, and as he stood to lean against the deck, wickedness gleamed in his eyes.

"Use your fingers," he commanded. "Clean up my cum and put it inside you."

Guinevere's eyes went molten, but she didn't hesitate. She captured his release on her fingertips, wiping it from her pink and hardened nipples, and then she spread her knees so he could see her. Her fingers slipped inside, her cunt still dripping with arousal.

"Good girl. I love filling you up." His smile froze on his mouth when instead of withdrawing her fingers, she pumped them inside her. Her skin flushed as her breathing heaved, and Arthur leaned further back against his desk to watch as she moaned. Within minutes, she was grinding on her hand, her orgasm building in beautiful waves. She never broke his eye contact, and he never moved. He simply watched with rapt attention as she pleasured herself with his cum, and when she came screaming on her knees before her husband, he came undone.

Chapter Twenty-Three

Arthur snatched up his discarded shirt and carried it to his kneeling wife. He crouched before her as his fingers slipped behind her neck, pulling her to his lips. His kiss lingered, full of every emotion he felt for this woman, and only when he could barely breathe did he release her. His hands reverently skimmed her thighs before he dragged the soft fabric between her legs. He cleaned her gently, sacredly, adoringly, and when she was dry, he tossed the shirt onto the desk.

"I love you." He scooped her into his arms and carried her to his chair where he sat, cradling her naked and beautiful body against his scarred one. She didn't answer him with words, but her arms coiled around his neck, her head resting against his thundering heart, and he understood her with resounding clarity.

"It worked to a certain extent, but his confession was still frustratingly vague." Guinevere finally broke the silence. "I'm sorry I asked you to humiliate yourself for so little. I wanted it to work, but instead, I have more questions than answers."

"Tell me what he said." Arthur brushed her hair back from her forehead.

Guinevere recited Lancelot's confession, and when she finished, she studied her husband's stoic features. Most couldn't read his expressions, but to her, he was a book. It was almost as if his mind cracked open to play on his face just for her benefit, and she watched as he worked her words from every angle.

"You will be pleased with the second traitor's identity?" Arthur asked, and she nodded. "That makes me nervous."

"Likewise."

"That clue brings your father to mind, but he has no money or standings other than your marriage to me. He has no army. Lancelot can't use him to overthrow me."

"I would also hope my father cares for me enough not to betray and kill the man I love," Guinevere huffed, and Arthur grunted his agreement.

"So, it aligns with your suspicions that it's someone in this castle that you are close with."

Guinevere nodded.

"Which means it is someone I care for, too."

She nodded again.

"Fuck." Arthur tilted his head back and pinched his eyes shut. "I don't want to say it."

"Please don't." She didn't want him to voice it either. She cared for all his knights, but there was one that she had grown surprisingly close to. A man that reminded her of her husband and who she trusted with their lives. If there was one person she wanted on her side, it was him, but if Arthur said it, if he labeled him a traitor, her heart might break. It couldn't be him. Anyone but him.

"But we don't know for sure." The words tumbled from

Arthur's mouth fast and desperate. "He wouldn't. Not after everything we've been through together."

"Maybe we are on the wrong track," she agreed. "Gawain is your man, through and through. Lancelot dislikes him, and if I am supposed to hate you, wouldn't he assume I also hated your shadow? You two are so alike. It can't be him. Right?"

Arthur nodded, barely able to breathe.

"Then it's settled." Guinevere cupped his angled jaw in her soft hands. "It isn't him."

"Even if it isn't Gawain, it's still someone I care about, and that kills me. A friend I trust is waiting to stab me in the back."

"I've watched you train, Arthur. I've seen men try to attack you from behind, take you by surprise, and it never works." He smiled at her as if she was trying to cheer him up with flattery, but she shifted so he could see the seriousness in her beautiful eyes. "On our wedding, Gawain told me you scared people and that he hoped I would never have to witness your violent side. He said it would terrify me, but he was wrong. I'm not afraid of you. I want that version of my husband to rip free because he is a savage. A warrior who won't be trapped or stabbed in the back by a coward. It doesn't matter who the traitor is. You know he is coming, and that's good enough. He won't survive you."

"You have a lot of faith in me."

"I will always have faith in you." She cupped his face and kissed his lips softly. "I will always fight by your side."

Arthur lost himself in her for a moment, kissing her deep as he drew her small body against his scarred chest. If only he were as invincible as she made him feel.

"So, I am going to commit a horrible crime?" Arthur re-centered their conversation before her beauty drowned him.

Guinevere nodded. "I was hoping you might have an idea what he means. Is something happening within the next few days that might ruin you? Is a foreign dignitary visiting? Killing someone important from another kingdom would start a war, one Lancelot could avoid by executing you as punishment. The wronged kingdom would view the power shift as justice, and Camelot would support Lancelot's efforts to keep us from war."

"I don't know of any visitors. That doesn't mean Lancelot hasn't set that in motion, but no, I cannot think..." He trailed off, and his body froze.

"What's wrong?" He didn't answer her. "Arthur?"

"Your involvement is over." His voice had gone cold and ruthless, terrifying her.

"I know," she whispered. "There is little more I can learn from him, but—"

"I'm serious," he cut her off. "I don't care what I have to do to protect you from him, whatever lie I have to weave so that he doesn't suspect you, but you are done. I'll lock you in the dungeons myself if I have to."

"Arthur, you're scaring me."

"Something that will inspire Camelot to hate me. Make my people no longer trust me?" The color drained from his face. "Something like killing my wife?"

"What are you talking about?" Guinevere bolted upright in his lap and stared at him.

"He wants to show me as a monster, and what is more heinous a crime than to kill my young wife? I practically assaulted you at breakfast, and you saw the horror in everyone's eyes, how their opinions changed of me. They don't know it was all an act. Imagine how deep the hatred would run if I murdered you, if I left your mangled corpse for all to find?"

"Arthur, stop."

"Maybe that is why he desires your love, to lure you away from me and murder you. I can't think of anything more horrifying than your death."

"Arthur, stop, please." She seized his face in her hands and kissed him roughly, silencing him. Her heart was pounding in terror, and tears pricked her eyes. "He won't kill me. He is in love with me. My death would devastate you, but it's not the worst thing to befall the kingdom."

"It is." His chest deflated, and she hated the look of despair on his face. "If you died, I would cease to exist. Camelot would die along with you because I couldn't continue. When I thought you loved Lancelot, it devastated me, but I told myself he made you happy. Even if it gutted me like a ravaged carcass, I would survive if you were happy. But if you die, if you suffer?"

Guinevere threw her arms around his neck, not caring to stop the tears choking her eyes. She held him tight, absorbing his fear into her body, and a panic she had never experienced flooded her veins. She believed she was a decent judge of character. The moment she laid eyes on him, she recognized Arthur was her future, just as she perceived Lancelot was wicked. She trusted Gawain, and so far, her instincts had led her true, even if this outcome was horrible. But was she wrong about Lancelot's affections? Did he mean to kill her?

"I truly don't think that is what he intends." She tangled her fingers in Arthur's hair, gripping it tight as she whispered into his neck. "But I promise you, I am done. I'll go to my father's if that is what you wish, or perhaps he can come here to guard me. I'll even scream and cry as you throw me in the dungeons for my infidelity—whatever steps you consider necessary—but I don't believe I'm in danger. He's obsessed with me enough to want my status as his wife. He wants to kill you and take your throne and your bride."

"I hope you are right."

"I am." She pulled back and brushed her fingers over his cheeks. "Don't worry about me. Worry about saving yourself. Remember what I said. You die, I die. I'm not staying on this earth without you, so figure this out. I'm sorry I have no more information, but figure it out. End this. Kill Lancelot."

"Yes, my queen." He kissed her lips, and then pulled her down into his arms, cradling her tight.

"Keep Excalibur on you at all times."

Arthur nudged her and then nodded toward the edge of the desk where the sword lay. Her eyes widened, and then she looked up at him with a sheepish grin.

"Was that there the entire time?" She blushed at the fact that it had been against her bare ass, and she hadn't noticed. Arthur waggled his eyebrows in a teasing motion, and she laughed, the sound easing some of the tension in the room.

"It never leaves my side. I just wish I could carry you around with me."

"You going to strap me to your back, too?" She kissed one of his scars.

"Don't tempt me, because I am this close to tying you there alongside Excalibur." She burst into laughter despite herself, and he jerked her closer. "Laugh all you want, it changes nothing."

"I love you," she wheezed through her laughs. "You always know what to say to make even the worst days better. I'm scared, Arthur. Absolutely terrified, but in your arms, my fears don't exist. You lied to me when you told me you weren't good with words. They may not be elegant, but you make me happy."

"And I will until the day I die." He looked her in the eyes, seeing the fear lingering behind her irises. It killed him to know she didn't feel safe. "I won't let anything happen to you; I promise. I will die before anyone lays a hand on you."

"I am not scared for myself," she said as she absentmindedly brushed her fingers over his chest. "I wanted to discover when he would enact his plans. Soon wasn't an answer, but the moment he told me a few days, it became real. I have faith in you, Arthur. You're the strongest warrior alive, yet, in days, people will rise up to kill you, to take you from me. I'm afraid to leave this room, to leave your arms because I'm nervous that once I do, I'll never feel them again. I'm not scared for my own life; I'm terrified for yours. I can't lose you."

She burrowed her head in his chest as she continued, "Five

years isn't long enough. We haven't had enough time. We're supposed to grow old together, have children together. I hate that all I can think about is if this is the last time you hold me. I don't want to be afraid, but I am."

"Then don't leave. Stay with me in this room. I'll make sure you escape unseen." Arthur pulled her closer.

She nodded, resting her head against his heartbeat.

"Sleep here with me." He stroked her hair lovingly, his heart breaking over and over as he watched her breathing steady. "But hear this, Guin. I didn't realize what love was until I met you. You taught me to be vulnerable, to be a friend, a husband, a lover. You changed my life because you saw me for who I was. I love you, and yet that phrase isn't enough to describe the way my heart beats for you, the way my body belongs to yours, the way my mind and soul and spirit have braided together with yours. You are my wife until I die, and even then, we won't be separated. I am yours in this life and the next. I love Camelot and my knights, but you? You are the beating heart that controls my entire existence, and if you are waiting for me, then I will not rest until I have returned to you. Lancelot won't kill me because I'm not done loving you, and I'll kill any man who tries to keep me from fulfilling my promise."

Arthur pulled her tired body closer and kissed her forehead. He didn't care that the chair beneath him was unforgiving. He would sit here all night with her in his arms if it made her feel safe.

"Sleep here with me, Guin. I have you. I'm never letting go."

CHAPTER TWENTY-FOUR

Guinevere woke alone in her bed, vaguely remembering Arthur carrying her to her room in the dark moments before dawn. It was a risk, but neither of them cared. This was the end, no matter the outcome, and they wanted every last moment together. It had been foolish to spend the night in his arms, but they both needed that calm before the storm. She felt guilty that he slept in an uncomfortable chair, his limbs cramping as he cradled her for hours, but the peace his heartbeat against her cheek brought her drowned out any regret. It had calmed her nerves, but as the day dawned on her solitude, the fear crept back.

The morning matured into the afternoon as uneventfully as the days before, but one difference nagged at Guinevere's brain. Lancelot. He had vanished. No one had seen or heard of him since yesterday, and the longer his absence grew, the more her gut twisted into painful knots. This was it. She could sense it. He was moving, planning, destroying, and she dreaded what would happen when he emerged.

Male voices echoed off the corridor walls ahead, and her skin pricked at the deep voice. A second later, Arthur, Gawain, and Tristan rounded the curve, their sights landing on her, but her eyes were only for the king as they stormed closer. She could tell by their expressions they were analyzing her clues, and she wondered if Arthur had told Tristan the truth, or if he and Gawain held the dangerous details locked away

"My king," she said as she passed the trio, and Arthur's glare shot to her. She stifled a grin at the look, and Arthur let his friends pull ahead of him. The hallway was wide, easily accommodating them all, but he pulled back as if it were too narrow, as if the sight of her caused him to recoil. His pace slowed as if he meant to hide behind his men, but she matched his decreased speed. Her maid stepped ahead, and for a split second, their companions were oblivious to what was happening. They continued to move, unaware that the king and queen had slowed, and Arthur leaned sideways. His hand drifted across the divide, and like the moon to the earth, Guinevere's lifted to its gravity. He gripped her fingers with a possessive claim, and she clung to him until the distance separated them.

Guinevere's skin tingled where his hand had graced hers, her heart pounding against the prison of her ribs. Worry clouded his eyes. Longing echoed in his hold, and she despised the trepidation on his face. She hated that he was unable to trust the very men his life depended on, and she couldn't stop the sense of failure from wrapping its boney fingers around her heart. She had promised her husband she was done meddling, but Lancelot hadn't been seen all day. He wasn't in the castle, which meant…

"I feel like tea in the garden," Guinevere said sweetly to her maid. "Be a dear and run to the kitchen. I will go straight outside."

"My Queen—"

"I am craving something sweet, too." Guinevere interrupted,

her face transforming into a beautiful expression, and the girl crumbled under the pressure.

"Of course, my queen. I shall fetch you tea and pastries immediately."

"Thank you," Guinevere called as the maid raced down the corridor, but the moment she disappeared from sight, Guinevere turned on her heels. She would not send Arthur into this fight blind. She would not let her husband stagger around in the dark waiting for a knife to sever his spinal cord. Lancelot wasn't here. This might be her only chance.

She raced for the knight's room, unsurprised to find the door locked. She reached into the pockets of her dress and pulled out a key. Lancelot had gifted her a copy after Arthur attacked him, so she might visit him unnoticed, and she conveniently forgot to return it. Throwing a look over her shoulder to ensure she was alone, Guinevere slipped inside.

She paused, scanning the room after she locked the door behind her. It looked the same, tidy and without clutter. She would have to be careful not to misplace anything, not that she knew what to search for. His room was sparse, draining her hope of finding something of significance, but she had to try. Arthur needed an edge.

With methodical care, Guinevere inspected his wardrobe, but his clothes offered nothing. She then leafed through the books and papers on his bedside tables, but they held little interest. She explored his deck last, and to her utter disappointment, it presented no hope. No out-of-place object was present. No correspondence appeared to be written in code. Everything was as it should be, and she slammed the desk drawer in frustration.

Something solid rolled against the wood, and Guinevere froze at the sound. She hesitantly pulled the drawer back open and was confronted by a ring that had not sat there seconds before. It must have dislodged from its hiding place at the force, and she snatched it up. Lancelot had never worn this, yet it was uncomfortably familiar. It bore an ornate 'M' on the seal, and the longer she stared at it, the more her heart shredded apart in bloody tears. It had been only in passing years ago—the seal of someone long dead—but she remembered where she had seen this 'M' before, and she thought she might be sick. She needed to get out of here, to warn Arthur. This was worse than she expected.

Male voices rumbled outside of the room, and Guinevere almost dropped the ring in fear. *Lancelot.* She thrust it back into the desk and gently closed the door as she wildly searched her surroundings. There was no escape, but perhaps she didn't need one. She rearranged her features and shoved the key down into her dress. She would tell him she missed him, that when she couldn't find him, she panicked. He would believe her. He had to.

A second voice answered Lancelot, and Guinevere watched in horror as Lancelot's shadow darkened the crack under the door. Someone she didn't recognize was with him, and panic circled its brittle and icy fingers around the base of her spine, tightening as if to shatter her vertebrae. She needed to hide.

Guinevere scanned the room. The bed or the wardrobe offered little protection. *Think, Guinevere.* A window at her back opened onto a small balcony. They would see her out there, but if she hung off the side?

She bolted for it, throwing it open as a key slid into the lock behind her. She pushed her body out onto the ledge designed for aesthetic purposes and closed the window, careful not to latch it. A stone design protruded from the castle wall, and Guinevere heaved a sigh of relief as she used it to balance out of sight. She berated herself for being so careless as Lancelot opened the door. She could fall to her death out here, and she prayed he was not retiring for the evening. Served her right for not listening to her husband.

Muffled voices sounded inside, but she couldn't understand them through the glass panes. They spoke in hushed tones, and while she recognized Lancelot, the second voice was shrouded in mystery. It didn't matter, though. She had seen the ring. She knew who it was, despite the impossibility. He was dead, yet he was the traitor she would be pleased to discover. Suddenly, everything made sense. Lancelot's behavior, his hatred of Arthur, his reason for believing she would approve of this development. Not because this newcomer was a friend, but because of the sheer power he possessed.

The voices continued, drifting toward the door. She should remain hidden until they were long gone, but Guinevere needed to see him with her own eyes. Lancelot had already left, but his companion still hovered in the doorway. His features were concealed as he exited, but she saw his clothing as she peered through the glass, his demeanor. There was no mistaking what he was. *A mage.*

Guinevere didn't know how long she hid outside that window, staring at the empty room. She should move, she should run, but horror had stolen her senses. It was impossible.

"Arthur," she whispered, and the sound of his name punched adrenaline into her heart. She climbed inside as fast as she dared and then ran to the door. No one stood outside in the halls, but she forced herself to walk calmly. She wanted to tear through the castle like a haunted banshee, but she couldn't attract attention. Not now. Not when she possessed this secret. No, she needed to find a necklace to signal Arthur.

The journey to her room felt like a decade, and she threw herself inside, finally able to breathe, but a flurry of hulking motion ripped a cry from her throat.

"Where have you been?" Arthur captured her face, scanning her with such intense concern, it was as if he expected her skull to be split open. "Gawain pays your maid to watch you closer than the rest. She told him she was supposed to bring you tea in the garden, but you vanished. He couldn't find you, and I lost it. I thought Lancelot took you."

"No… I'm all right." She was not all right.

"Where were you?" He sounded manic. "You can't do that to me. You can't disappear like that." He seized her hand and slammed her palm against his thundering heart. "Look what you did to me."

"I discovered who the second traitor is," she blurted, and Arthur froze.

"How?"

"It doesn't matter."

"How, Guin?" She recognized that tone. There was no fighting it.

"Lancelot wasn't here. I searched his room."

"Guinevere." Arthur ripped his hands free from hers and paced. "We agreed you were done. You are in too much danger."

"I'm fine…" she started

"But what if he had caught you?" He whirled on her, looming above her with such speed she flinched in surprise. "What if he found you? He could have killed you."

"He didn't catch me." She placed her palms on his chest, shocked at how rapidly his heart was beating, and he gripped her hands, holding them tight to him, afraid to let go.

"You scared me." The king was near tears.

"I'm sorry I alarmed you." She pushed her face into his chest. "But I'm not sorry I did it. I figured out who he is working with, and it's worse than we thought."

Arthur peeled her from his body to study her eyes, and he saw how terrified she was. He needed her to tell him. He didn't want her to speak.

"It's Mordred."

Chapter Twenty-Five

"What are you talking about?" Arthur looked genuinely confused.

"Lancelot is working with Mordred."

"That's impossible."

"I found his ring." Guinevere was insistent. "I recognized his seal."

"I killed him, Guin." Arthur didn't understand why conviction flooded her features. "Lancelot may have his ring, but he's dead."

"I saw him," she blurted. "He is in the castle."

"Where?" She shook her head at his question, and he gripped her shoulders, jerking her to attention. "Where?"

"Lancelot's room," she whispered.

"Damn it, Guin, I thought you said they didn't catch you." Arthur looked like he might explode.

"They didn't notice me, I promise, but I found his ring. I saw him with Lancelot. He's here."

"That's not possible." He dropped her shoulders and stepped back. "I killed him. I watched him die."

"He is a mage," Guinevere offered. "Could he have tricked you?"

"No."

"Are you sure?"

"Yes." The king sat on the bed in disbelief. "I don't know. If you asked me yesterday, I would have insisted Mordred was dead, but if you saw him... I don't know what to trust anymore. A man who I assumed loved me plots to steal my wife and throne and kill me for a crime I will never commit. I guess all things are possible."

"Think about it." Guinevere knelt between his legs, resting her elbows on his thighs. On instinct, he curled his hand around the back of her neck, weaving her dark hair through his fingers. "The day you killed Mordred is the day Lancelot entered your life. He appeared a godsend, and you welcomed him to Camelot with open arms. What if that was the plan? Mordred faked his death to get Lancelot close to you. Corrupt your rule from the inside out."

Arthur looked down at his wife in alarm as the possibility washed over him.

"Mordred couldn't defeat you on the battlefield. He always fled like a coward because he understood if he stayed, you would destroy him," Guinevere continued. "But with Lancelot crippling you from within, he stands a chance. They cannot win the war, so they will cheat their way to the throne."

"How will Mordred's involvement please you?" Arthur asked as he studied his kneeling wife. "You have no connection to him."

"With Merlin at your side, Lancelot is weak." Guinevere shrugged. "But Mordred's magic can battle Merlin's. Perhaps he meant I would feel safer with a mage defending us?"

Arthur swore, rubbing his mouth with his free hand. "And you saw him?"

"Only from behind, but after finding his ring, it has to be him."

"And he's in this castle now?"

She nodded.

"Everything confirms he is dead, but the panic in your eyes tells me you aren't lying." His hold on her neck tightened, his long fingers resting against her pulse. "I feel how frightened you are, and if you are this scared, then I need to ignore what I believed and listen."

"I wish I was wrong," she whispered. "But how else do you explain what I found?"

"Pack your things, necessities only," Arthur said. "Tomorrow, I'm sending you along with a protective detail to your father's." Guinevere opened her mouth to protest, but he pressed his fingers against her lips. "This is not up for discussion. You promised me that in matters of violence, in moments of life or death, you would heed my judgment. An attack is on our doorsteps if Mordred is here. If you are in danger, if you are even near the struggle, I won't be able to do what Camelot requires of me. Please do this for me. Go to your father, wait in safety, and if I die, he will protect you from Lancelot."

"You can't die." She cupped his jaw in her palms. "Say it. Say you won't die on me. Otherwise, I'm not leaving."

Arthur rolled his eyes and then leaned forward, capturing her mouth in a rough kiss. "I refuse to die if you're waiting for me. I will end this and return to you. I'll always return to you."

She kissed him with a hunger so fierce it gnawed at her soul. Her arms wrapped around his neck, desperate and all-consuming, like a flame licking at a dried forest. All of her ached for all of him. Body, soul, heart, spirit. This was greater than love. It was both the entire universe and the smallest molecule. Happiness was found in his embrace. Heartache bled from her veins when she left his arms. Marrying him was the greatest decision of her life, just as leaving him now would be her worst.

"I'll go," she whispered into his mouth, and he caught the words with a greedy inhale.

"Thank you." He leaned his forehead against hers, breathless and anxious. "Have your maid sleep here tonight. I don't want you alone. Promise me you won't leave this room or her side until my guards come for you tomorrow."

"I promise."

Arthur captured her waist, hoisting her into his lap. He kissed her, tasting her lips, her tongue, her mouth. Claiming her. Marking her. Devouring her. He did not let her go as he pulled her bottom lip between his teeth, drawing his tongue over the seam of her mouth, gathering her closer, ever closer, until all that existed was her scent, her touch, her taste. He loved her beyond words, beyond reason. She was a part of his soul, an extension of his own body, and her love was carved so deep into his heart that he would never be free of her. Guinevere owned him. She owned his life, his happiness, his every waking thought, and even though he had promised her he would survive, he kissed her with desperation in case he didn't. If this was the last time his lips ever tasted hers, he wanted to memorize her every moan, every caress, every curve. If he was going to die, he wished their final memory to be her in his arms.

"You will come back to me," she moaned against his mouth as if she could read his thoughts. "I love you too much to let you go. You die, I die, remember? So come back to me."

It took Arthur a long time to summon the courage to leave Guinevere, but as the sun set, he stalked silently through the castle until he found Gawain.

"Did you find her?" the knight asked, concern threaded through his brow. The king nodded. "Is she safe?" He nodded again.

"I'm sending her to her father in the morning."

"Did something happen?" he asked as he fell in step with his king.

Arthur felt sick, but he needed his friend now more than ever. So, with a hesitant tongue, he told him everything Guinevere had discovered.

"That's impossible." Gawain stared at his friend as if he had gone insane.

"I know." Arthur looked defeated. "Yet I trust her. She is telling me the truth."

"I don't like this."

"Neither do I."

"You can't possibly believe her." Gawain grabbed Arthur's biceps, yanking him to a halt. "This is absurd."

"Why would she lie about this?"

"I don't know." Gawain swallowed as if he had ingested poison, and then before he lost his nerve, he blurted, "Maybe she is in on it with Lancelot."

"Gawain." His name was both a threat and a warning.

"I know. I'm sorry," Gawain huffed in frustration. "It's just this is too far-fetched. We are supposed to accept that a ghost haunts these hallways."

"I don't want to believe it, but until we have definitive proof, it is wise to assume anything is possible."

"You don't think…?" Gawain paused uncomfortably.

"What?"

"Is it possible Lancelot knows she's playing him?" Gawain's eyes were wide. "That performance at breakfast yesterday was terrifying. If I wasn't in on it, I would have assumed you meant to harm her. I saw the rage in Lancelot's eyes. It was unsettling. I've never seen a stare so dark and full of venom. He fell for your act, but... she went to you last night. Is there a chance Lancelot caught you?"

"No."

"Are you certain, because if he saw, if he suspects where Guinevere's true loyalty lies, he could be setting her up? Baiting her with fall information so he can catch her lie when she relays it to you."

"I was careful."

"I hope so, for her sake. It's good you're sending her away. She isn't safe here."

Arthur looked defeated at that fact, and Gawain patted his king's back.

"She'll be all right. She's tough, and her father will watch over her. I'll get Tristan and the knights gathered. If Mordred is here, we'll find him."

"Be careful," Arthur warned. "Mordred shouldn't have been able to breach our defenses without Merlin's knowledge. If he is truly here, we are all in danger."

"We haven't had a good fight in a while." Gawain smirked. "Don't worry about us."

"I'll tell Merlin. Lord knows we need his magic."

Gawain bowed his head and left, leaving Arthur more unsettled than before. He hoped confiding in the mage would help ease his apprehension, but as the night wore on, his anxiety worsened. Merlin was nowhere to be found.

TWENTY-SIX

The knock was wrong. The way the knuckles rapped against the wood wasn't the right weight, the right height, and Guinevere bolted awake. That was not Arthur at her door.

"What—" her maid groaned, still half asleep, but Guinevere rolled over and slapped her hand over the girl's mouth, silencing her. At the king's request, her maid had slept in her room, and with a racing heart, Guinevere shoved her off the bed. The maid understood the Queen's urgency, sliding obediently to the floor, out of sight, and Guinevere lifted a finger to her lips. The girl nodded, and with shaking muscles, the queen answered the door.

"My love." Lancelot seized her hands in the pale light, and Guinevere had to fight her own body to keep from recoiling. How had he found her? Had he been watching? Had he seen Arthur emerge earlier? Her chest constricted sharply around her wild heart as the questions tumbled through her mind.

"It's time." He smiled, drawing her close with triumph on his lips. He hugged her, his arms trapping her with an almost painful force. Instinct begged her hand to slap him, to beat him bloody for touching her, but she forced herself to play along. Placate him. Make him happy. Make him believe. She had to survive until she reached Arthur.

"I cannot wait to crown you my queen," Lancelot said as they parted, and her relief that he didn't suspect her and the king was so strong that a genuine smile curved her lips.

"That day cannot come too soon." She pictured Arthur slaughtering him so that her voice oozed desire.

"That day is here." He shifted, and Guinevere saw two guards at his back. She had never seen the gargantuan men before, and her body turned to ice.

"Don't worry." Lancelot cupped her cheek placatingly. "They're here to protect you. I know it is early, but I don't want you here for this. The king may try to use you against me, and I cannot stomach the thought of him hurting you. These men will take you from Camelot until it's safe."

No. No. No. No. No. The word rang like a mantra in her mind. She couldn't let him take her. Arthur wouldn't know where to look. If he separated them, it could spell her death.

"Surely, I can be protected within these walls." Panic seized control of her muscles, poisoning them with its acid.

"My love." Lancelot's tone was iron, and she glimpsed the kind of king and husband he would become. A man demanding blind obedience. A man followed without question, even though he led his men into the pits of Hell. A husband requiring a submissive jewel, not a wife.

"This is for your safety," he continued.

"Of course," she lied her agreement, eyeing the guards at his back. Her refusal would only result in those brutes manhandling her. Perhaps going willingly would curb their suspicions, offering her an opportunity to escape.

"Let me dress," she said, gripping the door with white

knuckles. "It is still dark. Surely you can spare me a moment to make myself decent?" She looked pointedly at the guards and then down at her nightdress, drawing Lancelot's attention to how little she wore.

"Of course," he swallowed, his jealousy flaring. "Be quick. We cannot waste time."

Guinevere smiled obediently and shut the door, but before it could click closed, his fingers slipped between the doorframe. He didn't open it, but he let it stand cracked. Guinevere watched the sliver, dread dripping through her veins and bleeding into her stomach. Did he plan to watch her? But after a moment, nothing appeared at the crack, and her pulse slowed. It seemed he merely wanted her within earshot, and she cursed under her breath. There would be no instructing her maid now.

Guinevere grabbed a dress that didn't restrict her movements and stepped around the bed so her maid could see her. She shook her head slightly before peeling off her nightgown, slipping the dark fabric over her body. When she was done, she stared down at her maid. Neither woman spoke, but the girl understood the fear in her queen's eyes. She understood the silent plea, the instructions, and she nodded. Guinevere showed no sign that she had seen the girl's acknowledgment. She simply turned back to the door and pulled it open.

"I'm ready…" and then loud enough for her maid to hear, she asked, "Where are you taking me? Shall we go to my father's? He will keep me safe until this is over." If she went to her family, Arthur could locate her.

"Leave through the northern gate." Lancelot ignored her question as he shoved her at the guards. They were larger than she initially thought, and her heart plummeted. There would be no escape, no matter how viciously she fought. "You should avoid all conflict exiting the city that way."

They escorted her at a rapid pace through the empty hallways. Guinevere prayed they would happen upon a servant, a guard, anyone, but in the dark hours before dawn, the castle was a tomb. Not a single soul witnessed her danger.

They arrived outside uninterrupted, and three saddled horses waited in the darkness. Without a word, the two brutes mounted their animals, and Lancelot dragged her to the third beast.

"When we meet again, I will be king." He settled her before him, the vision of a man possessed. "I'll make you my queen, and your suffering will come to an end. Arthur's reign is over."

"The day I have been praying for." Guinevere wasn't sure how she kept her voice so steady, so convincing.

Lancelot yanked her close, kissing her hard, and she clenched her eyes, telling herself that today was the day that Arthur ripped out this man's throat. She had to obey for a while longer, and then she would attempt an escape. She would fight her way back to Arthur to warn him, and she would help her husband kill this monster.

"Go, now." Lancelot pulled back breathlessly. "Go before I cannot say goodbye to you. We will have a lifetime after today, and I'll finally be able to taste all of you, my beautiful bride."

Guinevere turned to the horse to hide her disgust, and with his guiding hands, she slid into the saddle.

"May God bless you and bring you all you deserve," she said. *"A mouth full of blood and shredded entrails,"* she added silently. She smiled at him, her lips curving beautifully. He thought she intended her excited grin for his victory, but as she rode away from the castle into the dawn, the smile was truly for Arthur and for how skillfully he would turn this beautiful traitor ugly.

Arthur's eyes were bloodshot, and they burned with exhaustion. The sun had yet to rise, but he and the knights had spent the seemingly endless night searching for Mordred and discussing every potential outcome of Lancelot's threats. They discovered no evidence of the mage, and nothing occurring in Camelot could be misconstrued as a heinous act. Arthur and Gawain agreed it was in their best interest to tell his most trusted knights of the plot. Lancelot's betrayal shocked them all, except for Tristan. He noticed Guinevere's behavior at his wedding and found the idea of Guinevere abandoning Arthur incomprehensible. He had watched her carefully, wanting proof before presenting the king with her infidelity, but his instincts had been right. She would never abandon her husband.

Lancelot's treachery, though, had come as a punch to the gut. The knights had been livid at the king for not seeking their help sooner, but after a yelled argument conducted with hushed tones, Arthur made them see. If Lancelot, the friend he loved and trusted, was capable of this level of deception, who else in this court wore a dangerous mask? The fact that Lancelot's plans threw their own loyalty into question stung like salt in an open wound, but in the end, they understood how one traitor's actions isolated the king. Regardless of the threats banging down their gates, they vowed to help him, but hours later, they had nothing to show for it. There was no sign of Mordred. No sign of any disturbances. It was the unbearable calm before the storm, and Arthur dreaded how quiet it was. The greater the silence, the greater the devastation, and as dawn crept closer, so did his doubt.

Arthur splashed cold water on his face. The darkness would give way to morning within the hour. He would give Guinevere till sunrise before he woke her. He hated the idea of sending her somewhere beyond his protective reach, but she was his weakness. One threat against her was all it would take for him to cave. A man could torture him within an inch of his life, beat him until he was no longer recognizable, and he would never yield, but one finger raised against her? Arthur shuddered at the image. He would abandon everything to save her. She needed to be far from the oncoming fight.

A commotion at the door sounded, and Percival barged in. His hair was disheveled, his eyes bloodshot and horrified. Arthur hadn't seen him in days, not since he tasked him with investigating the monastery's disturbance, but the man looked unhinged.

"My king." Percival practically threw himself against Arthur, gripping his biceps as his chest heaved. "You must come to the monastery immediately."

"What did you find?" Arthur asked as Tristan brought him water. Percival gulped it down, sloshing some onto his shirt, and then he stared at the king with disbelief.

"When I arrived, I found nothing out of the ordinary. No signs of a disturbance. I intended to return to the castle, but a mile into my trip, instinct urged me to go back. Why did we receive reports if everything was as it should be? Dread nagged at me. I missed something important, so when I returned to the monastery, I concealed my presence. I've been watching it ever since."

"What did you learn?" The knight's expression told Arthur he didn't want to hear the answer.

"It's Mordred, my king. They are harboring Mordred. He is still alive."

Arthur let go of Percival, and his gaze collided with Gawain's as he leaned over the table, his broad hands protesting his weight.

"Did you hear me?" Percival rushed to the king's side. "Mordred is back. He is alive."

"We know," Gawain answered for the king. "We had our suspicions, but you just confirmed it."

"We need to get her out of here." Arthur glanced at Gawain. "She was right about Mordred. She isn't safe here."

"We'll get her out." Gawain nodded.

"We must journey to the monastery. If we can catch him there now, we may sever their plans before they are in motion. Tristan?"

"My king?"

"Gather soldiers you trust."

"We need Merlin," Percival said as Tristan walked for the door.

"We can't find Merlin," Arthur said with a sinking in his gut. "He has disappeared."

Percival opened his mouth, but before he could utter a single word, Tristan pulled the door open and a feminine voice squeaked in surprise. The knight's heads collectively snapped to the doorway, and the moment Arthur saw her, he knew. His stomach clenched and his vision blackened at the edges. He stumbled, and if Percival hadn't caught his arm, he might have crashed to the floor. For there, with her fist poised to knock, stood his wife's maid, still dressed in her nightgown, her face ashen.

CHAPTER TWENTY-SEVEN

The sun had long since risen, its rays peeking through the trees as they rode, yet Guinevere had found no opportunity to escape. With each passing mile, her dread multiplied until it was a living, breathing beast in her chest. Her guards did not drive her at a fast pace, opting for a more leisurely journey, and at first, she hoped their slow speed would grant her a shot at freedom, but it had the opposite effect. Undistracted by a grueling race, their eyes had been plastered on her for every agonizing second.

Their pace initially confused her, but as they veered off the main roads and into the trees, she understood with a sinking heart. They were not delivering her to her father. They were not leading her anywhere. The guards simply aimed to keep her from the castle. If her maid found Arthur, he wouldn't know where to search. They weren't attempting to flee; they were hiding her, and if they had no predetermined destination, Lancelot intended this to be Arthur's last day on earth. He wanted her out of the way as he claimed the throne. Worry knotted her gut as they rode ever farther. Lancelot's confidence was unsettling. Unless there were lodgings and food on this unorthodox journey that she wasn't aware of, these knights didn't intend for her to spend days on the road. She fought the flood of tears clamoring at the gates. Whatever Lancelot had planned, he meant it to be fast and deadly. Could Arthur, despite his rage and unmatched skill, withstand such an assault?

"Please," she whispered to herself, her chest constricting as if a snake choked the life from her lungs. "Please, Arthur. Do not leave me. Don't come looking for me. Just survive."

"My queen?" one of her guards interrupted her prayer, and she jerked in her saddle. He studied her, and she quickly wiped the surprise and despair from her face. These men believed she loved Lancelot. They believed they were protecting her, not kidnapping her, and she needed to perpetuate the illusion. She had immediately recognized the kind of men they were. They wouldn't touch her now, not while she was the future wife of their leader, but if they expected she was a traitor? No one would hear her scream as they strangled her in the dirt.

"Are you well?" the man asked, and she forced a subdued smile.

"I was merely praying," she answered.

"Don't worry, my queen. Lord Lancelot will be victorious."

"How do you know?" she blurted. Maybe if she played their game, they would admit their plans. Despair whispered she would never warn her husband, but she had to try something. "Why are you so confident? How are you so certain King Arthur won't kill him and leave me a widow before I can even wed?"

"Lancelot has been planning his revenge for years. He will not fail."

Revenge? Guinevere squinted at them. *What revenge?*

"You won't tell me anything?" She blew out a breath of frustration, and then changed tactics. Arthur loved when she begged, and a similar technique might drag these men to their knees.

"Please." Her voice was sickeningly sweet, her youthful eyes wide and innocent, and she threw everything into her pleasing expression. "Can you not tell me a little? You must realize how much I love Lancelot, and being here without him, not knowing the danger he faces, is driving me to madness. I beg you, spare your queen, and give her hope to cling to."

The men exchanged a glance, and then the second shrugged. "She will learn of it, eventually. We should ease her suffering."

"Lancelot didn't want her involved," the first argued. "He wanted her shielded from this."

"Please," Guinevere purred. "Surely, he'll understand you did it to soothe my torment. I cannot imagine he wants me to be out of my mind with worry. Can you not feel my anxiety? I have to know he will survive the day."

"Swear to keep this conversation to yourself," the first man said. "Lancelot wanted you far from this, but I can see how worried losing your lover is making you, so I'll tell you only if you promise to keep my words silent."

"Of course," she blurted. "I would never dream of causing trouble. I am just frightened."

He nodded, accepting her assurance, and then he began, "Lancelot has spread rumors that a monastery outside the city limits is harboring Mordred."

"Mordred?" she repeated, feigning surprise. "He is dead. How could he be at the monastery?"

"He isn't," he answered, and she kept her face neutral, knowing full well the mage had been in the castle yesterday. "But the king doesn't know that, and the temptation will be irresistible. He'll march out to meet him, but all he will find are monks and orphans. Dead monks and orphans."

Guinevere paled, and Lancelot's words replayed in her mind like a curse. *Something so horrible, so unforgivable, that not even his own army will fight for him. Camelot will turn against him in a heartbeat, welcoming me to the throne.*

"We stationed a loyal soldier at the monastery," the man continued, oblivious to her faltering heart. "He'll be the sole survivor of the king's massacre and will run to the city bathed in blood. He shall scream of Arthur's madness, of how the king accused them of harboring a dead mage and then killed everyone because he chased a ghost. God-fearing men. Innocent children. Camelot will see the king for who he is. An insane brute."

"No one will believe he would stoop so low," Guinevere barely had a voice.

"Of course, they will." The man looked at her with suspicion. "He spent years hunting Mordred. He is obsessed, and his behavior as of late only supports his madness. Look at how he flew into a rage and almost killed Lancelot in training. At how he laid his hands on you in front of the entire court. The people will accept the narrative. They shall read the proof in the children's bodies, in your absence, in our man's bloody clothes. Don't worry, Arthur won't escape this."

Sickness churned in Guinevere's stomach. Her legs clutched her horse for fear she might pass out and fall off. Arthur had been acting insane… because of her. She had driven him to assault Lancelot. She asked him to act drunk at breakfast, calling his integrity into question, and now he would pay the price. Bile crept up her throat, hot and acidic.

"You shouldn't have told her," the second guard said. "She looks ill. Lancelot will be furious."

"No." Somehow Guinevere found her voice. "Thank you for telling me. It is a brilliant plan. One I am certain will succeed."

And it was a brilliant evil. She loved Arthur more than her own life. She had been willing to destroy everything to save him, yet if he slaughtered monks and children in cold blood, she wasn't sure she could stand by him. She knew this was a lie, that

Lancelot's sinners had violated those innocent lives, but if it had been her husband's doing, her loyalty would falter. And if the woman who adored him retracted her allegiance, Camelot would revolt with the speed and carnage of an avalanche. They didn't know him like she did. All they knew was a monk would deliver butchered children to their doorsteps and blame the king. They would scream for Arthur's head. They would crucify an innocent man because of this plan. Guinevere's vision blurred black. She had to get out of here. She needed to stop Arthur from going to that monastery.

"You are a God-fearing woman," the second guard said, scrutinizing her disgust. She couldn't hide the waves of nausea battering her. "Lancelot loves you dearly, speaks highly of your goodness and resilience despite the king's oppression, so I realize this loss of life bothers you, but consider it, my queen. Think of the lives Lancelot has saved in the end. There will be no war, no invasion. A few died, so hundreds might live."

Guinevere stared at him, shocked to see his conviction that murdering children was the best approach, but she understood her precarious position. If they harmed babes without guilt, what would they do to her?

"I understand," she whispered with a shaky voice. "Lancelot is wise. I am no soldier nor a king. If he says this is the way to save our people, I trust him."

"You are a good woman, my queen," the second man said. "I can see why Lancelot wishes to shield you from your husband and claim you as his wife as he rebuilds Camelot."

GUINEVERE FELL silent as they rode deeper into the forest, all sense of direction and hope bleeding from her broken heart.

She felt like a rabid wolf, lashing out at any thread of hope. This could not be how Arthur met his end, like a trapped predator hacked to pieces by his own kind.

The underbrush rustled, and Guinevere whipped her head toward the sound, but the trees were lonely and still. Her guards barely offered the noise a passing look. The logical part of her brain told her it was only an animal disturbing the foliage, but something inside her, a primal instinct, warned her to slow her horse. Guinevere pulled her mount's reins, forcing the beast to fall behind. But after an unbearable silence, nothing happened. She scanned the trees, hope and dread tugging her in opposite directions. A gentle breeze tossed the leaves in a graceful dance. Birds sang of romance and sunshine. Tree bark curled in knotted shadows, but they were alone, the wild their only companion. The sound meant nothing.

The first guard shifted in his seat to ensure she still followed them, and the moment their eyes met, she heard it. The sharp whistle of air was the only warning before the man's throat exploded in blood. Guinevere watched in horror as a crimson arrow tip broke through his skin, dripping and filthy, and then the man collapsed from the horse. She had never witnessed a person die before. Not like this, and her scream lodged painfully in her throat.

The guard hit the underbrush, and her horse flung itself sideways, almost knocking her to the dirt. She barely had time to throw her arms around the beast's neck when another arrow sang its death song and buried itself in the second man's chest. The brute went down hard, his flailing hand slapping her mount, and the horse bolted into a run.

Guinevere clutched his mane, his reins, anything she could find. Her thighs gripped the animal as he ran, and she wasn't sure if she should be afraid of the uncontrolled escape or the shooter at her back. She ground her teeth, waiting for the piercing pain of an arrow to rupture her skin. She prayed the archer's aim was true. That her death would be quick.

"Guinevere!" The firm voice broke through her panic with resounding familiarity. "Woah, there." The word grew closer, and she registered a second pair of hooves pounding the dirt.

Guinevere yanked on her mount, trying to force him to slow, but the animal only surged faster. She was a skilled rider, but on a manic horse, it was all she could do to remain in the saddle.

"Easy, boy," the commanding voice sounded again, and a strange horse pulled into her peripheral vision. "Guinevere." A strong hand reached across the distance. "Jump."

"I—"

"Jump now," the man cut her off as he surged forward, his fingers almost brushing her arm.

Forcing her mind not to think, Guinevere released her hold and flung herself sideways. True to his promise, the newcomer grabbed her waist and yanked her against his chest. The moment her legs cleared her saddle, he slowed his horse and pulled her into his lap.

"I got you," he said as she threw her arms around his neck, a sob falling from her lips. "You're safe now."

"How did you find me?" she sobbed, soaking Gawain's shirt with her fear.

"Your maid warned us." Gawain stroked her hair gently as he turned back to where the dead men had abandoned their mounts. "Arthur sent me after you, but it took me a while to pick up your trail. Your maid told me you asked Lancelot if he was sending you to your father's, but he only mentioned the northern gate, which confirmed my need to track you along a different route."

"I wanted to escape, but they never took their eyes off me."

"You did the right thing. You wouldn't be able to take them

yourself, and I was coming for you. Arthur would never leave you alone out here."

"Arthur." Guinevere pushed her face out of Gawain's chest. "Where is he?"

"Percival returned. Mordred was sighted at a monastery—"

"We have to go." She didn't let him finish that sentence as they reached the two remaining horses. Hers had vanished. He would most likely find his way home when his fear subsided, but they couldn't wait. She had to warn her husband.

"We have to stop him," she said as she climbed off of Gawain's lap and onto the first guard's horse.

"Why?" Gawain asked as she pushed the animal forward.

"I'll explain as we ride," she answered, urging the horse to pick up speed. "But Arthur is walking into a trap."

CHAPTER TWENTY-EIGHT

Their pace was brutal. Hooves pounded the ground with anger. Breaths panted in ragged heaves. Fear consumed all in its ravenous path. They pushed onward, the scenery disappearing behind them in a blur of color, yet it wasn't fast enough. They were too late to save the doomed, too late to stop Arthur from leaving the city. She prayed they were not too late to intercept his return to the castle. That was where Lancelot and his lies waited. The moment the king returned to the city limits, to the riots that surely had shattered the peace, he was a dead man. No, their speed was not fast enough.

Guinevere told Gawain of Lancelot's massacre, and with dread in his eyes, Gawain explained Arthur had sent him—his most trusted knight—after his wife while he and the rest rode out to investigate the monastery. Sickness curdled her stomach, tying her in knots. Her mind was of a singular focus. If they intercepted Arthur, they could warn him of the lies that would ignite a riot. They would keep him from walking into

Lancelot's waiting blades. She knew her husband. When confronted with the carnage, he would rally his army in search of the guilty, only his army was no longer his. They would hear the false events spewed from the mouths of wolves in monks' clothing, and they would hate their king. The man who fought and bled and suffered to provide his people with a better future, the man who wore his struggles and pain on his skin. They would see Lancelot's false evidence, and they would turn on Arthur. They would execute him and crown the true murderer their king, unaware of how in their plea for justice, they condemned themselves to tyranny and oppression. If Guinevere stopped Arthur from returning to Camelot, Lancelot would still seize the throne, but at least her husband would live to fight another day, survive to one day make things right.

Both their hearts broke as they rode over the empty land without opposition. They encountered no signs of the king or his knights, and as they drew closer to the monastery—sweating and breathless—she knew. She sensed it in her bones. They were too late. All her plotting and planning, her sacrifice, was for nothing.

They saw the smoke first, smelled the stench of death second. Determined not to allow orphans to suffer the childhood he'd had, Arthur had worked closely with this monastery at the dawn of his reign. He couldn't bear the thought of the motherless stealing food, the fatherless being kicked like rats. These monks gave the orphans of Camelot a home, a future, a life, and Lancelot had ripped it away in a single night.

Guinevere dismounted, and her delicate fingers clamped over her lips. A fire raged through some of the buildings. Bodies lay hacked and strewn across the blood-soaked courtyard, and she doubled over, heaving bile onto the ground at the sight. The small, dismembered corpses were too much for her to stomach.

"Guinevere." Gawain caught her as her knees buckled, and

he lowered her to the dirt. "Don't look." He grabbed the back of her head and press her face gently against his chest.

"I have to," she sobbed into his shirt, shaking uncontrollably. "I have to see what he did, witness what I allowed to happen."

"This isn't your fault. You risked everything to uncover his plans. My God, Guinevere, I went to Arthur, begging him to let me deal with you because I thought you intended to destroy the king. You put yourself in the line of fire to stop this."

"I should have tried harder, pushed harder." She beat his chest, and he let her. "I betrayed my husband's trust so I could help save him, but it didn't matter, not in the end. I failed, and now… now Lancelot is going to ruin the man I love."

"This isn't on you. You sacrificed yourself to the devil. Few women would be brave enough to do that for their king and country, and Arthur doesn't believe you failed him. Without you, he would be blind. At least now he knows who his enemy is, and I've seen him survive the harshest of odds."

"He had an army at his back then, soldiers who believed he would usher in a better future." Guinevere pulled away from Gawain, the fight bleeding from her muscles. "Now all they see is a madman. His own people will crucify him."

"His knights know the truth. They will defend him to the death."

"Then they are dead, too." Guinevere gripped the knight's shoulders and pushed herself to her feet. In a daze, she dragged her shaking body into the courtyard, the tears flowing unrestrained down her cheeks. She felt shriveled and dehydrated, but still, the tears came destroying her. She forced herself to survey the bodies, to witness their deaths, their mutilations. She was their queen, but she had failed to protect them. Now all she could do was pray for their souls to find peace.

A monk lay at the center of the courtyard, a heavy cross clutched in his hand, and Guinevere knelt before him, gently prying it from his grip. She folded her fingers around the wood and closed her eyes, his body her altar as she prayed. Her voice was low as her words blessed their souls, as she begged the Lord in heaven to offer them a place at his holy table. She asked for forgiveness and then finished with one last request on her tongue.

"Save my husband." Pain laced her voice. "Return him to me."

She returned the cross to the dead monk's hands, and pressing her palms to the dirt, she pushed off the ground only to freeze when something jutting out below the corpse caught her eye. She snatched it in her fist, holding it up to the light.

"What's that?" Gawain asked, and she jerked. She hadn't heard him approach.

"I... I don't know." She stood and moved closer to the knight. The curved metal in her hand had sharp edges, as if a violent force had shattered it. It was mostly unrecognizable, but some of its carvings taunted her.

"Does this look familiar?" she asked, her mind flipping through her memories like the pages of a thick tome.

"I think so," Gawain answered. "But I can't be sure."

"There is something." She twisted it in her hands, studying its every angle. "I... what am I missing?"

He shrugged as she shoved it into the pocket of her dress. Without another word, she stormed back to her horse, and after a confused second, Gawain followed.

"Where..?" he started.

"We need to get to the castle." Something about that shard ate at her gut, her memory, her instinct. She couldn't explain it, but she knew Arthur needed to see this broken metal. The pull was so strong, she had to force herself to move carefully instead of racing from this graveyard, manic and possessed.

"Absolutely not." Gawain caught her biceps and whirled her around. "The king's orders were explicit. I am to deliver you to your father's protection. I shouldn't even have brought you here, but the hope of intercepting him confused my judgment."

"I'm going to Arthur," she growled, the challenge returning to her eyes.

"Guinevere—"

"I am your queen," she said, and despite her twenty-five years, she suddenly looked older, more mature, like a feminine version of the warrior king. "You can either come with me or you can leave and explain to my father why you abandoned his daughter."

Gawain stared at her, a battle of wills waged silently, and then he bowed his head. It was slight, barely noticeable, but it was enough. Guinevere turned and mounted her horse, Gawain following her lead, and together they raced for the city.

THE NEWS HAD SPREAD. Chaos burned in scorching waves from every soul they passed, the city a hellish inferno of rage. People were fleeing for the monastery, desperate to prove King Arthur's guilt with their own eyes, and everywhere Guinevere looked, she saw brutish men dressed as commoners calling for Arthur's head. Lancelot's army had the crowd in a tailspin. Violence was on the brink of exploding. A brutality this kingdom would never survive.

Traitors in bloody monk robes spewed venomous lies about the king and his madness, about the nights and their torture. Their poisoned words were almost unbearable to hear, and if their stories of mutilation were not enough, they pulled carts of the disfigured victims behind them. It was a macabre display of Arthur's supposed depravity, and Guinevere had never felt such fear. Camelot was in turmoil. The death toll would be too large to count by the time the day was through.

"My queen." Gawain leaned close so she could hear him over

the volatile crowd. "We'll never make it to the castle. These people don't know you are supposed to be under Lancelot's protection. They'll skin you alive for Arthur's crimes if they catch you." She looked at him with terrified eyes but said nothing, so he pushed. "I did what you asked. I brought you here, but I swore to defend you with my life. If that is the last order King Arthur ever gives me, I will not fail him."

Guinevere urged her horse forward, but Gawain gripped her elbow, pulling her to a stop.

"I love him too." The knight looked distraught. "He is my best friend, and I would die for him. But there's no path into that castle that ends with you still alive. Don't make me watch them torture you. You don't want to know what this crowd will do if they capture you. It's why Lancelot sent you away. Until you are wed to him and under his protection, you belong to Arthur, and the people's hatred of him will spill onto you. I cannot protect you against an entire kingdom. Please, Guinevere," he begged, "don't make me watch them hurt you. Don't force me to listen to you scream."

Guinevere looked around, her mind spinning, spinning, spinning. She was going to be sick, and Gawain's words slipped into her brain, releasing their venomous fear. She wore a plain dress, her appearance disheveled, but eventually someone would recognize her. Gawain was right. The pound of flesh this angry mob would exact from their queen would be unbearable. A shiver rattled her spine, and she forced the horrifying thoughts down into her darkest recesses.

"What about the garden?" she asked. "Can you get me there instead?"

"I…" He looked around. "Maybe, why?"

"Please, get me to the garden," she begged. "I promise if we can't make it, I'll let you take me to my father's, but can we at least try?"

Gawain surveyed the crowd. The horde stormed through the

streets, aiming for the castle's entrances, and he paused. Smaller alleys led to the castle gardens, and it stood to reason that rioters would be more concerned with men and valuables instead of the carefully cultivated bushes.

"Get down." He leaped from his horse, and Guinevere followed suit. Gawain ripped off his outer jacket and flung it over her head, hiding her easily recognizable raven hair. "Wear this and keep your eyes down. Don't leave my side and do exactly as I say. If I say we can't make it, we can't make it. I won't take you unless you agree."

"I agree."

"Guinevere?" He glared down at her. Her headstrong nature had become so like the king's.

"I promise," she swore. "I will listen, but I have to try."

He nodded and gripped her biceps, dragging her into the mass. To her credit, she never once faltered, keeping up with his punishing pace, and as they wove through the throng, she kept her head down and her elbows sharp. They pushed and shoved their way through, and as they closed in on the gardens, the crowd thinned.

It took them longer than it should have, but they finally reached the outer wall surrounding the grounds. Gawain tugged her to a gate. Both of them were relieved it still stood locked, and the knight pulled the key from his neck. He shoved her inside and locked it behind them. It wouldn't keep the rioters out indefinitely, but he certainly would not make it easier for them.

The moment they were sealed in the peaceful garden, Guinevere launched into a run. Gawain grunted in surprise at her speed but fell into step beside her with ease. Neither of them spoke, and within minutes, they arrived at the wild part of the garden. Guinevere rushed for the wall, slapping her hand against the hidden lever. A confused Gawain opened his mouth, but the wall's groan silenced him as the door slid free.

"What in God's name?" He gawked as she stepped into the shadows.

"Come on." Guinevere beckoned, hands already on the internal lever. He obeyed without hesitation, and as soon as he stood beside her, she sealed them in the blackness.

"Where are we?" Gawain asked as the queen grasped for him in the darkness. He caught her hand, and she slid her fingers into his, and it struck him just how small and young she was. Protectiveness surged through him, and he pulled her closer. He was a fool for letting her put herself in so much danger.

"It's a straight shot. We can't get lost," came her disembodied voice. "Press your palms on the wall and go slow. We'll hit steps, eventually."

"Guinevere?" he asked as they shuffled forward, reminding her she had ignored his question.

"It leads to Arthur's study," she said, and he clutched her fingers tighter, not liking that he couldn't see her. "We can't leave the door open, so we'll have to walk this in the dark."

"Is this why he permits no one in his study?"

"Partially. But you know him as well as I do. He likes the solitude."

Gawain heard the love and fear in her voice, and it broke his heart.

"If we find him, we can get him out through this," Gawain said, needing to offer her hope. "We'll regroup and make a plan. Lancelot has Mordred, but Merlin is more powerful."

"How did this happen?" Guinevere asked. "I thought Merlin's power and Arthur's strength made them unbeatable."

"I don't know." He had been wondering the same thing. "We assumed Mordred was dead until yesterday. Merlin is powerful, but how was he supposed to protect us from a ghost?"

Guinevere grunted, tipping forward as her toes thudded against the stone, and Gawain yanked her to his side.

"Found the stairs," she said, trying desperately to sound hopeful. "He is still alive, right?"

"Trust me, if Arthur was dead, we would have heard about it outside." Gawain meant it as encouragement, but he felt the queen stiffen as they climbed the circular staircase. "If there is one thing I know about Lancelot, it's he loves eyes on him. He is beautiful, strong, and vain, and if he went through all this trouble to blame Arthur for his crimes, he will make sure the king's death is public. He wants an audience to view him as their savior, and since they are clamoring for his head, your husband is alive."

Guinevere didn't answer, and Gawain squeezed her hand.

"Arthur still lives. You have made me come this far. You can't give up on me now."

"Never," she said as they reached the end of the stairs. Guinevere groped the wall blindly until her fingers snagged the lever. It popped open easily, and light flooded their eyes. Both of them blinked as they burst into the silent study, and Gawain surveyed the sparse room with surprise.

"This is it?" he asked. Guinevere smiled as she nodded. If they survived this, she was serious about decorating this office. She would make it comfortable, and then she would never leave Arthur's side.

"Stay here." Gawain moved for the door.

"No—"

"Yes." He whirled on her. "I'll find Arthur and bring him to you. I'll try to locate the other loyal knights, and then we'll return. So please, wait here for us. The king will have my head if I lose you."

Guinevere nodded, too afraid to speak, and then Gawain drew his sword from his back and left her alone in Arthur's study.

TWENTY-NINE

Guinevere sat at Arthur's desk, her thumb absentmindedly rubbing the woodgrain of the armrest. How different this visit to his study was from her last. She had spent that night in his arms, pressed against his naked body, and now she didn't know if he was alive.

Anxiety launched her to her feet, and she moved to the door, pressing an ear against the wood. Silence. Here, in his solitary study, the conflict did not exist. She was alone in the quiet, and with every passing second, her worry morphed from a spark to a forest fire, determined to singe her from the inside out. Gawain was taking too long. Surely, he should have returned by now?

Unable to sit still any longer, Guinevere paced the small, bare room. She promised the knight she would stay, but as the minutes ticked by with no sign of him, she knew she wouldn't keep her word. Her husband was out there, his subjects screaming for his blood, but this was her fight too. Till death did they part, and if she had any say in it, today was not Arthur's end. She didn't care what she had to do, but he would survive. He would grow old and grey beside her, his last breath breathed in her arms as their children surrounded them. He would not die for crimes he never committed.

Guinevere paused before the door and stared at it before her hand shot out. Her fingers gripped the latch for a lingering moment, but then she yanked them back. She should give them a little longer. She should keep her promise a while more.

Her resolve lasted ten minutes before she barreled down the spiral staircase. She couldn't do it. She couldn't sit alone and wait for the news of Arthur's death. This urgency was the same pressure she had experienced the night she met him. She had paced in her room, fighting his call, his gravity, but in the end, she appeared at his bed, unable to resist. This moment? This was the same. He was pulling her into his orbit, and she dared not refuse. He needed her, and if death was his fate, then she would join him. She would rather end her life, her body wrapped around his, than do nothing.

The winding staircase dumped her into an empty corridor, and Guinevere listened as she crept forward. From the echoes reverberating softly off the stone, the streets still contained the riots, the castle walls remaining unbreeched by civilians, but the further she slipped unnoticed through her home, the more signs of chaos reared their ugly heads. Lancelot's army had made quick work of the castle. They must have stormed its defenses while Arthur and his knights rode out to the monastery, the trap for the king set with little resistance.

Guinevere paused, the stench of death and destruction stronger the further she slipped behind enemy lines. Gawain's words lingered like acrid smoke in the back of her mind. Lancelot wanted Arthur's execution to be public. He needed Camelot to witness his victory, to witness him plundering the throne, and she knew where she would find them. There was a grand hall on one of the upper floors, a lavish balcony extending from its double doors to view the city below. Arthur used the vantage on the rare occasions when he addressed his people, and Guinevere sensed the pull in her gut, urging her to that balcony. That was where Lancelot would slit the king's throat so that the spray of blood would drip onto those watching. Either the king or the knight would die there today, and while fear for Gawain, for Tristan and Percival, and all those loyal to Arthur plagued her heart, she had no choice. Her feet were already moving, carrying her unnoticed through the servant's halls.

As if an angel guided her steps, not a single soul crossed her path. She passed an occasional sign of a struggle, but it seemed Lancelot's plan to pollute the kingdom had been successful. The sounds of fighting drifted up from the floors below. The traitors no doubt engaged in vicious combat with Arthur's legendary knights, but the upper levels were a tomb. The empty halls offered her an uninterrupted route, but as she climbed the final set of stairs, she heard the clang of metal so brutal, the blow jarred her bones. She knew that sound. How many times had she watched Arthur train, listening to the way his blade rang with unmatched force as it struck his opponent's? She had been right. Arthur and Lancelot were here, and she wasn't sure if that knowledge brought her relief or dread.

The crash of swords drew closer, faster, harsher. A deep voice grunted, followed by a metallic ring so severe, the air vibrated in pain, and Guinevere's heart swelled. She recognized that rough tone. The way its sharp edges grated against her soul, shredding it raw so that it might seep into her heart and consume her whole.

She raced to the top of the stairs and peered through the cracked door. Gawain had warned her, had wished she would never have to witness her husband's brutality, but nothing prepared her for the warrior that filled her vision. Arthur was a monster, a savage, an avenging angel with a sword of vengeance. She had watched him spar with his men for five years. She thought she understood the man that slept beside her, the man she let grip her thighs, her waist, her throat, but she didn't truly know the killer she trusted with her body until that moment. Excalibur was one with his fist, and despite the blood oozing from multiple wounds, he was a terrifying sight to behold. His blade swung with perfect ruthlessness; his muscles danced to the song of death. He was death reincarnated. He was violence and anger and war wrapped around flesh and blood and bone. This was not the gentle husband who respected her, who cherished her. This was the devil made man, and Guinevere understood how a penniless boy from the streets had become the legendary King Arthur.

Yet she was not afraid. She watched in awe as Lancelot struggled to deflect the king's unstoppable blows. She felt foolish for her overwhelming concern for Arthur. His brutality was unmatched, his precision unwavering, and she should have been terrified. His eyes had gone black, his jaw rigid with murderous rage, and she should have felt a bolt of fear freeze her blood in her veins, experienced the horror that she ever let that man put his hands on her skin, but she couldn't bring herself to feel anything besides exhilaration and pride. This king, her husband, would not go willingly into that darkest night. He had promised her that as long as she was waiting for him, he would fight to return to her, and as he raised Excalibur for a blow that would carve Lancelot's brain in two, she knew he would be true to his word.

A blast of air collided with her face as Arthur flew backward. Guinevere watched in shocked confusion as her husband stumbled, and when he regained his footing, blood poured over his lips. Guinevere scanned the room, desperate for an explanation. No one had touched him. He had been seconds away from ending the traitor's life, yet he spat crimson onto the floor as if a man twice his size had tried to cave in his jaw.

Arthur wiped his mouth and raised his sword before his torso. Darkness flooded his features, the blood dripping from his teeth creating a savage of the king, and that was when Guinevere saw Lancelot's outstretched hand. She squinted at the knight's gesture, his palm extended as if his flesh could stop Excalibur from carving into his chest. For a moment, neither man moved, and then with a roar, Arthur lunged.

Excalibur swung down hard, but instead of raising his own sword, Lancelot threw his outstretched palm at the king. An unseen force knocked Arthur to the side, but he leaned into the blow, accepting its pain as he flew forward. Blood poured anew from a slash on his biceps, and his blade collided with Lancelot's.

Magic. Lancelot was using magic. He was a mage. Guinevere pulled further behind the safety of the door, a new and primal wave of fear torturing her. Arthur was the greater warrior. He should have killed Lancelot immediately, yet the knight still stood. Arthur bled from more places than she could count, and the gravity of her husband's situation almost made her collapse to her knees in dread. Excalibur was the only reason he still fought; the blade forged by magic for magic, but Arthur would not be able to withstand the onslaught forever. It was why Mordred had escaped the king's vengeance for so long. Even with the legendary sword, Arthur was merely a man. Flesh and blood and bone and mortality.

Guinevere looked around wildly, her brain screaming for her to think, to concentrate. How had she failed to see Lancelot was a mage? How had he kept his magic secret for all these years? Arthur was strong, the warrior forged by battle into a ruthless killer, but not even her beloved husband could survive magic's bloodlust. She needed to find help. She needed—

Movement caught her eye, and holding the men locked in combat in the corner of her view, Guinevere shifted toward the sight. A figure emerged from the shadows, his robes long and familiar. Her heart thundered in recognition as Merlin stepped out into the opening, and relief bathed her spirit. Merlin was one of the most powerful mages in Camelot's history. If he was here, Arthur was saved. She exhaled a deep breath, and then she was suddenly flat on her back, pain radiating from every cell in her body as the edge of her vision blackened.

CHAPTER THIRTY

Guinevere couldn't see. Her lungs refused to breathe. All she knew was pain. All she felt was agony. She had never suffered the effects of magic, but it was a heartless form of torment. The blood dripping from her husband was visible proof of its malice, but this? This blow was unnatural and ruthless. It was a hell like no other.

Struggling to swallow her cough so the sound wouldn't alert them to her presence, Guinevere rolled painfully to her side. She forced her eyes to focus on the scene before her, and when she saw Arthur's broken body sprawled on the floor, she clamped her hand over her mouth to hold back her scream. She clenched her eyes shut, unable to look at the awkward angle of his head, the unnatural rise and fall of his ribs. If her limbs hurt with such excruciating agony at the backlash, how much anguish must grip his muscles as the intended target of the magic's strike? That blow was no accident. It was not meant to disarm or unbalance the king. No, it had aimed to destroy him, to break him apart from the inside, and that he still lay breathing was only thanks to Excalibur absorbing some of the magic. Magic Guinevere recognized all too well. It was familiar, almost a comfort despite the pain blistering her body, and that made this attack unforgivable.

"Merlin?" Arthur coughed blood, and Guinevere wanted to scream at the way his words garbled over his teeth. She longed to run to him and take him in her arms, to protect him, but she could barely move.

"What are you doing?" Arthur asked, but Merlin said nothing. He simply raised his arm and then drew his fingers into a harsh fist. Arthur jerked violently, his massive frame forced to a weak kneel before his friend.

"Merlin?" Betrayal colored the king's features.

"I have been waiting for this moment, for the look on your face when you realized what I've taken from you," Lancelot laughed as he limped forward. Arthur struggled to stand, but Merlin's magic bound him on his knees.

"It has been a long five years in your court, but this victory makes my suffering worth it," Lancelot continued, his angelic voice tinged with something dark and venomous. "The moment where you realize that I have stolen your kingdom, your crown, your mage, and your wife. All of Camelot hates you for what they believe you did to that monastery. They are outside screaming for your blood, and when I spill it for them, you will know I stole everything you loved. Not even your most trusted mage or your beautiful wife stand beside you. They belong to me, and you will die with nothing."

"Merlin." Arthur's eyes shot to his friend. "Why are you doing this? Let me go."

"He won't answer you," Lancelot taunted. "It took time to exert my control over him. I would have conquered your throne long ago, but Merlin is far more powerful than I am. Challenging both him and Excalibur would be impossible, so I consumed him, integrating his mind with mine. I needed to be accepted into your court because my magic isn't as strong as his. To become one of your trusted knights. Once you loved me, Merlin relaxed his guard, and I poured my magic into him. After five years, your friend is no longer in control of himself. His body, his actions, his power. They belong to me, and with him at my side, I will finally rule Camelot."

"But Mordred." Arthur coughed blood. "You had Mordred's support. Why poison Merlin?"

"Oh, you foolish, barbaric man," Lancelot laughed. "Mordred is dead. He has been for years. You killed him when you claimed Excalibur from the stone."

"No..." Arthur trailed off.

"Did you enjoy hunting him after Camelot crowned you its ruler? Do you appreciate what I did to you, forcing you to fight a ghost?" Lancelot squatted before Arthur to meet his gaze. The king jerked forward with a growl, but Merlin's magic held. "Mordred was one of the men who stood guard over the sword, and you murdered him when you claimed Excalibur. My father has rested in the dirt for years." Arthur's eyes went wide, and Lancelot grinned his perfect smile. "Yes, Mordred was my father. I inherited some of his magic, and when you killed him, when you drove a blade through his gut, I vowed to destroy you. I swore on my father's grave that I would avenge him. I gathered an army and selected a puppet to portray him, but I realized that with my lesser magic, we would never win. I needed to corrupt your reign from the inside out, and I have done such a thorough job, even your wife is clamoring for your death. I want you to die knowing I will marry that pretty little thing and fill her with my child while your grave is still warm. She will scream my name as I fuck her in your bed, giving her what you never could."

"The man I killed when we met?" Arthur did not fall for Lancelot's taunts. He may be on his knees facing death, but he knew who owned Guinevere's heart. It beat in his chest beside his own, and both organs broke with the knowledge he would never see her again.

"A scapegoat I set up to die so that you might welcome me into your fold, and you fell for it. You believed I would save you, fight for you, and you opened your home." Lancelot sneered as he stood. "And now you will die for that. You'll pay for your mistakes, for my father's death." He reached down and grabbed the king roughly by the collar. "You shall pay on your knees before your people, and they will see the monster you truly are."

"Your father," Arthur groaned as he uselessly tried to resist Merlin's magic. "If he was guarding Excalibur, then he was one of the reasons Camelot withered into corruption. He was one of the cruel men who destroyed this kingdom. You don't have to follow in his footsteps. You don't have to allow his evil to corrupt your—"

Lancelot punched Arthur in the mouth so hard, the king's head flew back. Blood sprayed from his lips, and Guinevere watched in horror as he lost consciousness for a moment. Lancelot continued to drag him toward the balcony, Merlin's magic immobilizing him, and if Guinevere didn't do something, anything, she would have to watch them murder her husband. The pain slowly bleeding from her muscles, she stood with shaking limbs. Glinting metal caught her gaze, and she stared at Excalibur. The sword lay feet away from the door she hid behind. The blow had flung it across the room, and she gawked in disbelief. It resisted magic. It was what helped make Arthur nearly unstoppable. If she could return it to his hands.

She glanced back at her bleeding husband. His swollen face was almost unrecognizable. Only the true leader of Camelot could wield the sword. To all others, it was impossible to even pick up. The blade would not move, cemented to this spot on the tiles until someone worthy came along to give it purpose. Yet as she watched the men grow closer to the balcony doors, she couldn't focus on that. She refused to consider failure, and without a second thought, she slipped from the door's shelter.

Guinevere arrived at the sword in two steps, and with a fortifying breath, she braced for the struggle. Her fingers closed around the hilt, and she heaved with all her might, nearly toppling over backward when Excalibur lurched off the floor into her hands. Guinevere froze, the legendary sword protruding from her small fists. The blade was almost as big as her torso, and its weight was both heavy and light, her grip both steady and faltering. Her heart thundered in her chest. Her blood pumped so loud, it pulsed in her ears, vibrated against her skin, and she gave Excalibur a hesitant swing. It obeyed her like an extension of her arms, and a jolt electrified her nerves as the sword bonded with her. Excalibur answered to her heart, joined with her soul, just as it had Arthur's. Guinevere was a true ruler of Camelot.

With fire in her eyes and rage in her spirit, the Queen of Camelot raced forward on silent feet. Excalibur pulsed life through her veins, and with the grace of a dancer, she sailed over the floor. Even though the thought sickened her to her core, she had to do it. The king loved Merlin. She loved him in her own way too, but it was his magic that restricted Arthur, his magic that corrupted the kingdom. Without Merlin, Arthur would be free, and together, husband and wife would rip Lancelot to shreds.

"I am sorry," she whispered under her breath as she ran, and then she raised Excalibur high above her head and aimed for Merlin's skull.

THIRTY-ONE

Metal collided, and the assault ricocheted through Guinevere's skeleton, threatening to shatter her bones. She gasped at the pain shooting knives through her shoulders, at the blade halting her death blow. Her eyes trailed the stained sword resisting Excalibur down to the hilt, to the hands, to the arms, and her gaze lifted with defiance.

"Guinevere?" Lancelot's eyebrows pinched at the sight of her gripping Excalibur. Her muscles shook as his sword struggled to keep hers from cleaving Merlin's skull in two. "What are you doing?" All traces of his smug victory vanished from his features.

"What I have always done," she answered through gritted teeth. Tension coiled in Arthur's body as he watched helplessly from his knees, but she refused to look at him, all her concentration pouring into the sword clutched in her fists. She had spent hours observing Arthur train with this weapon, and while she had never set foot on the training field, images of his technique flooded her mind. If she glanced at his face and read the terror etched into his brow, she wouldn't survive longer than mere seconds in this fight. A fight she already had no chance of winning.

"Protecting... My... King." She enunciated each word slowly, reveling in the betrayal that danced over Lancelot's features as realization set in.

"No..." Lancelot pushed his sword against Excalibur as if his arms were disembodied limbs and not extremities attached to his torso. "You..."

"Played you like an instrument," Guinevere snarled. "I never loved you. I will never love you. You may have stolen Arthur's friend and mage. You turned Camelot against him, and you might yet steal his throne, but you never had me. I have always been and will always be Arthur's."

Lancelot twisted his wrist, tossing Excalibur from his blade, and Guinevere stumbled back at the unexpected force. Her eyes flicked to her husband for a fraction of a second, and his expression made her instantly regret it. Pure, unadulterated terror. She had never seen genuine fear in her husband's eyes before, and glimpsing it now shook her to her core.

"You've been lying to me this whole time?" Lancelot gawked at her incredulously, his beauty fading into an ugly snarl.

"Every word, every touch, every look." Guinevere raised Excalibur, just like she had witnessed Arthur do. "I was Arthur's spy, his confidant, his wife. You are unworthy of breathing the same air as my husband, and I love him enough to endure your treachery so I could save his life. I would have never married you. I will die before I let you touch me."

"I can arrange that, you fucking bitch." Lancelot launched himself at her, bringing his sword down with inescapable speed. Instinct flung her hands into the air, Excalibur absorbing most of the blow as she stumbled backward, almost collapsing to the floor.

"Guinevere!" Arthur screamed, and she tried to tune out his

voice. She had never heard that tone depart his lips before. Carnal fear, primal and soul-wrenching. His desperation gutted her. "Lean into the sword," he roared as Lancelot barreled down on her. "Let Excalibur guide you."

His words washed over her as Lancelot swung, and she leaned into the sword's will, letting it govern her muscles, her movements. It shielded her from the worst of the blow, but she wouldn't survive much longer. Not like this. Her smaller body couldn't withstand the force raining down on her.

"Good girl!" Arthur's intense voice rattled her soul. "Keep your hands up, Guin, move your feet." She pictured him on the training field as he yelled. She saw his steps glide, his blade swing, and she ducked, mimicking her memory of him, barely escaping a blow aimed at her skull.

"Don't stand still. Come to me, Guin. The sword will help you."

"Shut him up!" Lancelot roared as Guinevere let Arthur guide her, his words bringing her strength. Lancelot's blade came down so hard on Excalibur that she almost lost her grip as she crashed to the ground to avoid decapitation. Her eyes landed on her husband just as Merlin threw more magic against his face. Blood poured from his lips, his head lolling unnaturally to the side for too long before his neck pulled it upright. His pain distracted her from Lancelot's movement, and a scream ripped from her throat as his fist gripped her ankle in a suffocating hold.

"Get your hands off my wife!" Arthur thrashed against Merlin's bonds, terror rippling off him in palpable waves. "I will fucking kill you." His fear was too much, poisoning her with nausea. "Let her go!"

Lancelot dragged her on her stomach before flipping her onto her back as he pulled. Guinevere swung her free leg in a graceful arc, smashing her heel into Lancelot's groin. His grip on her ankle loosened as he doubled over, and she kicked him in the nose. His head snapped backward, and she scrambled to her knees, clutching Excalibur in her fist as she crawled for her husband. Their gazes collided as her palms scraped over the tiles, and for a moment, she was safe. She was alive, as was he, and she was so close. She was almost to his side.

Arthur's widening eyes were the only warning before the outside of her left thigh exploded in agony. She screamed as metal carved through her muscles, and her ribs smacked the ground as she fell. Tears clouded her vision, pain laced her voice, Arthur's fear rattled in her ears.

"Let me go!" Rage vibrated the king's chest as he bellowed at the deaf Merlin. "Guinevere, get up!"

His words sparked her adrenaline, and she pushed herself to her knees, clutching the sword.

"Leave her alone! Do not touch my wife, or so help me God, I will kill you." Arthur's eyes met hers, and she saw his suffering. Chained to the floor by magic, he was helpless to save her. All he could do was watch, and Guinevere's chest heaved. She didn't want him to have to observe this. He shouldn't see this. No husband should.

Pain exploded in her body as Lancelot's blade sliced over her ribs, and she collapsed, sobbing as her blood spilled onto the floor. Her husband was screaming, writhing in anger and horror, and she gritted her teeth so hard she thought they might crack. She had to get to him. She refused to die without kissing him one last time.

Determination consumed her, blotting out the pain, and clutching her weapon, she crawled on her hands and knees for her husband, her blood leaving a trail of gore behind her. The room was spinning, spinning, spinning. Arthur was yelling. Maybe she was the one yelling? She couldn't be sure. All she knew was Arthur was so close. Too far. She had to get to him, to keep moving.

"Guin!" The warning in the king's voice was unmistakable,

and the air at her back shifted. She took a deep breath, waiting for Lancelot to close in for the kill. She saw his shadow fall over her, heard his heaving as he readied the death blow, and she inhaled. With all the strength and rage and terror left in her body, she flung herself backward to her knees and swung Excalibur behind her. The blade connected with Lancelot's side, and the man howled as he stumbled, falling hard on his ass. She could tell by the resistance that the wound wasn't fatal. He would keep coming for her, but she had made her peace with death. All she craved was Arthur's arms around her as they both departed this world.

"Stop the bitch," Lancelot roared as she dragged herself toward Arthur, and absent control of his mind and body, Merlin whirled on her and grabbed her neck in one swift move. She yelped as the mage slammed her to the ground, but it was the only sound he allowed her as he squeezed. His larger frame pinned her to the floor. His fists closed over her throat, and the more she flailed against him, the more she beat and pounded and raged, the more pressure he exerted until the corners of her vision dimmed.

"Get your fucking hands off of her." Guinevere concentrated on Arthur's voice as the darkness encroached. His tone was heartbreaking, striking unimaginable fear in her as he thrashed against the magic, but it was all of him she had left. She vaguely registered Lancelot limping across the floor toward the king as her husband spit every obscenity he could think of at the man.

"I love you," she choked, her voice silent as Merlin killed her. "I love you, my king."

Just as her vision gave its last shuddering breath, something fell from Merlin's cloak to dangle above her throat. The haze in her brain cleared for a split second as she saw his pendant. It was cracked, a large section of the outer curve missing, and like lighting against her bare heart, adrenaline bolted through her. It matched the fragment she had found under the monk. Merlin. Merlin had been at the monastery.

With all the strength she had in her, Guinevere shoved her hand into her pocket and pulled out the broken fragment. With one swift motion, she clutched the jagged piece in her fist and slammed it down hard. The metal punctured Merlin's side, the shard still sharp from where it shattered. The mage jerked as she ripped it out, and she mercilessly plunged it back in.

The heat of his sticky blood washed over her fingers, but she kept going, recoiling and stabbing as fast as she could, and suddenly Merlin's hands were gone from her throat. Blessed, glorious air flooded her deprived lungs, and Guinevere coughed violently as her vision cleared. Merlin collapsed with a thud beside her just as Lancelot dove for the king.

Arthur growled, launching himself at the knight, and Guinevere watched in a daze, struggling to breathe as her husband and the traitor toppled to the tiles. Stabbing Merlin had released Arthur from his magical chains, and he was on top of Lancelot in seconds. The chained animal gone, the feral lion in its place.

"I told you I would kill you for touching my wife." Arthur's voice was low and steady, menacing enough to terrify the devil himself, and then he began.

Guinevere watched as her consciousness slipped in and out as her husband used his hands, not his sword. Lancelot tried to fight back as he lay pinned beneath the king, but something had snapped inside Arthur. He had witnessed a torture no husband should have, and it woke the beast. There would be no mercy.

Arthur used his fist, and it was not quick. It was painful. It was horrifying. It took time for Lancelot to die, but when he finally wheezed his last breath and departed this world, he was no longer beautiful. He was hideous.

ARTHUR PULLED himself off of Lancelot's corpse and limped on unsteady legs to Guinevere. With tears in his eyes, he collapsed to his knees and scooped her into his arms, clutching her frail and battered body to his chest.

"Stay with me, Guin." The pain in his plea was unbearable. "Don't you dare leave me."

She could barely move. Her voice refused to obey her commands to speak, to assure him she would never abandon him.

"Please, stay with me." He was begging, pleading. "I love you."

"Arthur?" a confused voice echoed through the room as Merlin struggled to his knees. "Is the queen well?"

"Don't you fucking touch her," Arthur growled, shielding his wife with his body, and Merlin recoiled before yelping in pain. He pressed his hand to his side where Guinevere had stabbed him. The shard was too small to inflict lasting damage, but the mage suddenly ached.

"My king, what happened?" Merlin's question was tinged with panic as Arthur snarled at him. "What happened to the queen?"

"He..." Guinevere wheezed, the word barely audible, but Arthur heard it, his gaze snapping to her lips. "Wasn't in control," she forced out. "Don't think he remembers."

"Remember what?" Merlin blurted, the concern on his face genuine. "What did I do?" He was on the brink of hysterics.

"I should kill you for what you did to her." Tears ran down Arthur's cheeks as he clutched his wife to his chest. "I should rip your head from your goddamned body, but she is right. This wasn't you, and I need your help."

"Anything." The mage shifted close to Arthur, but he recoiled, hoisting Guinevere further into his lap.

"Lancelot slaughtered a monastery of monks and orphans," Arthur said, graciously omitting the fact that Merlin had a hand in the carnage. "He blamed it on me, planning to use the crime to incite violence and take the throne." The mage jolted in shock and disgust. "I can explain when this is over, but right now, the kingdom is calling for my head. We need your magic to calm the rioting."

"Of course, my king." Merlin stood up, the loyal friend and ally back in control of his body, but he stumbled from the pain in his side. He wiped the blood and glared at his crimson-coated fingers. "What happened to me?"

"She did." Arthur gave a humorless laugh. "This glorious, fearless woman. She did that. She saved my life."

Merlin stared in confusion at the bleeding queen, but the violence churning the air told him it wasn't the right time. If they survived this day, the king would tell him everything. Everything he was terrified of learning. He had lost his mind so slowly, he barely remembered when he ceased to exist. He expected hearing his sins would be nearly unbearable, especially since Arthur's rage was so vicious, but now was not the time for answers. Now was the time to fulfill his pledge. Serve his king.

"I told you to stay away." Arthur curled Guinevere against his heart, whispering into her hair. He needed to find the physician. He needed her to stop bleeding. His own body was battered and destroyed. He could barely stand now that the adrenaline had run its course, but he refused to let his wife die in his arms. It took him long minutes, and a few tries, but he eventually staggered to his feet, Guinevere cemented to his chest.

"You promised me on our wedding day that you would listen to me in times of danger, that you would stay safe," he groaned in her ear as he began the agonizing journey to the physician's quarters. He didn't know if the man would be there, but the supplies needed to save Guinevere were. Lord knew he had bandaged himself enough to know what he was doing.

"But thank you for saving my life." He kissed her head gently as he leaned against the wall for support down the stairs. "I will forever cherish you for it, even though seeing you like this destroyed me." He kissed her again, hating the purple necklace blooming around her throat.

"I'll never leave you," she wheezed, her weak fingers clutching his blood-soaked shirt. "My king."

Chapter Thirty-Two

Guinevere's leg ached, but the sun felt glorious against her skin, kissing her with its warmth. She had been confined to a bed for almost three weeks, and when the physician finally approved her request to use her own two legs, she had practically run outside, Gawain hard on her heels as he swore under his breath at her recklessness. When he caught her, he forced her pace to the speed of a snail, insisting she sit often as they moved throughout the gardens, and despite her protests, she genuinely didn't mind the protective father act. She had grown close to Arthur's most trusted knight, and unlike her own father, who had always viewed her as a commodity, Gawain saw her as a fearless warrior, a woman deserving of his respect and trust. She had found another family member in him, even if his ever-watchful gaze was excessive. When he discovered that Lancelot and Merlin had nearly killed her after she fled his protection, he had been nearly inconsolable. He half expected Arthur to exile him from court for leaving her unattended, but the king knew her actions had saved his life. He couldn't be angry at her for defying every one of their requests when he still breathed air because of her.

Guilt plagued the knight, though. Guinevere read it in his eyes, and so she remained silent when he spent most of his time watching over her. He volunteered to care for her in Arthur's absence, which had been often. They had beaten her husband worse than her, but the stubborn man was on his feet within days of the attack. Lancelot and Merlin's actions had almost broken Camelot, and there were a few terrifying days where the king hadn't been sure the kingdom would survive, but fate offered them her favor. Merlin recalled enough of his memories to provide the people with proof of the king's innocence. The evidence against Lancelot was overwhelming, and after a public trial, the remaining traitors were executed. Merlin wanted to submit himself to such a trial, but Arthur refused. Instead, he called his knights together and let them be the judge of the mage's fate. When they heard Merlin's shame on his voice and how his consciousness had been screaming, trapped inside the prison of his own mind, unable to break free to the surface, they judged him innocent of his crimes. It was punishment enough for the mage to recall evils his magic unleashed, to learn of the blood on his hands. Lancelot's influence had been so slow, so gradual, that no one noticed him slip away until it was too late. Merlin himself hadn't even realized until he woke up one day staring out of eyes he no longer controlled, moving in a body he did not command. He had spent five years disappearing behind Lancelot's confinement. He suffered alone, and the knights of Camelot determined that horror retribution enough.

Merlin threw himself into helping the king regain his good standing, and after the first initial days where Camelot had been on the brink of collapse, peace slowly permeated the kingdom. Unable to defend herself, Arthur and his men had shouted Guinevere's praises. Her betrayal was his salvation. Her sacrifice, her pain, gifted him a future. Her love gave him hope, and he stood—Excalibur strapped to his back, the crown on his head —because of her. He made sure Camelot knew it.

"Would you like to stay here a little longer?" Gawain interrupted her reverie, and Guinevere's eyes turned toward the setting sun.

"I should go inside before Arthur sends a search party for me." She smiled at Gawain's extended hand, letting him pull her to her feet. Her leg protested slightly, as did her ribs, and sensing her discomfort, Gawain threaded her arm through his.

"Thank you." She clutched him tight, leaning on him for support as they drifted inside.

"Are you in pain?" he asked. "I could carry you."

"They wounded Arthur worse than me, and I never saw you offer to carry him?" Guinevere teased.

"The only way I could carry that man was if he was unconscious, and even then, I expect he would find a way to protest."

Guinevere burst out laughing and then winced as it pulled at her healing ribs. "He is too stubborn for his own good."

"He's stubborn?" Gawain laughed, deep and infectious, as he pinned her with his stare.

"Quiet." Guinevere smirked, slapping his arm. "Still, he needs to rest. I'm worried he'll push himself too far. He would barely let me get out of bed, yet he has been running himself ragged trying to restore the kingdom. I want him to heal, too."

"I expect he is purposely keeping himself busy so that he doesn't have to face his own thoughts," he said, and when Guinevere gave him a questioning look, he added, "He watched you almost die. Our king is resilient, but watching them attempt to kill you. It broke something inside him. I see it when he doesn't realize anyone is watching. The fear. I think in the quiet, all he sees is you bleeding on the floor."

Guinevere went still, but her heart thundered. Arthur had spent every day worrying about her pain that she hadn't stopped to consider the agony he was enduring in silence.

"My queen." Gawain nudged her. "Stop that." She looked up at him with confusion. "The guilt. I see it brewing. He has a difficult time opening up to us, his friends. Always has, probably always will, but he opens up to you. He is different with you, and now that you are on the road to recovery, I know you will take care of him. You won't let him drift aimlessly in his pain. It's one reason he loves you so much. You see him, all of him, and you love every facet, every dark corner and kind bone. I should have recognized that sooner. I'm sorry, but I recognize it now. You are the person who loves him most, and because of that, he will heal."

They stopped at her bedroom door, and Guinevere took a steadying breath. She had not set foot inside since she heard Lancelot's plans that fateful night, and standing here brought tears to her eyes. She missed sleeping beside Arthur so much the ache in her heart was almost worse than the pain pulling at her thigh.

"Goodnight, my queen." Gawain released her arm, and she turned her head to look up at him.

"He saw me first," she said simply, and Gawain smiled. She didn't need to elaborate. He understood.

Guinevere pushed into the room, the sunlight still peeking through the windowpanes, and she contemplated asking her maid to bring her food. She wanted to wait and eat with Arthur like she used to, but she was sore and hungry and exhausted, and his work kept him from her side until late. Walking, even as slow as snails dragging their slick bodies over the plants, had worn her out.

"Arthur?" She jerked in surprise as she looked up, finding the shirtless king leaning against the headrest of their bed. The swelling had gone down, and his wounds were healing nicely, and Guinevere's thighs clenched together at the sight of his bare skin. Their injuries had only allowed them stolen kisses amidst the chaos, and seeing him leaning there, his strong thighs spread just enough to exude dominance over the room, had her core clenching.

"What are you doing back so soon?" She smiled at him, and his eyes darkened as they drank her in.

"If you thought for one second, I was going to miss your return to our room, you are insane." His voice was rough, so rough and low she wanted him to drag it over every inch of her skin.

"You slept next to me in the infirmary," she teased.

"That's not the same, and you know it. Someone was always watching, and I spent every night worried you might stop breathing." A pang of sadness shot through Guinevere at his words and, seeing her mood fall, he added, "I finally get to have you all to myself. You're never leaving this bed again."

"I have had enough sleeping without you. Enough to last a lifetime."

"How do you feel?" Arthur asked, shifting to the edge of the mattress. His bare feet hit the floor, and his thighs fell open as he settled. Guinevere almost groaned at the movement. She knew he wasn't doing it on purpose, but the way his legs spread as if he owned every molecule of air in this room, as if he was pure sex and addiction, made her breath falter. He was male perfection, her male perfection, and she could see the concern on his face for her, but all she could think about was how delicious it would feel to drag her palms up his muscled thighs.

"Are you in pain?" he continued, mistaking her distraction for discomfort.

"A little," she answered honestly. "But the physician said I'm healing well. As long as I'm careful and rebuild my strength, my limp should eventually disappear. Or at least mostly."

"That's good." His dark eyes stared at her with such adoration, her heart nearly exploded. "How's the limp now?"

"I'll show you." Guinevere raised her eyebrows, and he nodded, not understanding her meaning until she gripped the shoulder of her dress. She watched his Adam's apple dip as he swallowed, and her nipples hardened. Desperate for relief, she dragged the fabric down over her breasts, and Arthur groaned loud and rough as it pooled on the floor.

She stood motionless, letting him drink in the sight, and his eyes feasted on her every curve as if he was a starving man. He didn't move. He didn't speak, he just made love to her with his eyes, and she lost all control. She stepped forward, limping until she stood between his spread legs, and he caught her hips in his large palms.

"That was good." His voice sounded like whiskey weaving over gravel, and she inhaled with an audible gasp. "Pretty soon you will be running all over this castle, making us all crazy again."

"I can make you crazy even with this limp," she teased, lacing her fingers in his dark hair.

"Lord, have mercy," he chuckled. "That you can." He pulled her hips closer, and she obeyed the call, dipping her head until their lips met. The kiss was soft and reverent, like a prayer, and when they broke apart, Arthur looked solemnly up at her.

"I love you." His voice shook. "I'm afraid to shut my eyes. I worry you'll disappear on me, and I'll wake up to find you lifeless on the floor, choked to death in your own blood."

"It's all right to be afraid," she soothed, running her fingers lovingly through his hair. "I am too, but we have each other, so close your eyes, trusting that if you descend into madness, I will pull you out." She kissed his forehead and noticed his gaze fall to the scar marring her left ribcage.

"I hate that he did that to you," he whispered. "That I have to see how I failed to protect you. I let you almost die, and that will haunt me until my death. I never want to experience that again, to watch you suffer like that again."

"Don't hate them." Guinevere grabbed his jaw and tilted his gaze to hers. A seriousness lingered behind her eyes, and she gripped him as if she could force him to believe her. "I gave myself willingly to save you. You would do the same for me. We are married. We're no longer two people, but one soul, and I'll never abandon you to the darkness. I don't hate your scars. You always worried I would find them off-putting, but I love them. I love every inch of you. You are perfect for me, so please don't hate any part of my body, especially the scars that saved your life." She kissed him gently. "Love them because of what they mean, not because of what happened."

Arthur wrapped his arms around her waist and pulled her to his chest. His kiss was searing and possessive. He claimed every part of her mouth, her heart, her skin as he poured his love into her, and when they parted, wetness dripped down Guinevere's thighs. Her breaths heaved, and she watched with flushed cheeks as her husband's gaze dipped to her breasts, drinking in the sight.

"Besides." She pulled back and seductively twisted her torso from side to side. "Now we match." He rolled his eyes at her comment, and she laughed. "We do. Now we both have scars."

Arthur leaned forward and kissed the one on her ribs tenderly before trailing kisses over her breast. Guinevere's breath hitched as he sucked her nipple into his mouth, teasing it with his teeth before he let it go with a wet pop.

"I guess we do." His smile returned to his full lips. "And I could never hate any part of you. I'm furious it happened, but you are as beautiful today as you were the night I met you. Maybe more so." He slapped her ass lightly, and she yelped, falling further into his arms.

"I was thinking," he said as he took her other nipple into his mouth. He dragged his tongue over the stiff peak before sucking it, and she pulled his hair so hard as she moaned it stung his scalp. "You can wield Excalibur," he murmured against her breasts. "You should know how to defend yourself. You clearly paid attention to my trainings, but it isn't the same as hands-on learning, and since my sword is now your sword, I want you to wield it well."

"I..." She gasped as he nipped at her breast. "I would like that."

"Good." He smiled up at her lust-hazy eyes. "I want you to be my queen in every way, so when you are strong enough, I'll teach you. Plus, the thought of you wielding Excalibur makes me so fucking hard." She raised her eyebrows at his comment, and with a wicked growl, he snatched her hand from his hair and pressed it against his cock. His hard length strained against his pants, and with greedy fingers, Guinevere began to undo their lacings.

"If that is the case." Her fist found the silky-smooth hardness, and she swallowed his groan with a kiss. "Then we should train in private." She stroked him torturously slow, her thumb dragging over the pre-cum beading at his head.

"Fuck." His voice rattled his chest, and he clamped his fingers around hers, forcing her to stroke him faster. Together, they fisted him, and arousal slammed into her so hard, Guinevere thought she would come just from the feel of him in her hand.

"You need to stop, pretty girl, or I'll lose control," Arthur growled. "I don't want to come in your hand. I need to be inside you, to feel that tight little pussy wrapped around me."

Guinevere stroked him faster, biting his bottom lip as she kissed him. "I want you to beg for it." She moaned into his mouth, repeating his words back to him.

"Fuck." He ripped his hand away from hers and shoved it between her legs. His knuckles dragged through her wetness, teasing her once, twice, three times before he thrust two fingers inside her. "You're so wet for me."

"Beg me, please." She was so close. She couldn't take much more, the nerves in her body already coiled painfully tight.

"I need you, Guin," Arthur groaned into her mouth as he

added a third finger. "Please, I want your pretty little cunt wrapped around my cock. I want to be so deep inside you that you never forget how much I love you."

Guinevere released his dick and gripped his shoulders. Her nails marked his skin as she dug them in, but she couldn't stop herself. Her body was out of control, her pleasure not her own, but his.

"My king," she screamed as her orgasm ignited her body. It rolled through her in unending waves of bliss, and her legs buckled. Arthur steadied her, fucking her through her climax, his movements sending shocks to her core.

When the haze of lust receded, Arthur pulled his fingers from her and brought them to his lips. She watched with hooded eyelids as he sucked them into his mouth, and instantly she was on fire. She wanted more of him, all of him.

"Delicious," Arthur growled as he dragged his fingertips over his lips. "Come here." He grabbed her hips and roughly yanked her against him. His hand slid up her bare back, and his fist tangled in her hair as he pulled her to his mouth. "I want you to taste yourself on me, to see just how beautiful you are." He kissed her roughly, her arousal heavy on his tongue as it invaded her mouth. His kiss was a drug, the taste of her pleasure driving her wild, and she shifted against his chest, desperate for relief. Arthur chuckled into her mouth at her movement and pressed her further against his body.

"Get on my cock now, Guin."

She didn't need to be told twice, and she climbed into his lap, straddling his half-clothed thighs. Arthur was oblivious to everything except his aching desires, and he grabbed her hips and slammed into her in one thrust.

"You feel so good," he roared, trying desperately not to come as he sank in to the hilt.

"I love you." She seized his face and stared into his eyes, her wetness already dripping onto his legs.

Arthur's chest constricted, and he wrapped his arms around her waist, pushing her down harder onto him. He kissed her as he thrust deep, and her core clenched in pleasure.

"I love you, my queen," he said against her mouth, and his term was not lost on either of them. "My queen, my wife, my best friend." He found the scar on her leg, and his fingertips dragged delicately over the uneven skin, just as hers had done to his on their wedding night. He traced it reverently, and when he came to its end, his fingers trailed up to the scar on her ribs. "I love every part of you. Every inch of you. All of you."

"Don't stop," she moaned, throwing her head back to offer him her breasts. He obeyed immediately, sucking her pink nipple between his teeth as she rode him. "I'm so close."

"Good girl," he praised against her skin. "Come on my cock, I want to feel you."

"My king."

"Come for me now, pretty girl. Come with me."

His words pushed her over the edge, and she screamed, not bothering to be quiet. She wanted all of Camelot to hear how much she loved her husband.

Arthur's control snapped with exquisite force, and he joined his wife, roaring as he filled her. For a moment, nothing existed besides their pleasure. They rode the blissful after waves together, bodies shaking, hearts pounding, breaths heaving, and when they finally slowed, Arthur pulled Guinevere forward to meet his gaze.

"You are stunning. I love the way you look after you have been fucked, my queen." He kissed her and lay back on the bed, pulling her on top of him. He stayed inside her, his cum dripping out, and her heartbeat quickened at the sensation.

"Do you like how full you are?" he asked. "Do you enjoy knowing how hard you make me come?"

"I love it." She kissed a scar on his chest so tenderly, he reflexively tightened his hold on her.

"Guin?" His voice was hesitant, not resembling the dominant king who had made her see stars. She propped herself up on his chest, and he brushed her hair behind her ears. "Did I hurt you?"

"No." She shook her head. She felt euphoric, too blissful to notice the pain, but when his concern didn't fade, she cupped his jaw. "What is it?"

"I love you, and I would give you the world. You know that, right?"

"Of course."

"What if…" He paused, grief passing over his features, and Guinevere couldn't stop herself from pressing a reassuring kiss on his lips.

"You can tell me anything," she whispered. "We promised no more secrets."

"What he said." Arthur couldn't bring himself to say Lancelot's name, but he didn't need to. She knew. "We've been married for five years, and I haven't given you children. I know you want a baby. I do too, but I'm afraid I won't be able to give that to you, and you'll be unhappy."

"Don't let his words bother you." She held his gaze so she could see just how serious she was. "Of course, I want a family, but if that is not our destiny, my happiness remains unchanged. You are my family, and if we never have a child, you are enough. You're all I need."

"And you are enough for me."

"So please don't worry. Lancelot was a mage." She would not let his name have any more power over her. "He wanted me for himself. For all we know, he cursed us to keep us from having an heir. It would have been difficult to steal the throne if you had a son."

"You think that's possible?"

Guinevere shrugged. "Or maybe I cannot have kids. Maybe you can't give them to me, but whatever the reason and whatever the outcome, I am happy as long as I get to grow old and grey bothering you."

Arthur laughed, and the sound filled her chest to overflowing. "Please bother me," he said. "For as many years as I have left."

"I promise." She stole a kiss as she continued, "Excalibur chose you to be king. It bonded with me as well. If we don't have children, the sword will choose the next true ruler of Camelot. Don't worry about me or the kingdom. We will be all right." She looked down at him with a twinkle in her eye as she wrapped her arms tighter around his neck. "But..." she dragged the word out as she kissed him seductively, coaxing a moan from his throat. "It doesn't mean we should stop trying for a baby."

Arthur flipped her onto her back with a growl, kicking off his pants so that he could be fully naked with his wife, and that was how they spent their first night in their room together. Trying until neither of them could move a muscle, and then the king tucked his queen against his side, whispering to her until they fell asleep, utterly spent and satiated. Just as they always had since the beginning of their marriage. Just as they always would.

Thank you for reading A Loyal Betrayal. If you enjoyed this book and feel comfortable, please consider leaving a review. It goes a long way in helping authors like me!

Also by N.R. Scarano

The Pomegranate Series

A Gender-Swapped Hades & Persephone Reimagining

*As Nicole Scarano

Pomegranate

Pitchfork

Pandora

The Competition Archives

A Survival Dystopian

*As Nicole Scarano

There Are Only Four

There Was Only One

There Will Be None

(Coming Soon)

There Have Been Many

(Coming Soon)

ABOUT THE AUTHOR

Nicole writes steamy fantasy & sci-fi romance as N.R. Scarano and fantasy, sci-fi, & mystery as Nicole Scarano. She doesn't like to box herself into one genre, but no matter the book, they all have action, true love, a dog if she can fit it into the plot, swoon-worthy men & absolutely feral females.

In her free time, Nicole is a dog mom to her rescued pitbull, a movie/tv show enthusiast, a film score lover, and sunshine obsessive. She loves to write outside, and she adores pole dancing fitness classes.

For all links & to sign up for her newsletter visit:
linktr.ee/NicoleScarano

instagram.com/nicolescarano_author
tiktok.com/@nicolescarano_author
twitter.com/nicolerscarano
facebook.com/nicolescaranoauthor

Made in the USA
Middletown, DE
06 September 2024